DARK
SUNSET

Peter McGarvey

Cliff House Publishing

Cliff House Publishing
Huntington, New York

cliffhousepublishing.com

Cover design by Lesley Stodart

ISBN 978-0988139619

IN MEMORY OF

Mike Magee

Books by Peter McGarvey

NON-FICTION

Baffled by Travel Guide to Toronto & Niagara Falls
The 10 Second Guide to New York City

ACKNOWLEDGMENTS

Special thanks to

Amy Mark, my editor who examined each word with a crafty eye.

Thanks to …

Robert J. Sawyer for his generous guidance and advice;

Don Hutchison for his friendship and support;

Helena Aalto and Anne Marie Robert for pointing out the errors of my ways;

and finally to

Lesley Stodart for the wonderful cover design.

DARK
SUNSET

From the darkness without
To the secrets inside
The night will reveal
What the shadows hide.

Aubrey Colgate Jones
American Poet (1895 – 1963)

PROLOGUE

Shadow Lake, Michigan, July 26, 1963

This was the night Aubrey Colgate Jones had chosen to die.

His words were irrevocably gone, stolen.

He could not recreate them. He had tried for weeks but they would not come back to him.

> "A war today or tomorrow, if it led to nuclear
> war, would not be like any war in history."

He took a last look around the cabin. His father had built it in the 1920s. He had felled the trees himself and shaped the logs. It had taken him an entire year to finish. His parents were gone now but he could still feel their presence in the cabin. He blinked back the tears remembering them brought.

He could see his father there in the armchair next to the Philco listening to Jack Benny, tendrils of pipe smoke drifting lazily in the air above his head.

His mother would be in the kitchen. She loved it there. The fragrance of her baking mingled with the pipe smoke and made Aubrey feel warm and protected.

The only reminder of them was a grainy black and white photograph on the mantel. In it they stood in front of the cabin, his mother cradling him in her arms.

> "A full-scale nuclear exchange, lasting less
> than 60 minutes, with the weapons now in
> existence, could wipe out more than 300

> million Americans, Europeans, and Russians,
> as well as untold numbers elsewhere."

Tonight, instead of Jack Benny, President Kennedy's voice came from the radio and filled the living room. All day there had been brief announcements about an important speech which would be broadcast that evening. It reminded Aubrey of a similar announcement which had preceded the Cuban missile crisis last fall. The world had come to the brink of annihilation until calmer heads prevailed. It sounded now, from the tone of the speech, that Kennedy was taking steps to make sure it never happened again.

> "And the survivors, as Chairman Khrushchev
> warned the Communist Chinese, "the
> survivors would envy the dead"."

Envy the dead.

Aubrey certainly did.

He walked onto the porch and looked at the lake.

The night air was dry and pleasantly cool, scented with the faint perfume of wood smoke. The blood-stained moon rose large over the pines at the edge of the lake. Their jagged tops reminded him of a predator's teeth.

Haley.

The moon was crimson from the forest fires burning far to the north over the Canadian border. Winds had spread the smoky haze across most of upper Michigan. Aubrey thought the moon's color was a harbinger of impending evil and he felt helpless to stop it.

But that would soon be over.

He stepped off the porch and began to unbutton his shirt as he headed toward the lake. By the time he reached the rocks at the shore Aubrey was naked. Without hesitation he strode into the water.

He heard the radio faintly from the cabin. Kennedy's speech had been replaced by music as the station resumed its regular schedule. The song was sad. The singer mourned the loss of her lover while the world went on oblivious to her pain.

> "Don't they know it's the end of the world ... "

He sank up to his shoulders. The summer had been a hot one and the water was warm. He put his head down and swam out into the lake. When he sensed it was deep enough, he paused and dog paddled in place.

Above him the stars seemed to grow brighter. In the fullness of the night the universe was coming to life. The sky was filled with brilliant points of light – suns which had died millions of years ago. He continued to gaze at the celestial vista in wonder.

He stopped paddling and let the lake gently pull him down. As the water closed over his head, Aubrey took a final breath.

Apprehension and fear faded. Now, in the embrace of darkness, there would be peace.

He felt a tug of regret as abstract became reality. As he sank deeper he thought of the stars above him, of his cabin by the lake, of his parents.

Death would not be a release. Death would bring only nothingness. The thought of that terrified him more than anything else ever had.

I don't want to die!

He began to thrash in the water, burning up precious oxygen as he fought his way toward the surface. A brilliant golden light guided him from what seemed like miles above.

He clawed his way upward. It was an impossible distance. The last of his air was gone. His lungs felt like they were filled with burning razorblades.

He had to breathe.

I can't. I'll die.

His head broke the surface and he drew in gloriously cool night air. He continued to breathe greedily. Panic gradually subsided as he floated.

Orange and gold flared off the water.

Strange.

Aubrey twisted around to see what was causing it.

A hundred feet away his cabin was on fire.

Smoke began to drift across the lake, thickening as the fire grew in intensity. The dark tops of the pines undulated with its orange glow. There was a beast loose in the night.

He swam desperately toward shore.

The fire was already stabbing through holes it had eaten in the roof. Superheated sap exploded inside the log walls, throwing brilliant streamers out into the darkness.

Aubrey reached the shore and ran toward the conflagration. As he passed a patch of darkness something stirred and moved forward. He didn't notice.

The volunteer fire department would never be able to stop it. His cabin would continue to burn while they looked on helplessly.

Aubrey's only legacy was gone. He should have felt something but didn't.

He sank to his knees before the fire, a supplicant, and laughed uncontrollably at this final absurdity.

The porch roof collapsed forward sending blazing cedar shingles cascading onto the lawn. Small fires started in the dry grass around him. Air flowed violently past. A vortex formed in the fire's center.

A brilliant spiral of flame burst through the roof and reached into the sky. It was mocking him with its determined fury, chewing at the core of his being, hollowing him out.

Aubrey was not alone.

Someone had moved from the darkness of the woods and stood near him. Completely absorbed by the fire he didn't sense that person's malevolence and unbridled hatred as it reached out toward him.

Out of the corner of his eye he saw something move. He started to turn.

A sharp flare of pain in his right temple was the last thing Aubrey felt. He didn't hear the sickening crunch as the axe blade caved in the side his skull and sent slivers of bone deep into his brain.

Death was instantaneous.

The killer looked down at the axe and then threw it into the heart of the fire.

Aubrey's eyes were frozen open in death, their sheen gradually fading. The figure knelt beside his body.

Off in the distance came the sound of sirens.

In the flickering darkness, the killer dragged Aubrey into the woods, leaving a faint trail of blood in the grass.

Aubrey Colgate Jones' cabin collapsed in on itself throwing up a massive shower of sparks.

Tiny points of light rose into the night sky and winked out one by one.

Glimpsed deep in opiate's red flame
Come dreams from the fire
Dreams of the day's bright breath
And fear of night's dark desire.

~ Aubrey Colgate Jones

ONE

Sunset Michigan, today

Barry Elkins stepped into the darkness under the bridge. An icy wind knifed down the channel and found him. He shivered and huddled deeper into his parka. It might be mid-April but it felt like January.

Real brass monkey weather.

He had been in a deep sleep in his hotel room when the phone call came. Still groggy, it took him a few minutes to comprehend what the voice was saying. Finally he made sense of it. He was to meet the caller in a half hour.

That would be midnight.

He started to protest, to demand that they meet the following morning at the hotel. The caller sharply cut him off and read a few lines from the page. He grabbed his page from the table and followed along, his excitement rising as each word the voice recited matched his copy exactly.

The caller had the answers he was looking for.

He agreed although his common sense told him this wasn't a good idea. Meeting a total stranger in a dark place in the middle of the night was something that happened in spy fiction and it usually turned out badly. But he had no choice. This was his first solid lead since he'd arrived here two days ago.

He thought about the other promising clues he'd followed.

The old man who'd known Jones had been a frustrating waste of time. He babbled on, telling a story that never seemed to end or even have a point.

Another lead, the library director, had been annoyingly enigmatic and was no help whatsoever. Still, Elkins had the strong feeling she was hiding something.

Well fuck them both.

This was the real thing. He didn't really care about the bitter cold or the unpleasant smell of urine and damp cement – or even the lethargy he couldn't seem to shake. He yawned and looked at his watch again. It was now fifteen minutes after midnight.

He felt a faint stirring of nausea in the pit of his stomach.

Maybe I got the time wrong.

It was possible. He'd been disoriented after the phone woke him. It had been the first good sleep he'd had since he arrived here. The other two nights he'd alternated between excitement and doubt. The excitement came from the possibility of discovering a treasure. When his search had been fruitless he began to doubt whether or not it even existed.

Above him he could hear vehicles crossing the bridge. Although there weren't many at this time of night the metal structure creaked and groaned alarmingly from their weight.

It was a lift bridge. Twice now he'd been forced to wait after it was raised to let the ferry go through. When it was up it split the town of Sunset in half. To the south were shops and restaurants, most of which were closed during the off season. The pristine beaches to the north made Sunset one of Michigan's most popular summer tourist destinations.

Elkins looked at the harbor where the ferry rocked gently in its berth. It was illuminated by harsh sodium lights which turned the black water to silver. He turned and gazed down the channel to the blinking navigational beacons marking the entrance into Lake Michigan.

He wondered what the town would be like in the summertime and then realized he didn't really care. All he wanted was to find what he had come here for and get back to Toronto as fast as he could.

If this trip turned out the way he expected, it would be life changing. No longer would he be forced to toil in academic obscurity. He would be a star – the man who had made the most important literary discovery in fifty years. He would be able to write his own ticket and have his choice of the finest university postings.

It was this possibility that held him here, almost against his will. Every fiber of his being told him to flee back to the safety and warmth of his room and the sleep he so desperately needed. Instead, he yawned deeply and continued to wait.

He looked at his watch one more time: 12:20.

A shoe scraped on the pavement behind him.

At last!

He started to turn.

"It's ... "

His words were choked off as something was twisted around his neck. He couldn't breathe. His eyes bulged and his head pitched forward as the blood to his brain was cut off.

The garrotte loosened and he swam back into consciousness.

I have to fight.

The noose slipped as he struggled. Elkins desperately tried to work his fingers underneath it. It slid further up his neck, under his beard, and the pressure increased.

He hurtled into blackness.

When he came around a voice was speaking softly in his ear. Disoriented and oxygen deprived, the words made no sense.

He's playing with me.

All Barry Elkins wanted to do was breathe, to take a single gulp of cold night air, and bring everything back into focus.

A shoe pressed against the middle of his back as his attacker applied more pressure. It crushed his windpipe.

Three minutes and five seconds later his heart stopped beating.

The attacker waited an additional two minutes and then let the inert body flop forward. It hung loosely over the railing with its head pointing down toward the water. Elkins' killer removed the noose and, with little effort, tilted the body the rest of the way over the railing. It splashed into the channel eight feet below.

The corpse floated face down and was gently tugged by the current out into the center of the channel. It began a slow journey toward Lake Michigan.

Breathing hard, the murderer leaned on the railing and listened intently to the sounds of the night.

Somewhere in the north end of town a dog barked and a baby cried. Down the street a woman laughed. The rhythm of normal life.

With a final glance down the channel toward the vague outline of the body, the killer moved out of the darkness and up the stairs leading to the street.

TWO

Molly Parsons rocketed out of sleep.

There's someone here.

She couldn't catch her breath and she was soaked in sweat.

Molly tried to claw her Beretta off the night table.

Where the hell is it?

She knocked the TV remote and the alarm clock onto the floor.

Jesus.

Her hand closed around the hard rubber handles of the pistol and she swung it up to cover the doorway.

Heart pounding, she stared into the darkness. The pressure in her chest was intense, like she was being squeezed in a vise. She couldn't hold the pistol steady. It wavered in her quivering hand. She held it tighter.

What had woken her?

The creak of a floorboard?

The sound of someone breathing?

Something was wrong; she knew it.

But there were no shadows, no out of place noises.

The house was still.

It had all been in her mind. Nothing was out of place.

Molly took a slow deep breath trying to control her panic with the technique she had been taught. She closed her eyes and concentrated on the word she'd been given. It would help break down the irrational wave of fear which gripped her.

Her rapid breathing began to slow as she focused, repeating the word over and over in her head, visualizing it. She felt the panic slipping away. Molly's taut muscles began to relax, tension uncoiling.

She lowered the pistol to her lap and opened her eyes. She could see the clock glowing on the satellite receiver across the bedroom: 2:05.

Terror had shredded her sleep once again.

She knew from experience fear would be her companion until dawn. Exhausted, she would drink a pot of strong coffee and question the wisdom of her decision to return to Sunset. It had been like this every night since she came back. She'd considered getting help but she knew she wouldn't and the cycle would just keep repeating.

Molly was startled by her BlackBerry —two quick buzzes, followed by a longer one. The department was trying to reach her. She grabbed it off the nightstand.

"Molly?"

It was Paul Booster, one of the deputies.

"What's up, Paul?"

"Sorry to bother you so late, Molly, but we have a body down at the mouth of the channel. It's up on the rocks. Looks like a drowning but you probably should have a look."

"Okay, I'll be there in twenty. Better let the Coast Guard know."

"Already have."

Of course you have, you efficient little shit.

"Good, I'll see you then."

Molly dressed quickly in jeans and a heavy sweater. She put the Beretta into its nylon holster along with two full magazines and clipped her badge to her belt.

In the kitchen she turned on the outside lights which led down to the boathouse. She pressed a toggle switch on the wall beside the backdoor to remotely lower the Zodiac into the water.

She jumped into the boat and turned the ignition key. The powerful outboard roared to life. Unhooking the bow line she pushed away from the dock and opened up the throttle.

She looked across the lake toward Sunset. At this time of morning only a few lights from the town sparkled on lake. Molly raced across the dark water.

Damn! Why did it have to be a drowning?

THREE

The wind coming down the channel built up a fair chop on the surface of Little Lake Bay. Molly's fifteen foot Zodiac Commando handled it with ease. The boat's 75 horsepower Evenrude drove it through the waves at high speed.

She rounded the bay and turned into the channel's entrance. Slowing down she chugged toward a small group of people gathered at the far end. Illuminated by portable halogen lights Molly could see the unmistakable shape of a body under a blue tarp.

Ten feet from the beach she gunned the engine and then cut its power. The forward momentum of the boat carried it up onto the sand. She hopped out with the line and set the anchor to hold it.

She saw Paul Booster climb down from the pile of boulders that formed a breakwater on this side of the channel. The stones kept the channel from eating away at the delicate beaches that flanked either side of it.

Booster was tall and thin with the severe angular features of a Puritan. He reminded Molly of Anthony Perkins in 'Psycho' because of his nervous anxiety.

He shrugged.

"Sorry, Molly, I didn't want to call you but I couldn't get Chief Sharpe."

That didn't surprise her. She figured Chief of Police Kenton Sharpe was likely passed out in his recliner with a bottle of bourbon keeping him company. Nobody bothered trying to reach him after 10:00. That meant Molly, who was next in the chain of command, would automatically get the call for anything serious.

She stood over the body as one of the EMS guys lifted the sheet. The corpse lay on its right side, the face turned toward her. She could see it was pale and drained of blood but not gray and waxy like many of the drowning victims she'd seen.

A fresh one.

It looked like it had been in the water less than an hour.

"Who called it in?" she asked Booster.

He nodded at a young man standing nearby. She recognized Tony Huffner, the son of local Coast Guard Commander John Huffner.

"Tony spotted the body floating down the channel and snagged it with a rescue pole before it drifted out into the lake," Booster told her.

Molly took out her notebook and walked over to Tony. "You okay, Tony?"

He shook his head. "Never saw a dead body before."

"Sorry. I know it's not a pleasant sight," she said. "Can you tell me what happened?"

Tony took out a pack of Camels. "Okay if I smoke?"

"Sure, no problem."

He nodded and lit the cigarette. Tony inhaled deeply and blew out a long stream of smoke.

"I saw him floating in the water, so I went and got the pole from the rescue station and climbed down to get him. I dragged him up the rocks and called 9-1-1." His voice wavered. "He wasn't moving or nothing so I figured he was probably dead."

Molly looked over to the body and nodded. "Yeah, he's been in the water for at least an hour. Recognize him?"

"Nope." Tony shook his head and took another long drag on the cigarette. "Do you?"

"No, I don't."

As Tony continued to smoke Molly notice a tremor in his hand.

Cold or frightened?

"What brings you out here this time of night?" she asked.

Tony looked away for a split second and she knew he was going to lie to her.

"I had some drinks at the Villager and I wanted to sober up a little before I went home."

"You live over on Park Street right?"

"Yeah, just below Cufflink Hill."

"Your dad'll give you shit for coming home drunk."

"Yup, he's a real tight-ass about that stuff."

Molly smiled. She'd worked with John Huffner a few times and he was a real no nonsense person. He would definitely be pissed off at Tony for coming home drunk.

"Can I get going now?" Tony asked.

She looked at him again.

He's definitely lying about something.

"Sure and thanks for calling it in, Tony," she said. "But you'll need to come by the station in the morning and give us a full statement."

"Sure," he replied.

"Can I have somebody take you home?"

"No, I'll be okay. At least I'll have a good excuse for being so late." He threw his cigarette into the channel. "Anything else?" he asked.

"No, that does it for now, Tony. We'll see you in the morning."

She watched as he walked down the beach.

One of the paramedics caught her attention and pointed to the body.

"Hey Molly, okay to release?" he asked.

Everyone was cold and wanted to get out of there.

"Yeah, take him," she nodded.

They would take the body to the hospital for a post-mortem although this looked pretty cut and dry.

Well, maybe not so dry.

Molly saw water dribbling out the corpse's mouth.

Funny, the eyes are open.

Drowning victims usually had their eyes shut.

The EMS guys rolled the corpse into an open body bag and zipped it up. They carried it over the icy rocks to the ambulance. After they drove off, Booster joined her.

"See if we can get an ID on the body," she said.

"I can hang around for the PM if you want," Booster offered.

Molly shook her head. "No, Kolmenn's in court in the morning so he won't do the cut until sometime after lunch."

She and County Coroner Ronald Kolmenn were scheduled to testify in the morning. Molly had been looking forward to it. Dr. Kolmenn always kept things lively.

"Sorry, Molly, I forgot," Booster said.

She knew he hadn't forgotten and wasn't really sorry. Booster was happy he had the opportunity to disturb her sleep the night before an important court appearance.

She smiled at him. "No problem. I'm going home now to catch some ZZZZZs."

Molly lied.

There would be no more sleep for her that night and she would be exhausted in court.

Perfect.

FOUR

Jonnie Blatz was the worst lawyer in the state of Michigan. In fact, Jonnie Blatz might have been the worst lawyer in the entire nation. His only redeeming qualities were that he dressed well and worked cheap. He also took any legal aid case which floated over his transom.

A meth cooker of modest means facing a second degree murder charge had limited options for legal counsel in Sunset. That's how a Class A burnout by the name of Theodore "Tweak" Brown had come to be Blatz's current client.

Tweak lived in the woods north of town and supported himself by cooking up large batches of crystal meth. Unfortunately he smoked most of his own product, leaving his brain functioning like a bowl of polenta.

Tweak could have been a poster child for the horrors of meth. He was only twenty six but looked like a man in his eighties. The drug had cost him most of his hair and a good number of his teeth. His skin was the color of a cadaver's and that was after Blatz had applied a generous amount of makeup in a failed attempt to make him look healthy. It only added to Tweak's overall ghoulish appearance.

Blatz had also arranged for a sedative to counteract the fidgeting which came with meth withdrawal. The result was that Tweak now had the appearance of something which had stumbled out of 'Dawn of the Dead'.

The case was a typical Sunset County murder – stupid and tragic.

Tweak and his best friend Odie Cox had stolen an old Airstream from a trailer park south of Petoskey. They hauled it along a state access road deep into the woods north of town. It was the perfect place to set up shop.

Tweak was clueless about how to make meth but Odie had a basic high school grasp of chemistry and a few more brain cells. Miraculously they had managed to cook up a large amount without blowing themselves into South Dakota.

The boys spent most of the winter cooking and smoking. When the snow melted they came out of the woods to stock up on Sudafed and other supplies. They drove their pickup down to Sunset and ended up at Oleson's supermarket on the south end of Main Street.

They had gallons of model airplane fuel which they used to make the meth. Odie thought it would be alright to fill the truck's tank with it instead of gasoline. It wasn't. When Tweak parked the truck there was a small explosion and flames shot out from under the hood.

In the hallucinatory world of Tweak and Odie this wasn't particularly alarming and they strode off toward the store. It was at that point that Tweak believed the Coke machine by the store's front entrance had suddenly come to life and was going to attack him. He whipped out his Glock and began shooting at it. One of the bullets went wild and hit Odie in the back. It splattered his heart against his ribcage, killing him instantly.

With his gun empty Tweak seemed oblivious to the fact his best friend was lying face down on the pavement. He just stepped over the body and walked into Oleson's to do his shopping.

When Molly arrived Tweak was piling packages of cold medication and hot dogs into a shopping cart. She walked up to him and asked for his pistol. Handing it over without a fuss, he was surprised to learn he'd killed his best friend when Molly cuffed him and read him his rights.

~

On the witness stand Molly described the scene the day of the murder along with Tweak's confusion at the time of his arrest. During his cross examination Blatz focused on Molly's lack of medical qualifications to declare Odie dead at the scene.

"You are not a medical professional licensed by the state of Michigan," he stated and paused dramatically.

Unperturbed she looked down at her notes.

"Are you?" he asked.

Molly smiled at Blatz. "No, but I've seen a dead body before."

"Yes, and how did you determine the victim was dead at that time?"

"He had no pulse, his eyes were fixed and dilated, and he had a wound the size of a softball where his heart should have been. I think it was a pretty good bet he was deceased."

"But you are not a qualified medical professional, are you?"

"No, but I know a corpse from a square dancer and Odie Cox was definitely not doing a doe-see-doe."

Blatz pushed forward. "Did you call an ambulance for the victim to be transported to the hospital emergency ward?"

"No, I called EMS and requested they pick up the body and transport it to the morgue for a post mortem."

"And again, Miss Parsons, you are not a qualified medical professional, are you?"

"And again, Mr. Blatz, I state Odie Cox was very dead when his body left the scene."

"No further questions of this witness, Your Honor."

As with most of his cases, it was obvious Jonnie Blatz had no defence strategy. He was notorious for changing tactics several times during the course of a trial, hoping something would stick and lead to a not guilty verdict. Up until now this tactic had produced miserable results for most of his clients.

When she was off the stand Molly decided to stick around. She wanted to enjoy Kolmenn in action with Blatz.

~

If anyone in the courtroom looked worse than Tweak, it was Dr. Ronald Kolmenn. He'd been the county coroner since Molly was in elementary school. He was a tiny man, not quite a dwarf, but close. Kolmenn reminded Molly of the mummy in that Boris Karloff movie.

In order for Kolmenn to be seen while he testified, the bailiff slipped a copy of the 1968 New York City Yellow Pages onto the chair in the witness stand. After being sworn in Kolmenn slowly climbed up onto the thick book.

The District Attorney started by asking the coroner to state his professional qualifications. Kolmenn highlighted his impressive career and credentials.

The DA led Kolmenn through the specifics of his post-mortem on Odie Cox. Supplementing his words with graphic autopsy photos, Kolmenn described in detail the entry wound, exit wound, and trauma to the heart caused by the bullet. When asked how long after the shooting the victim had died Kolmenn stated, "Death was instantaneous."

Sitting at the defence table Blatz made notes on a yellow legal pad. Kolmenn watched him, a slight smile playing on his lips.

~

Jonnie Blatz rose on cross, buttoning his double-breasted charcoal suit jacket. He completed the impression of being a successful defense attorney with a pale gray shirt and bright yellow tie. Consulting his notes he walked to the stand, careful to keep a clear line of sight between himself and the jury.

"Now, Dr. Kolmenn, you just testified that in your opinion death was instantaneous. Is that correct?"

Molly, along with everyone else in the courtroom, could see where this was heading.

"Yes, that's what I said," Kolmenn sighed.

"And were you present at the scene?"

Molly looked over at the prosecutor.

Isn't this the time to leap to your feet and yell 'objection'?

However, the DA was calmly leaning back in his chair with an almost blissful look on his face.

"No, at the time of the murder I was enjoying my dinner. Double thick pork chops as I recall, cooked with apples and garlic."

"Doctor, I don't think your dinner menu is relevant to this trial."

"I'm not so sure. It's probably just as relevant as this line of questioning."

Blatz stiffened and whirled to face the jury. "Move to strike, Your Honor!"

Judge Pomm looked over at Blatz and shook his head.

"Please remove the witness's last response," Pomm wearily instructed the clerk. "Can we move this along, Mr. Blatz? I'm taking my grandson out for his birthday lunch today."

Satisfied, Blatz walked closer to the witness stand until he was only a couple of feet from Kolmenn.

"How many post-mortems have you done on dead people, Doctor?"

Kolmenn thought for a moment and smiled. "Actually, all my post-mortems have been performed on dead people. I'd get into trouble if they were still alive."

There was a smattering of badly stifled laughter in the courtroom. Kolmenn's smile broadened. He was enjoying himself. He had an audience – one that was breathing for a change.

Blatz ignored him and straightened his tie. "So, Dr. Kolmenn, what time did you start the autopsy?"

Kolmenn leafed through his notes. "At 7:35 that evening."

"And Mr. Cox was dead at that time?"

"No, he was sitting up on the table talking to his health insurance company on his cell phone to make sure he was covered for a post-mortem."

More laughter rippled through the courtroom. It was louder this time and prompted Judge Pomm to use his gavel. Jonnie Blatz turned his back on Kolmenn in obvious contempt.

He faced the jury. "Dr. Kolmenn, I think we can do without the sarcasm. This is a serious proceeding."

Judge Pomm pointed at Kolmenn. "Please, Dr. Kolmenn, this is painful enough."

Blatz returned to his line of questioning. "Before you performed the post-mortem, did you check Mr. Cox for a pulse?"

"No, Counselor, I did not."

"Did you check Mr. Cox's blood pressure?"

Kolmenn shook his head. This was getting ridiculous. "No, Mr. Blatz, I did not."

Blatz pounced. "So, Dr. Kolmenn, it is possible that Mr. Cox was still alive when you began the post-mortem?"

"No, it was not."

"And how can you be sure of that, Doctor?"

"Because his brain was in a dish next to his body on the table."

"And there's no possibility that Mr. Cox might still have been alive at that time?"

Kolmenn wrinkled his brow theatrically. He pretended to think. Finally, he nodded slowly.

"Well, there was a slim chance that he might still have been alive. There are a few recorded cases of patients surviving after their brains has been removed. As a matter of fact, several of them have gone on to become defense attorneys."

The spectators and the jury exploded into laughter. Judge Pomm shot Kolmenn an angry glare and tried to gavel order back into his courtroom.

Tweak, jolted out of his fugue state, jumped to his feet and screamed at the judge, "Your Holiness, I want a new lawyer!"

He tried to climb over the defense table to get at Blatz cowering near the witness stand but the bailiff restrained him.

Kolmenn shuffled his notes and smiled at the chaos around him. He winked at Molly.

The guards dragged the still screaming Tweak from the courtroom and Judge Pomm declared the proceedings over for the day. He summoned the District Attorney and Jonnie Blatz to his chambers to try to sort out the mess.

To salvation denied
And fraught with heaven's domain
To fall into ice and fire
And thereafter remain.

~ Aubrey Colgate Jones

FIVE

Sunset County Sheriff Arnie Voxx sat in The Villager Restaurant on Main Street and waited for Molly to arrive.

She'd called the previous day and asked him to meet her for lunch. It had been fifteen months since he last heard from her. Molly sounded matter of fact, as if the passage of time didn't matter.

When he got off the phone Arnie was disturbed by the cold flat hollowness in her voice. He wondered what she was feeling. Whatever it was, she hadn't shared it with him nor was she likely to.

That was her style, to keep her emotions hidden from the world. She was an enigma to everyone who knew her, including Arnie who had known her the longest.

Her father had been a dry drunk who reinvented himself as a preacher and started his own ministry in a decrepit building on the edge of town. The family was dirt poor and lived on handouts from the few people who were attracted to their church.

The old man also had a terrible temper. Arnie suspected he beat his children. At the very least he deprived them of anything close to a normal life and kept them locked away in that tiny shack.

Her parents had insisted on home schooling. This caused an ugly confrontation with the board of education. Sheriffs' deputies, including Arnie, were sent to enforce a court order requiring the children to attend the local school. His most vivid memory was of a little girl peering wide-eyed around a doorway. She was curious about who was standing up to her daddy. He smiled and waved and she ducked back into the room. Arnie liked to think he'd played a small part in her eventual escape from the strict discipline of her family.

Years later when she returned to Sunset as a confident and capable young woman, they had become close – or at least as close as Molly would allow.

Arnie had hired her as a deputy in his department. There was no doubt Molly was a brilliant and intuitive investigator. She was smart, tenacious, and relentless – characteristics which made her an excellent cop.

However, she was also a moody and insular person and became more so after her husband's death two years ago. Their marriage had been the closest thing to happiness Molly had ever known and on one horrible night it was gone.

For a few months she struggled to carry on and rise above her personal tragedy. It was a struggle not helped by the lack of support from her boss, Chief of Police Kenton Sharpe. Sadistic and cruel, Sharpe seemed to enjoy her pain and added to it whenever he could. He was smart enough to do it so he wouldn't be detected. The effect subtly eroded her self-confidence.

When it finally became too much for her she took a leave of absence from the department. Originally it was to be for only six weeks but had stretched out to fifteen months.

Arnie felt her problems with Sharpe had somehow been his fault. She'd been a great deputy when she worked for him. He just didn't have the opportunities for her that she needed. She wanted to be a criminal investigator but his department already had one, Bert Small, who Arnie had inherited when he was first elected sheriff. Bert was a nice enough guy but inept as an investigator. However, he had seniority and it would cost too much for Arnie to get rid of him.

Molly had been approached by Mayor Floren Cooper and several members of the town council. There had been a rash of break-ins and they felt the police department needed an investigator. Impressed by her abilities, they asked Molly to apply. Kenton Sharpe protested loudly saying they had superseded his authority but, much to his chagrin, he was overruled.

Molly discussed it with Arnie and they both agreed it would be a good move for her even though she would have to work under Sharpe. Arnie and Sharpe had butted heads in the past, mostly to do with jurisdiction. Arnie thought the man was a self-righteous prick.

Sharpe had always made it difficult for Molly but he was doubly tough on her when she returned. He'd been happy she was finally out of his hair for good or so he thought. Then she unexpectedly popped up and refused to say where she'd been.

Her silence about her absence was the source of much speculation around town. Everyone had a theory.

She had been in a private clinic receiving shock therapy for depression ...

She had joined a religious cult ...

She had been on a really long bender ...

Molly heard these rumors and all the others which had circulated around Sunset. She maintained her silence. Where she'd been was just one more secret she kept buried deep inside.

Arnie was hurt that she hadn't confided in him or even bothered to call after she got back. Then yesterday, out of the blue, she phoned and asked him to meet her for lunch.

He drank his coffee while he waited for her. The Villager was filling up for lunch. He saw several familiar faces and had a brief conversation with Bob Castle, the manager of Oleson's supermarket.

The Villager was the place where the town came together. More important decisions were made here than in City Hall. The century-old establishment had passed through many hands. The latest owner, Hank Summerville, had been the proprietor for the last four years.

Although he stood an imposing six four and was built like an armoire, Hank was a gentle man. After serving twenty years in the Marine Corps he'd drifted around for a while. He ended up in Sunset in the mid-nineties and worked as a bouncer at The Villager. Back then it catered to a rougher clientele.

Hank had looked beyond the dingy interior and saw real potential. With its colorful history he decided it should be more than a dive bar and closed it for a month to renovate. Upon reopening it took no time at all for The Villager to become the center of Sunset's social life. During the summer months the line-ups for a table stretched out onto the sidewalk. Even now, in early April, the dining room was packed.

Hank gave Molly a big hug when she came through the door. His display of affection made her uncomfortable.

"This place hasn't changed," she commented as she looked around.

"And neither have you," Hank said. "It's good to have you back."

He led her to the table and Arnie rose to greet her.

"Hello, Kiddo," he said affectionately.

She hated it when he called her that and he knew it.

"I missed you too, Arnie," she said with a warm smile.

"Fifteen months is a long time … " he let his thought trail off, not sure how far to push it.

Sensing his discomfort she changed the subject. "You hear about court this morning?"

He chuckled. "I heard Judge Pomm was furious at both Blatz and Kolmenn. He hates anyone messing with his court."

Molly smiled at the memory of the morning's festivities. "Kolmenn knows he's untouchable and Blatz is an asshole. Blatz was trying to float some silly bullshit theory that Odie Cox was still alive and the autopsy actually killed him. I don't blame Kolmenn for playing with him."

"They should have disbarred Blatz years ago," Arnie said. "His only talent is for wearing good suits."

They were interrupted when their waitress appeared at the table with menus in hand.

"Afternoon, Sheriff."

"Hi, Desirée," he greeted her and nodded toward Molly.

"Desirée Platt, I'd like you to meet Molly Parsons."

She smiled at Molly and extended a hand.

"Pleased to meet you, Molly. I've … " Desirée stopped abruptly.

"Heard all about you," Molly finished in her head. She smiled at Desirée and shook her hand.

"It's nice to see Hank has more help in here," Molly said. "Business must be good."

A quick look around the dining room told her all Hank's changes had paid off; The Villager was packed.

Molly smiled up at Desirée. She was in her mid-twenties. Dressed in faded jeans and a beige turtleneck wool sweater, she wore thin wire-framed glasses and just the right amount of makeup. From the enthusiasm of her greeting, Molly guessed Desirée had the kind of personality that made her a popular waitress.

Arnie ordered the meatloaf special and Molly asked for a Cobb salad. Desirée hurried off to give their order to the kitchen.

"She's a great singer," Arnie said. "Hank lets her perform a couple of evenings a week. I think she could be another Shania Twain."

Molly didn't care for country music; rock was more her style. They lapsed into silence again.

"You're not going to tell me are you?" he asked.

"Let's just leave it off the table for now, Arnie."

More silence.

She leaned forward. "I want to thank you for looking after my place and everything."

While she'd been gone Arnie had driven out to the lake two or three times a week to check on her house. He'd arranged for the driveway and roof to be shoveled during the winter and for the grass to be cut in the summer.

"Mike Bloom was asking if you wanted to sell."

Mike, the local Century 21 broker, was always on the lookout for a new listing.

"I don't know," she said. "I don't think so. I'm not ready to do that yet."

Molly took her napkin and spread it neatly in her lap. Arnie knew this was her way of signaling that she no longer wanted to discuss this topic.

"How's the re-election coming?" she asked.

He frowned. "I think I've been doing this job too long."

As he said it Molly thought he looked weary. Arnie had been sheriff for over twenty years. She wondered if the fight had gone out of him.

That was too bad because Sunset County owed him a lot. He put people first and politics second. He'd never worried about re-election in the past. Arnie had done his job the best he could and let the people's wisdom prevail.

But things had changed.

Over the past few years a much nastier form of politics had crept into the county. A new group, the Citizens for Accountable Government, had crawled out from under a rock. Instead of uniting the electorate it preached a more black and white philosophy designed to divide them. 'You're either with us or against us' was the new mantra of political discourse. The middle ground was now a gaping chasm.

Molly suspected Arnie would never choose sides. He would continue to follow his own path and do what he thought was best.

And they would eat him for breakfast for doing that.

"Come on, Arnie, you can't let those shits take you down."

"Why not? They seem to call the shots on everything else around here these days."

The CAG was making no secret of the fact it was drafting a list of possible candidates to run against Arnie in the upcoming election. Molly figured that asshole Sharpe had to be somewhere near the top of the list.

As chief of police Sharpe had a less than stellar on-the-job record. He was stupid and a bully who measured every situation by the damage or good it could do for him. He seemed to resent the department in his charge, like it was beneath his grandiose aspirations.

He wanted to control a much larger force. The Sunset Police Department was tiny – consisting of just three regular deputies and Molly. There were also a couple of part time dispatchers and an administrative assistant. During the summer season when the population swelled, the Kenn brothers were added to the roster of deputies. They weren't all that bright.

The department's main function was to keep traffic flowing smoothly through town and investigate the minor property crimes that popped up now and then. The challenge for Molly as lead investigator was to match a crime to one of the local bottom feeders. It normally didn't take much effort. Even when they had an occasional murder it was usually the result of intoxication or jealous rage, or a combination of both.

Increased meth addiction had become the biggest menace the town was facing. Because it was cheap and easy to produce with ingredients found in any drugstore, it was responsible for the sharp rise in crime. It had caused a rash of burglaries in the expensive vacation homes on Cufflink Hill as crank heads looked for a quick score.

Recently there had been debate in town council meetings about the cost of a police force especially when they already had a sheriff's department. Molly had wondered about this herself. It was plain to see that with budget pressures the future of the department was in doubt. No wonder Sharpe was considering running for sheriff but it would be bad news for the county if he won.

~

Molly picked at her salad listlessly while Arnie devoured his meatloaf.

"Betty not feeding you anymore, Arnie?" Molly cracked.

"I wish Betty could make gravy like this." He held up a piece of the meatloaf which dripped with brown goodness.

Arnie's wife of thirty five years was an excellent cook. She had shelves of cookbooks and loved to experiment with new cuisines. The last dinner Molly and her husband Steve had enjoyed at their home had been during Betty's Thai phase. She'd prepared multiple dishes, each one more fragrant and spicier than the last.

As Molly finished her salad the BlackBerry vibrated on her belt. She looked at the display – Ronnie Kolmenn – and took the call.

"Nice show this morning, Ronnie. One of these days Judge Pomm is gonna toss you in a cell for contempt."

"What the hell does Jonnie Blatz think, that we're all as stupid as he is?" he snorted.

"Anyway, I've got interesting news for you," he continued. "I'm pretty sure the drowning vic they brought in last night was murdered. I'm just finishing up the cut right now. Come by in a half hour and I'll take you through it."

"Okay," she said, "I'll see you then."

"Good. See you when you get here."

Molly disconnected and told Arnie what Kolmenn had discovered.

She took out some bills to pay for their lunch but Arnie waved her off. "You get it next time," he said.

"Drop by the office later and fill me in," he added.

"Thanks, Arnie, and please give Betty my best."

Feeling like a worried parent, Arnie watched Molly head for the door. He thought about the familiar spark of enthusiasm which had flash into her eyes while she'd been talking to Kolmenn.

Too bad it took a murder to put it there.

He thought back to the night her husband died. Arnie had felt so helpless in the ambulance. All he could do was comfort Molly and hold back his own tears.

While she appeared to have recovered some of her old verve it was clear to him she still had a long way to go. He was worried about the deep blue smudges under her eyes and the tremor in her hands. Molly obviously hadn't been sleeping well.

Fifteen months away from Sunset hadn't been long enough.

Arnie drank the last of his coffee and signaled for Desirée to bring the check.

SIX

The body looked different this time. Laid out flat on his back under the glare of halogen lights, the victim had a waxy unnatural appearance.

The clothes had been removed and bagged for forensic examination. Kolmenn treated every corpse as a possible murder victim. If that turned out to be the case, the investigators involved appreciated that he had preserved evidence. In spite of his caustic personality Ronnie Kolmenn was widely admired in the law enforcement community.

"So, Ronnie, did you check his pulse?" Molly asked with a grin.

Kolmenn smiled and shook his head.

"That boy needs a good disbarring," he responded.

Molly agreed. "So what do you have?"

Kolmenn pulled on disposable latex gloves and handed another pair to Molly. He tilted the victim's head back so she could see clearly under the chin. There was a narrow bluish mark across the throat just below the beard. Kolmenn pointed at it with a pen.

"Looks like something thin, maybe fishing line."

Kolmenn lifted one of the victim's eyelids. Molly could see the pupil was fixed and dilated with tiny pinpricks of blood in the white of the eye.

"See it?"

"Petechial hemorrhages," she said.

Kolmenn nodded, impressed.

She knew the distinctive red dots were an indication of strangulation, caused when pressure on the neck veins ruptured tiny blood vessels in the eyes.

"You must've been doing some reading while you were away," he joked and pointed at the mouth. "I checked the throat. No mucus and foam martini."

Sunset was a tourist town and saw its fair share of drownings. Foam in the throat was the first thing Kolmenn would've looked for. None meant death occurred before the victim had gone into the channel.

"Can you fix a time of death?" Molly asked.

Kolmenn frowned. "It's hard to say. He wasn't in the water very long, maybe an hour or less. Dinner was still in the stomach so he must have eaten about three hours prior to death."

He shook his head, "Looks like he had a hamburger and fries. Too much fat and sodium for a guy his age. Bad for the heart – but then so is being strangled," he chuckled. "Anyway, if you can find out when he ate that'll help establish TOD."

Molly wrote in her moleskin notebook as he talked.

"Other than the ligature mark around the throat there isn't much in the way of trauma. There's a small bruise on his right ankle but from the color it looks like it's at least five or six days old. His liver tells me he was a drinker, most likely more than just a couple a day. I asked for a full tox screen so we can see how much he'd had to drink."

Kolmenn held up two evidence bags containing the victim's clothing.

"Looks like you have homework."

Molly picked up the bags. "Thanks, Ronnie. Fax me a copy of the preliminary when it's ready."

Kolmenn touched the blue mark across the throat. "I'll try to get an accurate measurement on this. It might help to narrow down the kind of line the killer used."

~

When she got back to the office Molly set the evidence bags next to her workstation. It was located in the corner of a large open room which held five other desks. Two were occupied by administrative staff; three were for the deputies.

She typed her notes in a Word document and saved the new file as 'Doe, John_2012-04-04'. Molly was confident they would have the victim's actual name for the file once the personal effects had been examined.

She sensed someone looking over her shoulder. Paul Booster.

"Chief Sharpe wants to see you," he said.

She turned to face Booster and noted the smirk on his face. He wasn't trying to hide the depth of his resentment toward her.

Prick.

While she'd been away he'd been top dog in the department. Her return had forced him back to his hated regular duties.

She closed the Word file and went to see Sharpe.

~

Kenton Sharpe didn't bother to look up when Molly entered his office. He flipped over page after page, pausing now and then to read something. It was a delaying tactic to waste her time, his not too subtle way of reminding her who had the power.

She stood patiently and watched as he finished whatever he was pretending to do.

Sharpe tried to project the image of a serious lawman. He was a shade over six feet and well-muscled. Each morning he shaved and polished his bullet-shaped head and put on a freshly ironed shirt. Molly wasn't sure if his dark red eyebrows were artificially colored or natural but she found it distracting when trying to have a conversation with him.

Sharpe looked up.

"So?" His expression was cold.

"You wanted to see me," she said with a hint of scorn.

He frowned.

Sharpe thought he'd seen the last of her when she'd gone on leave. He'd objected when she returned and wanted to resume her former position. He argued that she'd abandoned the department and didn't deserve reinstatement. Mayor Cooper and the council had overruled the chief and ordered him to take Molly back. This increased the existing tension between the two of them.

"Yes. I heard it went badly in court this morning." The tone of his voice made it sound like it was her fault.

"It could've gone better." She added, "My testimony was fine though."

Why did I say that? It makes me sound defensive.

She resented that he made her feel this way. She had nothing to be sorry about.

"I thought you should know our drowning from last night is actually a murder. Looks like he was strangled and then pushed into the channel."

That got Sharpe's attention. There weren't many murders around here and this might mean press coverage.

Press coverage is good for my political career.

"You sure?" There was a faint edge of distrust in his voice.

32

"Dr. Kolmenn is. There's a ligature mark on the throat."

He looked at her grimly. "Anyone we know?"

"No one's recognized him so far. He might be local but I don't think so," she said. "I should have an ID once I get his effects to the lab."

Sharpe resented the fact they didn't have the budget for their own crime lab. They had to pay a fee to use the sheriff's and he hated having to give anything to Arnie Voxx and his department.

"Okay," he said, "keep me up-to-date." He picked up a handful of papers from his desk and began to read, signaling their meeting was over.

Sure, I'll wake you up when I have something.

"I'll keep you posted," Molly replied.

Sharpe didn't bother to look up as she left.

~

With the build and intensity of a Navy Seal, Kurt Harbou didn't look the part of a crime tech. He was six two and as thick as a linebacker for the Packers, the kind of guy you'd want on your side in a bar fight. But when he handled evidence his gloved fingers worked with a delicate precision and he had a sharp eye for detail.

Kurt removed the victim's clothing from the bags Molly handed over. He folded the clear plastic bags and set them aside. He would examine them later for any trace evidence that might have come off during transportation.

He arranged the socks, underwear, pants, undershirt, shirt, sweater, parka, mittens, and a pair of waterproof Rockport shoes on a stainless steel bench. Next these he set an Omega wristwatch, an expensive fountain pen, a pair of reading glasses, and a small notebook.

"I'll need to dry this stuff off first to see if I can lift anything."

Kurt picked up the pants and removed a damp wallet from the right rear pocket. He pulled a room key card from the front pocket and showed it to Molly.

'Property of Great North Resort' was embossed on it.

Kurt continued his search. He found a ring of keys and held up a thick black one with a stylized 'T'.

"Toyota. Late model," he said.

Molly made notes as he itemized the rest of the contents from the victim's pockets.

"Canadian Passport, four gigabyte flash drive, Canadian and U.S. coins," he continued.

She wrote 'Canadian' and resisted the temptation to add 'eh'.

Kurt opened the wallet, revealing credit and other cards. She saw an Ontario driver's license in a clear window. Kurt flipped it over to show a government issued health card. The pictures on both matched the victim.

She wrote down the name – Barry Elkins.

Elkins' wallet was filled with Canadian and U.S. bills. She estimated there was a couple of hundred dollars of each currency.

From the amount of cash and the expensive watch, Molly didn't think robbery had been the motive.

Kurt held the notebook up by its edge and set it aside.

"I'd like to freeze dry this before I open it."

From the book's soggy appearance Molly figured anything written in it was probably illegible.

She wondered about next of kin. Molly couldn't remember if Elkins had been wearing a wedding band. She made note to ask Kolmenn.

They couldn't find a cell phone. It was possible he didn't carry one but she doubted it. She'd look when she searched Elkins' hotel room. She had enough to get started for now.

"I'll dust everything and lift prints for you," Kurt said. "If I find anything else that's odd or interesting, I'll let you know right away."

Molly nodded. "Open the passport for me again would you. I want to copy the emergency contact info."

Kurt showed Molly the front page.

> Name: Barry Elkins
> Nationality: Canadian
> DOB: 5 July / 58

He flipped the page over. Elkins had listed his brother as the contact. *No wife?*

Molly wrote down Richard Elkins' Toronto phone number. She'd need to notify him of his brother's death. This was the part of the job every cop hated. Unfortunately it had to be done – and this was the only way to obtain a positive ID.

Molly would make the call when she got back to the station.

SEVEN

"Campbell, Lloyd, and Barnes." The receptionist's voice was professional and efficient.

"Could I speak to Richard Elkins, please," Molly said.

"Mr. Elkins isn't taking calls right now. Can I take a message?"

"Sorry, but it's an urgent family matter. Please, let him know Molly Parsons from the Sunset Michigan Police Department is calling?"

A few seconds later Richard Elkins picked up. "Yes?" His voice betrayed a hint of trepidation as if he knew bad news was coming.

"Mr. Elkins, my name is Molly Parsons. I'm an investigator with the Sunset, Michigan, Police Department. I'm afraid I have some bad news concerning your brother Barry."

"Has there been an accident?" he asked anxiously. "Is he hurt?"

Molly didn't drag it out. "I regret to inform you that your brother has passed away."

Silence.

"Barry's dead?" His voice was shaky.

"Yes, Sir." She paused. "He was the victim of a murder last night here in Sunset."

The silence was longer this time.

"What?" His voice was choked with emotion. "Was it a robbery?"

The reality of the situation was hitting him. The numbness of grief would follow later. Molly knew that kind of grief. It was a pain he would carry with him every day for the rest of his life.

"We don't think so," she said. "The only thing which seems to be missing is his cell phone. Could you tell me what type of phone he carried?"

"A BlackBerry, I think." There was a catch in Elkins' voice. "He had it out at dinner last week. I'm certain it was a BlackBerry. One of the new ones with a touch screen."

"Was your brother married?"

"No, he was divorced a long time ago."

"Is there someone else we should contact? His ex-wife or children?"

"He didn't have any children," he replied. "I'll call Linda."

"We need you or someone from the family to come here and make a formal identification."

"Where did you say you were located?"

"Sunset, Michigan. We're on Lake Michigan about an hour north of Traverse City."

"Is there an airport near there?"

"Yes, Sir," she answered. "We have a small commuter airport right here in town. You can get an American Eagle flight from Detroit. They fly here twice a day."

"I'll try to get a flight in the morning," he said. "I'd like to start making arrangements to bring him back home."

"I can't say for certain when he'll be released. That's up to the coroner."

More silence.

Molly glanced down at her notes.

"Campbell, Lloyd, and Barnes. Is that an accounting firm?"

"No, we're a legal firm. I'm a senior partner. We specialize in corporate law."

Oh great, a lawyer.

"Is there anything else, Officer Parsons?"

"No, Sir, not right now. However, I may have some more questions for you tomorrow."

There was a long silence and she thought he'd hung up.

"Thank you for calling," he said softly and disconnected.

As Molly set the phone down she noticed Booster was heading towards Sharpe's office. She waved him over.

"You heard our drowning last night is a murder?"

Booster nodded. "The Chief told me."

Yes, of course he did since you're his little lap dog.

36

She wondered what they were up to but decided to give it a pass. She needed Booster's help with this.

Paul Booster had been a friend. They once had a great working relationship and shared a mutual respect. However, when she'd returned to Sunset she found him petulant and resentful. She tried to empathize with him. He'd taken over her responsibilities and, from all reports, had done a good job. By the time fifteen months had gone by he'd assumed the position was his. Her return drove a huge wedge between them. It was a wedge Kenton Sharpe used to his advantage.

Booster was a thorough investigator but lacked imagination. Although too quick to arrive at conclusions he was good with crime scenes. He took his time and didn't miss small details. She'd get him working on finding out exactly where the killing had occurred.

As soon as murder had been established she'd ordered deputies to put crime scene tape across the entrances to the walkway and the stairs leading down from the bridge. Hopefully they'd been quick enough to prevent any evidence from being lost.

"He was strangled and ended up in the channel," she explained. "I need you to go down there and take a look around. Figure out where it happened and then lock it down for forensics."

"That's a big area," Booster said. "He could have gone into the water anywhere in the harbor or along the channel."

She smiled.

"That's true but I think it most likely happened along the walkway. It's close to his hotel and it's also deserted at that time of night."

"I'll take a look," Booster muttered with little enthusiasm.

He stopped by his desk and grabbed his jacket off the back of the chair. He looked across at Sharpe's office. The door was closed. It appeared as if he was contemplating going in to see the chief but thought better of it and walked out the door instead.

Molly realized she hadn't asked Richard Elkins what type of car his brother drove. She was still rusty and should have written out a list of questions in advance. She'd been anxious about the distasteful task of notifying him of his brother's death and it had slipped her mind.

Don't worry. You'll find your groove again.

She thought about motive. The quickest way to solve a murder was to discover the reason. To Molly the most likely reasons for killing someone were greed, lust, or being in the wrong place at the wrong time. She'd already ruled out robbery.

A crime of passion might make sense. She wondered if Elkins was involved with someone from town.

Why the hell would he come here at this time of year – a long distance romance, a married woman?

This didn't feel like a crime of passion. From her experience that kind of murder normally happened in the heat of the moment and was usually fueled by emotion and alcohol.

This was different. The method was calculated and clinical.

Maybe wrong place, wrong time?

Perhaps he naively stumbled onto something. She knew some of the local fishermen smuggled in dope from Canada. The Coast Guard had made a large bust just a couple of months ago, seizing several hundred pounds of pot and thousands of tabs of Ecstasy.

Unfortunately Barry Elkins couldn't tell them what he saw. However, there was someone who might be able to – Tony Huffner. Before he fished Elkins' body out of the water he'd been hanging around the entrance to the channel. If Elkins had seen something there was a good chance Tony would've seen it as well. She'd have to ask Tony about this when he came in to make his statement.

From their conversation last night she was already convinced he wasn't telling the whole truth. His story was flimsy.

Tony Huffner definitely had more to tell her.

EIGHT

The Great North Resort was located just off Main Street, a few hundred feet north of the bridge. It was booked solid from the end of May through to Labor Day. At this time of year, however, there were only a couple of cars in the parking lot and the place looked sad and lonely.

Who the hell would book in here during the off season?

Molly made a quick sweep of the parking lot and noted one of the cars was a late model Toyota Camry with an Ontario plate.

The lobby smelled of burnt coffee. Someone had tried to mask it with a strong pine-scented spray but that obviously hadn't worked. The carpet was salt-stained from the front door to the reception desk. It needed a thorough cleaning. The information racks on the counter had only a few brochures left over from last summer.

Peggy Galligan, the desk clerk, looked up and smiled as Molly entered. She set down the paperback she'd been reading to cut the boredom. Molly recognized the cover of 'The Girl with the Dragon Tattoo'. She'd read it herself a couple of years ago but had been turned off by its brutality. She saw enough of that in real life.

Peggy had been a grade ahead of her in school and had never left Sunset. Her husband Patrick was a butcher at Glen's Market. They'd gotten married right after they graduated when Peggy discovered she was two months pregnant. Molly didn't know them all that well. They'd been part of the crowd who ignored her.

"Afternoon, Peggy."

"Molly," Peggy replied looking at her warily. She knew this wasn't going to be a social visit.

"I'm hoping you can help me out. I need to get some information about one of your guests."

"I'll get Daryl for you," Peggy replied.

Daryl Simms was the general manager. Molly had been on the library committee with him a couple of years ago and she knew he embodied fastidiousness. She guessed this was a good trait in a hotel manager but probably a pain in the ass for her as an investigator.

Daryl had changed since she'd last seen him. His cocky arrogance was gone, replaced by defeat. She knew the Great North was owned by a large conglomerate and Daryl had been sent here to generate more profit from the property. While most of the other resorts and hotels in Sunset closed for the off season, Daryl's bosses had insisted he find ways to create new revenue in the winter months.

He'd tried a number of different promotions over the past two years, starting with a romantic Champagne and Roses Weekend Special around Valentine's Day. This was killed off by an intense blizzard which made the highway impassable. During the Snowmobiler's Special the following winter, the weather conspired against him again by producing the highest temperatures and least amount of snowfall in over fifty years.

It seemed like everything he tried didn't work.

Daryl had come to Sunset as a stepping stone for his career. It now appeared to be his permanent backwater. She imagined he must hate northern Michigan by now.

"Molly, I understand you want to know about a guest. Would it be Mr. Elkins?"

"That's right."

He nodded. "Our housekeeper mentioned his bed hadn't been slept in when she went in this morning. We heard about the drowning last night. I figured it might be him."

Molly was annoyed. "You should've called me, Daryl."

"Well, you know … " he replied wearily.

"That his Camry out in the parking lot?"

"Yeah." Daryl consulted the computer on the desk. "2010 Camry, gray, Ontario plate number ACDH415. He checked in three nights ago and took a suite for a week."

Molly made notes and underlined 'a week'.

"Did he mention what he was planning to do while he was in town?" she asked Peggy and Daryl.

Peggy shook her head. "The room was booked through Expedia and he checked in after I went home. We close up at five this time of year."

"So how did he get into his room?"

"We sent him an email to let him know his room key would be in the mailbox at the side entrance. We gave him the access code to unlock that door."

"You mean there's no one here at night?"

"That's right," Daryl replied. "It doesn't pay to have someone on the desk."

"Is that safe?"

Daryl held up his hands. "We have a state-of-the-art alarm system and monitored cameras throughout the property. The security company sends someone down from their Petoskey office twice a night to make rounds inside the hotel."

Molly asked for the name of the security company. She made a note to contact them for the CCTV footage from the last few nights.

"I'd like to have a look inside his room."

Daryl hesitated. "I'm not sure I can do that, Molly. We have to protect our guests' privacy here."

"Mr. Elkins is dead and we're pretty certain he was murdered," she sighed. "We need to have forensics check over the room."

She let the implication hang in the air. She could see Daryl was weighing it — demand a search warrant to protect a guest's privacy or be seen as interfering with a murder investigation.

"Give me a second and I'll get the master key," he said and went into the back office.

~

In the hall outside Barry Elkins' suite Molly slipped on vinyl gloves and disposable booties. Daryl handed her the key card. She slid it into the slot above the handle and pushed the door open with her fingertips. From the entryway she looked into the bedroom. The bed, as housekeeping had mentioned, was undisturbed.

Cautioning Daryl to stay in the hall she walked through the bedroom into the living room/kitchenette area. It was cold in the suite; the heat was turned way down. The coffee table in front of the couch was piled with books. She didn't recognize any of the titles or authors. The remotes for the television and DVD player were still on the credenza under the flat screen. It didn't look like he'd watched much TV.

The room overlooked Main Street. It offered a great view of downtown and part of the harbor. This would be an expensive suite in season, at least three or four hundred a night. She wondered what it went for at this time of year.

A laptop sat on the table with a yellow legal pad and a bowl of popcorn. The kitchen looked unused. A half full bottle of single malt scotch was in the cupboard along with a pound of dark roast coffee. In the refrigerator was a container of hazelnut flavored coffee cream.

There was nothing out of place in the bedroom or bathroom. Elkins' clothes hung in the closet. Socks and underwear were neatly arranged in the top dresser drawer. His leather toiletry bag was still zipped.

She opened it carefully. It was filled with the kinds of items any traveler would carry – deodorant, toothpaste, after shave, shampoo. There was also blood pressure medication and a small package of Advil PM.

There was no BlackBerry. He may have left it in the car. Although she doubted it, she would look anyway.

Molly backed out of the suite and shut the door. She stuck an official crime scene seal across the door jamb which she signed and dated.

Daryl looked at the large sticker in dismay. He wondered if the frame and door would have to be repainted.

Molly smiled. "Don't worry, Daryl. The glue will come off with soap and warm water."

He looked relieved.

Of course she had no idea whether or not soap and water would remove the glue.

"Kurt Harbou, the crime technician from the sheriff's office, will be over in a little while. He'll probably take some things back to the lab. We'll also tow the car to the impound garage."

"Will he damage the room in any way?" Daryl asked.

"No. He'll just photograph everything and then have Mr. Elkins' personal belongings removed," she explained. "Kurt will dust for fingerprints we'll also need to take prints from anyone on your staff who had access to the room."

"That should be no problem. I'll let the staff know."

He paused for a second.

"How long do you think it'll be before we can use the room again?"

"I don't know, maybe a couple of days," she replied. "Why? Are you expecting a lot of business?"

"No," he said wistfully.

Molly removed the booties and gloves and they walked back to the lobby.

Daryl and Peggy looked shaken. This was probably the first time violent death had touched either one of them.

It was always an unwelcome visitor.

She thought again about the missing cell phone.

Where are you and what can you tell me?

Molly suspected it was at the bottom of the channel.

NINE

It was Whitefish Special Night at The Villager and the place was packed. Hank Summerville dropped by Molly's table to say hello. She showed him a picture of Elkins which had been enlarged from his driver's license photo.

"Recognize him?" Molly asked.

"Yeah, he was in a couple of times," Hank replied. "Is that your victim?"

Molly nodded and passed him the photo.

"Could you show it around to see if anyone else recognizes him?"

Hank's daughter Jennie appeared beside him with a menu. She waited tables part-time after school. Hank's only child was the center of his life after his wife passed away several years before. Molly remembered Jennie had been a handful when she was younger – the proverbial spoiled brat.

At eighteen she had matured into a pretty young woman. She was five eight, the same height as Molly, with auburn hair and sparkling green eyes tempered with just a hint of sadness. They flashed with recognition as Hank showed her the photo.

"He was in on Sunday for dinner. Desirée waited on him. I think he ordered a cheeseburger and fries." Jennie struggled to remember. "And a couple of pints."

"What time was that?" Molly asked.

"Well, I was here through the dinner rush and he came in a little after that. Maybe 8:30 or 8:45. I left at 9:00 and he was still here."

"Thanks, Jennie. That's a real help."

Molly ordered the special with a side salad and a pint of Wolverine. *What the hell, I'm off duty now.*

Earlier she'd gone by the office to pick up Kolmenn's preliminary report. He had written 'enjoy' on the cover page.

God, he's such a ghoul.

Molly started to read the report while waiting for her meal to arrive but stopped when she heard a soft twang from a guitar. Desirée Platt sat on the small stage Hank had set up at the back of the restaurant. The note was flat at first, changing into something more pleasant as she twisted the peg and tightened the string.

Molly walked to the stage and held up another photo of Elkins.

Desirée looked at the picture. "He was in for breakfast a couple of mornings ago."

"Was it Friday or Saturday?"

Desirée thought for a moment. "I'm pretty sure it was Saturday. I remember he looked like crap. You know, like he hadn't slept much."

"Was he alone?"

"Yeah, he was," she said. "Just had coffee and toast. Spent a lot of time checking his email."

"On his cell?"

"Yup."

"Can you describe his phone?"

"It was one of those with a sliding keyboard. I'm not sure what kind it was." As an excuse for not knowing she added, "I don't have a cell phone."

"Did he stay long?"

"No, not long. Maybe half an hour. He looked like he had somewhere to go."

"What time did he leave?"

"Well, he came in after the breakfast rush around 9:30 and I think he was gone a little after ten. I didn't see him leave. The money was on the table."

"Jennie mentioned that you also waited on him on Sunday evening."

Desirée smiled. "That's right he came in for dinner."

"Do you remember what time he left?" Molly asked.

"It was just before we closed."

"How was he when he left?"

"He seemed fine. Wasn't drunk or anything."

Desirée finished tuning her guitar and set it down in its stand.

"What time are you playing?"

"In a few minutes," Desirée said. "Are you going to stick around?"

Molly saw Jennie come out of the kitchen with her dinner.

"Yeah," she replied, "I'm looking forward to hearing you."

Molly thanked Desirée for the information and went back to her table.

~

Molly was thinking of ordering another pint when an excited Paul Booster rushed into The Villager.

"Looks like you could use a beer," she offered.

Booster shook his head and she remembered he didn't drink.

"I wouldn't mind something to eat though," he said.

She asked for another beer for herself. He ordered the house burger, heavy on the cheese and bacon, with fries and a chocolate milkshake. At twenty five he was in peak condition but it wouldn't last if he kept eating like this.

In ten years he'll have a pot belly and be cruising into coronary alley.

Molly could tell he was anxious to reveal what he'd learned.

"Well?"

"Okay, so Elkins is a big guy, right? At least two twenty five?"

She nodded.

"He could've put up a real fight. So whoever killed him got the jump on him."

Molly agreed with his logic.

"It means the killer was hiding close by and sneaks up behind Elkins and loops the cord around his neck. Then he puts his knee in Elkins' back and uses the guy's own weight to strangle him. That would explain the small bruise at the base of Elkins' spine."

What small bruise on Elkins' back?

Molly was confused.

How did he know something she didn't?

Then it hit her.

Son of a bitch. He read the post mortem on my desk before I picked it up.

Obviously, Ronnie Kolmenn had found a bruise on the victim's back.

Molly felt a stab of anger in her gut but pushed it down.

Better not to let him know he just fucked up.

"Where's the best spot for someone to hide along the walkway and not be seen?"

She was already ahead of him. "Under the bridge."

"Right," he replied eagerly. "And there are some scuff marks on the walkway and a scrape on top of the railing. Some of the paint was scratched off. Could've been a zipper or maybe a fingernail."

"It would take a lot for someone to scrape away paint with a fingernail," she said. "I'd bet on the zipper."

She made a mental note to call Kurt in the morning and ask him to take a close look at the victim's parka, especially the zipper.

"Anyway, the coroner thinks the body had been in the water for about an hour. That would make sense. It's about a quarter mile from the bridge to the mouth of the channel. With the strength of the current, it would take about that long to make it to where Huffner fished him out. He must have been murdered under the bridge."

She had to admit Booster was smart and thorough. There was no doubt in her mind that he was right about where the murder took place. Now they just needed to learn why Elkins had been killed.

Desirée began to play.

Molly was impressed. Desirée's voice had a raw sweetness which reminded her of Joni Mitchell. Molly glanced at Booster. Captivated, he'd set down his burger.

Desirée was the whole package. She had the looks, the talent, and the drive. Molly could imagine a time years from now when she would tell people she'd seen Desirée Platt performing in the back of a small-town restaurant.

She noticed Booster's eyes never left the stage. When the set ended half an hour later he went over to talk to Desirée.

Hank brought Molly coffee and a piece of fresh baked apple pie.

"I got people asking what nights she's performing," he said. "Best of all, I only pay her to waitress. She begged me to let her play."

Hank's eyes shifted to the front door as two men entered. "Shit," he muttered.

Molly saw what caught his attention. The first man through the door was Brian Haley. The second was Tony Huffner.

Haley was trouble – drunken brawls, DUIs, petty mischief. He was a bad news package from a wealthy family.

"I thought he was at State," she said.

Hank shook his head. "He got kicked out just after the semester started."

Haley reminded her of one of those Abercrombie and Fitch models. He was all rugged good looks; six pack abs, and not much else.

Haley's grandfather had come to Sunset in the late nineteen fifties. He'd developed most of the prime resort and vacation property around the area. Molly remembered hearing about Lucas Haley when she was a child. He had a reputation as a ruthless bastard who bullied his way into power. When he died in the late nineties more than one person around town had suggested they drive a stake through his heart just to make sure he stayed dead.

Lucas had two children, Jake and Ruthie. Jake, Brian's father, took over the family business after the old man died. Ruthie married Foster March, the drunken scion of one of Sunset's wealthiest families.

Jake Haley worked hard to be the antithesis of his father. While Lucas Haley had been cunning, Jake was intelligent. People liked and respected him. After expanding the family business into lumber and other interests, Jake decided he wanted to give something back. He entered politics and had been a state senator for the past fifteen years.

Brian, his only child, was one apple who'd fallen far from the tree. He was typical of third generation wealth. Brian had a nasty sense of entitlement and privilege. The rules didn't apply to him. He inherited all of his grandfather's meanness and none of his father's intelligence. He moved like a disease through Sunset, leaving wreckage in his wake.

His father bailed him out of scrape after scrape and grieved that somehow he'd failed Brian. In reality Brian Haley was just a mean little prick.

Molly watched as Haley stood at the bar and downed his beer in a few gulps. He picked up a second one and did the same. His feral eyes locked on Desirée, who was sharing a joke with Booster. Hank positioned himself behind the bar and motioned his bartender not to serve Haley any more drinks.

Haley slammed his empty glass onto the bar. He started to move toward Desirée and Booster.

Molly stepped in front of him.

"Not a good idea to pick a fight with someone carrying a gun."

"Fuck you, Bitch," he growled at Molly.

The Villager went silent around them, like a barroom did just before a brawl in a John Wayne movie.

Grabbing his left ear and pulling him forward, Molly slammed her knee hard into his groin. Haley doubled over in pain with a howl. Still pinching his ear, Molly walked him from the restaurant into the cold night air.

Molly leaned over Haley and said quietly, "The next time you talk to me like that I'll rip your balls off." Then she shoved him away from the entrance.

Still holding his crotch, Haley straightened up. Tony moved to his side, trying to take his arm and guide him away. Haley shook him off.

Booster came out of the restaurant and stood behind Molly.

"You cunt!" Haley pointed at Molly. "I'll have your badge for police brutality,"

"Police brutality," she laughed. "You don't even know how to spell it. Now, get the hell out of here or I'll throw your ass in jail."

Desirée stood next to Hank in the doorway.

Haley jabbed his finger in Booster's direction. "And stay the fuck away from my girlfriend you ass wipe!"

Booster moved up beside Molly. "Time to leave," he ordered.

Tony grabbed his buddy's arm and pulled him toward a red Ford Expedition. Haley leaned hard against the driver's door as he tried to unlock it.

Booster put his hand on Haley's to stop him. "You get behind the wheel and it'll be my pleasure to arrest you for DUI."

Haley turned toward Booster and cocked his fist.

"Brian, don't be an asshole," Desirée pleaded.

Haley allowed Tony to take his keys and guide him to the front passenger side. He got into the vehicle and turned his head away from the crowd on the sidewalk, staring defiantly in the other direction. Tony looked embarrassed as he slid behind the wheel. He started the truck and they drove off.

As Molly watched them leave she wondered about the relationship between Tony Huffner and Brian Haley.

Perhaps Tony hadn't been alone when he found Elkins' body.

TEN

The next morning Molly piloted her Zodiac across Little Lake Bay toward the town dock. As she got close she could see a lone figure holding two take-out coffee cups. He looked familiar and she tried to place him. Cutting the engine, she let the boat glide alongside the dock. She jumped out with the bow line in hand and tied it off to a cleat. With the Zodiac secured, she turned to greet the stranger.

Now she knew why he looked familiar.

"Mr. Elkins?"

Richard Elkins nodded. "They told me at the police station you were on your way."

He handed Molly one of the cups. "I didn't know how you take it. I have cream and sugar," he said taking the packets from his jacket pocket.

"Thanks," she said gratefully. "Just black is fine." She removed the plastic top and steam rose into the chill morning air.

"I managed to get an early morning flight out of Detroit," Elkins explained in a modulated, even tone.

Richard Elkins was dressed in expensive slacks and a turtleneck sweater. He wore a green waxed cotton coat. It reminded her of an old-fashioned hunting jacket. He had the same build as his brother, even a similar graying beard. However, he was a little thinner and looked like he worked out.

Elkins said. "I have a rental car just over there."

~

On the way to the hospital Molly called ahead so the attendant would have things prepared for the formal ID. Unlike in the movies, identification wasn't a process of sliding open morgue drawers and lifting sheets. The body was on a table and an overhead camera broadcast the image to a monitor in a private room. The next of kin could ask for a personal viewing, but most preferred the distance this process allowed.

Molly flipped a switch and an image filled the screen.

Richard nodded with a pained expression. "That's Barry," he said quietly.

Molly turned off the monitor. She wrote down the date and the time before making a short note the victim's identity had been confirmed by his brother.

"You look alike," she said.

"We're twins," Richard said. "I'm about fifteen minutes older."

"It must have been hard to tell you apart."

"Oh, we're different all right … ," his voice trailed off uncomfortably. He turned and moved toward the door. "I'd like to get out of here now."

"We can go back to the station," Molly suggested. "I need you to sign a statement."

"Could we get breakfast first?" he asked.

~

The August Diner had the best breakfast in town. Located in a small strip mall off Oleson's parking lot, it was just a block from the police station. The August liked to brag it hadn't changed a thing since nineteen sixty eight – except the prices, of course. It was still crowded, hot, and narrow. None of the vinyl upholstery on the stools lining the counter was intact. Costas, the owner, just kept repairing them with red tape. The once white Masonite tabletops in the booths were now an ugly shade of gray. The passage of years had been marked in coffee cup rings and mustard stains.

The breakfast rush was in full swing when they entered but Molly found a booth in the back. Costas appeared with a coffee pot and filled two mugs. Molly asked for dry rye toast and orange juice. Elkins ordered the special: eggs and bacon with home fries.

"I'm surprised you have an appetite," she said.

"They didn't serve breakfast on the plane. I'm starving."

He asked about the Zodiac and she explained it was the fastest way for her to get into town.

"It's ten minutes by boat but twenty if I drive."

"What do you do in the winter, use a snowmobile to get across?"

"No, I can't. Little Lake Bay has to be kept open for the ferry and Coast Guard vessels. The city uses a small icebreaker to keep it clear. I just drive in."

Costas brought their breakfast and walked away.

Elkins cleared his plate in ten minutes. Molly, always a slow eater, was still nibbling the toast on which she'd spread homemade raspberry jam.

Elkins put his coffee down. "If my brother wasn't robbed then why do you think he was murdered?"

"Well, we have some evidence which seems to indicate he was ambushed by his killer. I'm not sure, but it looks like he might have seen something he wasn't supposed to. We have a fair amount of drug smuggling on this part of the coast."

Molly took out her notebook. She wrote the date and time at the top of a new page.

"It would help if I knew why your brother was here in the first place. April is an odd time to visit. Most tourists come in the summer."

"Yes, I was surprised about it, too. When we talked last week, he didn't mention he was coming up here."

"Did he know someone here?" she asked.

Elkins shook his head. "Not anyone I'm aware of. He never mentioned this place."

"How did he seem when you last talked to him?"

Elkins thought for a few seconds. When he spoke there was a catch in his voice.

"He was excited. He was about to begin a year's sabbatical from the university. I think he was planning to write another book. Maybe he was looking for some place quiet to do his research."

Dr. Barry Elkins had been a professor of literature at the University of Toronto. She had Googled him after Kurt Harbou sent over a scan of the faculty ID card which had been in his wallet.

"It's at least a seven or eight hour drive from Toronto. It seems like a long way to go for solitude."

Elkins shrugged. "My brother had his reasons for doing things. They didn't always make sense to me, but that's who he was."

She caught a note of disapproval in his voice.

"But you got along okay?"

"We did, but we were very different people. He didn't approve of my corporate career. I was a sell-out in his eyes. Of course, I never understood how he could spend his life teaching bored students the meaning and relevance of contemporary poetry."

For some reason Molly found herself underlining 'poetry' in her notes. Something about the word had resonated in her subconscious.

"Can you think of anyone who might've wanted to harm him – his ex-wife, a student, a lover? Someone like that?"

"No one he mentioned. I'm sure he failed students. He had extremely high standards. The university might have some record of students who complained."

There was a flurry of shouted Greek. Costas bashed the side of an ancient toaster which was jammed with burning toast. Black smoke poured out of the slots.

"Is there any update on when I can take him home?"

"We can't release the body until the coroner signs off on it. I'll ask Dr. Kolmenn when he thinks he'll be ready to do that. It should be within the next few days."

More loud Greek came from the kitchen area. Costas seemed to be losing his battle with the toaster.

"Will you be going back to Toronto right away?" she asked.

He shook his head. "I've booked a hotel room until the end of the week."

"At the Great Northern?" she asked.

"That's right. It must be a popular place."

"At this time of year it's the only place," Molly said with a grin.

Elkins didn't return the smile. Instead he took a small notebook from his jacket pocket and flipped through the pages. "And his car?"

"Our crime tech is going over it today. If he doesn't find anything I'll sign it over to you tomorrow."

Satisfied, he put the notebook away.

"Can you tell me a little about your brother?" Molly asked. "Sometimes it helps if I can get a better picture of who a person was."

Elkins gave her a strange look. This wasn't an odd request but he seemed to hesitate. She could see he was calculating what he should say. She remembered he was an attorney.

Typical lawyer – always trying to anticipate the next line of questioning.

"We were close as children. Twins tend to be like that, as if they're one person shared between two bodies. When we got older Barry was determined to split that bond. If I did something, he would do the opposite."

"Sounds painful."

Molly thought of her own family. She had four brothers and was the youngest. Her father had been strict, especially with her. Everything in her family revolved around winning approval from him. This had crushed her mother and two of her brothers. After her mother died, the family had fragmented. Now they were strangers. They never made an attempt to see each other. It helped keep the bad memories at bay.

"I didn't understand why," Elkins continued. "By the time we got to university we had moved even further apart. I chose law and Barry decided to study literature. I graduated and took a job with a large corporate firm.

"After Barry graduated, he threw himself into sex and drugs for a while. He eventually settled down, got married, and went to grad school. Barry really became passionate about twentieth century literature, poetry in particular."

Again, something stirred in Molly. It nagged like a popcorn husk stuck between her teeth. She couldn't quite get to it and she had to force herself to focus on what Elkins was saying.

"He took his thesis and rewrote it in less academic terms. When the book was published it was so well received it became a popular text for literature courses. With that success the university offered him a teaching position.

"Even though Barry joined the establishment, I still represented everything he didn't believe in. Whenever we got together, it turned into an argument. Usually over the latest evil the corporate world had committed. I represented the ultimate in conformity. It scared him."

"Scared him? How so?"

"No matter how wide he felt the chasm between us was, he couldn't break away. I think he wanted what I had. Maybe I wanted some of what he had."

He paused.

That would explain the beard.

As if sensing her thought, he ran his thumb along the bottom of his moustache.

"We mellowed a bit. We were both successful in our careers but the tension was still there. I respected that he became a university professor …"

"But he didn't respect you," she finished his thought.

Elkins nodded. "I don't think so."

She detected a note of bitterness in his answer. Maybe it was regret. Either way, he would always carry that feeling with him.

"I'm going to do everything I can to find out who killed your brother but I need all the help I can get," she said gently.

He looked at her gratefully.

"I would like your permission to get his cell phone records so I can see who he was in touch with after he arrived here."

"It shouldn't be a problem. I have power of attorney. I'll make a call and get the records released."

"Thanks it would save a lot of time."

Molly gave him her card and told him he could call anytime.

Elkins paid the bill and they went their separate ways.

Molly walked back to the station. On the way she made a quick call to Kurt Harbou. The Camry had arrived at the garage and he was going to begin examining it in a few minutes. She asked him to hold off until she got there.

She considered Richard Elkins' relationship with his brother for a few seconds. There was a definite distance between the two brothers. But from the way he acted it didn't seem to be murderous animosity. It was more like sibling rivalry pushed up a few notches.

While she didn't seriously consider him a suspect, she would ask Customs and Border Protection to run a search on Richard Elkins' name to see if he'd entered the country over the weekend. In her mind, however, it was just a T which needed crossing.

ELEVEN

Kurt Harbou had removed the Tom Tom GPS unit from the center console of Elkins' Camry. He handed the bag to Molly.

"It's likely that it's still charged."

She held up the bag, examining the contents. "What about prints?"

"I'll dust it now so you can take it with you."

They walked back to his office. Taking the unit out of the bag, Kurt placed it on the bench. He angled a light to reveal fingerprints on the touch screen. He set up his camera and shot a series of photos from different angles.

Using a fiber brush and soft strokes, he applied white powder to the screen and other surfaces. Kurt lifted the prints with a special tape and applied each piece to a dark backing card to make the swirls and ridges stand out. He flipped them over, filled out the identifying details form, and signed each one to preserve the chain of evidence.

He put the GPS back into the evidence bag and handed it to Molly. Then they returned to the garage.

"He kept his car really clean," Kurt said.

Molly glanced in and could see there was none of the usual debris people tended to accumulate in their vehicles. The center console contained a couple of unmarked CDs. She guessed they were music discs and wondered what Elkins' preferred. If she accepted the stereotype of the pipe smoking professor, it would be classical or modern jazz. At his age, however, it was likely to be sixties and seventies rock. To satisfy her curiosity she asked Kurt to give her a list of their contents.

There were several gas receipts in the glove compartment; one from a BP station in Flint, another from a station in Sunset. The one from Sunset was dated three days ago. There was nothing in the trunk other than a couple of reusable shopping bags from a store called 'Loblaws'. There was a grocery receipt at the bottom of one of the bags. Junk food and frozen dinners seemed to be his regular diet. She would take a closer look at the autopsy report to see what kind of shape his heart was in.

~

When Molly returned to the office it was just after noon. All was quiet. Everyone was out for lunch except for the lone dispatcher eating her sandwich.

At her desk, Molly turned on the GPS. As Kurt Harbou predicted, the battery was fully charged. She touched the screen and a menu appeared. She selected 'Navigate To' from the options and opened a submenu. Under 'Recent Destinations', a list of addresses appeared.

She began writing down the addresses.

Interesting. The three most recent were right here in Sunset.

One on State Street, another on Popular Street, and the third was a lot number on Shadow Lake.

The first two addresses she recognized. She would have to use the GPS in her cruiser to locate the third one out on the lake.

TWELVE

After lunch Molly drove to the first of the addresses on Elkins' GPS, the one on State Street. She knew the address well. It was the Sunset Library.

The library had been built with federal government stimulus money in 2010. It was huge, out of proportion to a town the size of Sunset. Molly had been on the library board at the time it was proposed Sunset replace their aging Carnegie Library with something modern. The result was an attractive brick building almost a block long. The main reading room ran the length of the library and felt like the inside of a church. Large windows filled the space with natural light. Arts and Craft style wooden detailing made the space warm and intimate. Running right angle to the reading room was a series of smaller spaces dedicated to the area's history and literary tradition.

If Molly could describe any memory from her childhood as fond it was the hours she'd spent in the nurturing environment of the old Sunset Library. It was her place of escape. Here she felt safe and protected surrounded by thousands of books. Her father had preached against the evils of the printed-word and the free-thinking it inspired. The only book they'd had in their house was the bible.

As Molly entered the building she realized what had been nagging at her – the poet Aubrey Colgate Jones. He was the closest thing to a celebrity the town had ever produced. His poetry was still studied in many college courses and one of the side rooms had been dedicated to his memory.

Julia Harre, the library director, was waiting for Molly at the main checkout desk. They had known each since childhood.

"You finally got around to visiting us," Julia said with a warm smile.

Tall and lithe, she'd been a champion volleyball player in high school. She had married her college sweetheart, Tim, who owned the drug store on the main street.

This library was Julia's life. She had succeeded her mother Barbara and was fiercely protective of her domain. Julia was driven by a need to bury the stereotype of a librarian as a bookish old maid. She did not like the term 'head librarian'. Her official title was 'Director of Libraries for Sunset County'. She was forthright in her opinions, which had gotten her into trouble from time to time. However, she was adept at using her considerable charm to get what she wanted and to defuse conflict.

"Sorry, I've been really busy since I got back," Molly apologized. "By the way, how's your mom?"

From the expression of dismay on Julia's face, Molly regretted asking.

Barbara Harre had been one of the pivotal figures in Molly's childhood. In the safe haven of the library Barbara had welcomed and encouraged her, suggesting books which ignited Molly's lifelong curiosity about how the world worked both in a natural sense and in a human one. Reading was still her favorite escape and she had Barbara to thank for it.

"They're trying her on a new medication. We'll see how it goes."

Julia's mother had been diagnosed with Alzheimer's several years ago and had been steadily slipping away. Molly remembered Barbara as a vibrant person and had a hard time imagining her in the grip of this insidious living death.

She changed the subject.

"I need your help." Molly handed Julia a photo of Barry Elkins.

She studied it and nodded. "He was in a couple of days ago and spent a lot of time in the A.C.J. Room."

A.C.J. – Aubrey Colgate Jones.

She had been right.

"He requested access to our special collection of Jones' correspondence and notebooks. We don't normally do that, so I got involved. He showed me his academic identification from the University of Toronto. Turns out we have a couple of his books in our collection."

"So he spent time looking through the notebooks and letters then?"

"Well, no. We have a lot of items in storage. They need to be properly preserved. I made arrangements to have it brought up from the archives in the basement. He was going to come back today to look it over. He said he was working on a book about Jones. It was going to be some kind of literary biography. He offered to put us in touch with his publisher in New York if we needed confirmation."

"Did he mention who his publisher was?"

"I wrote it down. I can look it up for you."

"You said you had a couple of Elkins' books in the library. Could you get them for me?

"Sure, if they haven't been checked out."

Julia asked the young woman at the desk to see if the books were in the stacks and get them if they were.

~

The office was immaculate. Julia's formidable oak desk conformed to the overall Arts and Crafts style of the library, as did the two comfortable chairs facing it. Off to the side, was a small workstation next to a large bookcase, also in the same style. Windows ran the full length of the room. The space was inviting and comfortable. Molly knew this was deliberate. It was all about creating the right atmosphere. Julia's office was often the scene of tense negotiations with the staff union or the library board.

Julia opened her diary and showed Molly the notation she'd entered – Kepling and Sons. The telephone number beside it had a New York City area code.

"Thanks," Molly said.

"So what's going on? Is this guy legit? Julia asked. "Should I let him look at the material he requested?"

Molly told her about the murder and Julia's eyes widened at the news.

"How did he act when you were talking with him?"

"I don't know. Normal I guess. He talked a little fast, like he was a bit excited, but there was nothing strange I can remember."

There was a soft knock at the door and the librarian entered carrying two books. Molly could see a picture of a much younger Elkins on the back cover of one of them.

She had another thought. "Do you have anything by Jones?"

Molly had never read Jones' poetry. Her father would never have allowed that 'heathen fornicator's' works in his house.

"Not likely," Julia replied. "We have a long waiting list for his books."

"That's kind of unusual for a poet isn't it?"

"Not Aubrey Colgate Jones. If anything he's more popular today than ever before."

The young librarian spoke up. "His poems speak to our times. His vision was unique. He personified fear and loathing … "

"I thought that was Hunter Thompson," Molly commented facetiously.

The young librarian ignored her and continued enthusiastically. "Jones painted the landscapes with dread. He made nihilism almost beautiful."

"Thanks, Heather," Julia said dismissing her. After the girl left the room Julia raised her eyebrows. "Jones definitely inspires passion."

"Sure seems like it," Molly almost laughed.

"Greenwood's Bookmark usually has a good selection of his books," Julia said. "The tourists eat it up. There's nothing like reading a little Aubrey Colgate Jones at the beach. It counteracts the sun and fun really fast."

They walked from Julia's office to the entrance of the library.

"We should get together for dinner some evening," Julia said. Molly could tell she really didn't mean it.

Molly lied that they would. She wasn't going to be socializing any time soon.

She found it intriguing that Elkins had been planning a book on Aubrey Colgate Jones. Having vanished fifty years ago, he was Sunset's greatest unsolved mystery.

If, by dumb luck, Tony Huffner hadn't snagged the body when he did …

THIRTEEN

Sunset was normal for a town its size. It had at least one of everything. On the outskirts there was a Glen's Supermarket. It shared a parking lot with K Mart, the Co-op, a discount pharmacy, and a dollar store. Closer to town were the usual high-cholesterol joints – McDonald's, Wendy's, Pizza Hut, Dairy Queen – along with local favorites like Fletcher's Drive-In and King Kone.

This was where the highway became Main Street. There were a few blocks of houses and a public park next to the harbor. The downtown was three blocks long and ended at the bridge over the channel. On the other side of the bridge Main Street became Highway 31 again.

Most of the downtown businesses were seasonal. During the summer they sold a lot of T-shirts and ice cream. This time of year they were closed; their owners off somewhere sunny. The only stores which stayed open all year round were Burke's Hardware, the Rexall Drugstore, the Party Package Liquor Store, and Greenwood's Bookmark.

Molly parked across the street from The Bookmark. Ted Greenwood stood on the sidewalk outside his shop smoking a cigarette. He had been a fixture in town since Molly could remember. Ted had been a hero during the Korean War. There was a rumor he'd single-handedly killed an entire patrol of enemy soldiers. Molly had a hard time imagining it; Ted had the kindest eyes she'd ever seen. She saw his hand shake and wondered if it was early-onset Parkinson's.

He held up his cigarette. "Be right there, Molly."

"Take your time, Ted."

The shelves, which were crowded with paperbacks and hardcovers, hadn't been dusted in the last decade. There was a stale mustiness to the place and Molly detected the faint odor of fuel oil from the furnace in the basement.

Jones' books were part of a special display of local writers on a table in the back. She chose a couple and took them up front, adding a copy of that day's edition of The Sunset Examiner. She spent a few minutes catching up with Ted before returning to her Blazer.

~

The second address from Elkins' GPS was the grand Victorian home which housed the Sunset Historical Society. The Society's offices were only open to the public on Thursday afternoon during the off season. However, there was a local number to call to arrange an appointment.

The phone was answered on the second ring. "Yes? How may I help you?"

There was no mistaking Jonathan Drake's elegant voice with its cultured smoothness.

"Hello, Mr. Drake. It's Molly Parsons."

"Hello, Miss Parsons. I presume you would like to talk about the unfortunate Dr. Elkins."

Molly glanced down at The Examiner beside her on the seat. **MURDER** filled the top of the front page. Below the headline was the driver's license photo of Barry Elkins.

"I am just finishing my lunch. Why don't you come here at 2:00. We could talk then."

He didn't offer directions to his home. He didn't need to – everyone in town knew where Jonathan Drake lived.

"That would be fine, Sir. I'll see you then."

~

Following the last of Elkins' GPS coordinates, she drove north on Highway 31 and continued for a few miles until the unit instructed her to turn right onto a side road. She knew this road followed the north shoreline of Shadow Lake; it was the same road she lived on. Two miles beyond her place, the GPS indicated she had reached her destination.

Turning the Blazer onto a short road, Molly faced a serious looking gate. A sign announced 'No Trespassing' and that the property was monitored by security. The GPS map showed that beyond the gate there was a small point of land jutting into the lake. She got out of the Blazer and walked along the fence. It cut off the entire point and was at least a quarter of a mile long.

It must have cost a fortune.

The view beyond the fence was blocked by a thick grove of cedars.

The best way to see the point was from the water. Knowing she didn't have time before the meeting with Drake to get her Zodiac Molly decided she would swing by to take a look on her way home that evening.

She called Paul Booster and left a message asking him to run a check with the county records office to see who owned this parcel of land. The county office would confirm it, but Molly already had a good idea who it was.

Stone lain over water
Hastens the flow
Stones lain in the water
Make it deep below.

~ Aubrey Colgate Jones

FOURTEEN

Cufflink Hill was the only Frank Lloyd Wright house in this part of Michigan. It had been built for the Drake family as a vacation home in the late 1940s. Named for the high perch of land where it sat, the house was magnificent. Wright had designed it to make the best use of local wood and stone. Similar to Fallingwater in Pennsylvania, Cufflink Hill was built into the grade of the land, not imposed on top of it.

The house took its name from the business which had made a fortune for the family. The Drake Company was the largest manufacturer in the United States of cuff links and other men's fashion accessories. By the time their company was sold to a British clothing designer in 1975, it was worth hundreds of millions of dollars. Although their home and business were located in Boston, the Drake family had been spending their summers in Sunset since the 1920s.

Jonathan Drake moved to Sunset permanently in the late 1950s and was the closest they had to true aristocracy. He was rarely seen, except at the historical society where he gave occasional lectures on aspects of local history.

Drake answered the door and invited Molly in. He led her to a large comfortable living room. Golden panels of thick-cut pine gave the room a cozy ambience. A huge stone fireplace took up almost an entire wall. It was tall enough to walk into and there was a log as large as a tree trunk burning inside it.

Along the back of the house, floor to ceiling windows gave a spectacular view of Lake Michigan. From this vantage point you could see for fifty miles. Today, the lake looked dark and evil under a gunmetal sky as a storm moved in from the Wisconsin side. A few miles offshore Molly could see a freighter heading north toward Mackinaw at full steam, trying to stay ahead of the bad weather.

"Can I offer you anything? Coffee or a cold drink?" he asked.

"No thank you, Sir."

Molly liked Drake. In spite of his wealth he was unpretentious and set a person at ease.

The house was quiet. Molly noticed a small pile of hardcovers sitting next to a leather ottoman. She guessed Drake didn't get much company.

"I don't want to take up too much of your time, Sir." Molly took out her notebook. "Please tell me about Dr. Elkins' visit the other day."

"Dr. Elkins came for lunch on Saturday." Drake's voice was soft. "He wanted to ask me about Aubrey Colgate Jones. Apparently Elkins was preparing to write a book about Aubrey."

"Yes, so I understand." Molly said. "What did you discuss?"

"He wanted to know about Aubrey. I knew him personally, you see. In fact, I believe I am the last of Aubrey's friends still alive."

"Jones died sometime in the 1960s, didn't he?" Molly asked.

"Yes," Drake sighed. "He disappeared in the summer of 1963. It was a tragedy."

"I guess it was." Molly kept the impatience out of her voice.

"Perhaps a little background might help."

Drake motioned to a wooden bench running the length of the front window. She sank into the comfortable throw pillows covering it.

Casual elegance.

Drake settled into a leather armchair facing her. His clothes hung loosely on his thin frame. Faint wrinkles fanned out from the corners of his eyes but his forehead was still smooth. His nose and chin were drawn downward and elongated, reminding Molly of a half moon. His hair was cropped closely and gray, not the white you would expect for someone his age. Drake had to be over eighty but it was hard to tell. He could easily pass for sixty.

For the next hour and a half Drake told Jones' story in great detail. After World War I, the young poet left Sunset to seek fame. He found it for a time. Jones was acclaimed by the critics and hailed as the new Walt Whitman. By the beginning of the Great Depression, his poetry had fallen out of fashion and he returned to Sunset a broken man. He spent the rest of his life writing cheap fiction for pulp magazines. When that work dried up at the end of the 1950s, he was reduced to doing odd jobs around town.

"I did not realize he was virtually a hermit when I first went to his cabin. I was a teenager and keen to be a writer. I had written a few short stories and wanted his opinion. I was so naive ... " Drake looked sad. "After reading them, Aubrey suggested I focus on my family's business."

Drake turned his head to look out over the lake. Dark clouds were building across the horizon and seemed to underscore his regret. Molly followed his gaze. The temperature had been dropping all day and she guessed they would have snow before dark.

"It was a kindness really," he continued. "However, we did become friends. When I came here each summer we would spend many hours together drinking and arguing."

"Arguing?" Molly asked.

"Politics, literature, current events, philosophy. The subject didn't matter. Aubrey had a unique point of view on everything."

After a few minutes of silent reflection, Drake turned back to Molly and continued. "In the early sixties, I-75 was completed and the tourists discovered Sunset. So did the developers. They started buying land along Lake Michigan.

"It was during this period Lucas Haley first arrived in Sunset. He purchased large amounts of property as quickly as he could. He even tried to convince my father to sell Cufflink Hill. My father, of course, refused his offer.

"Another property Haley wanted was the point on Shadow Lake where Aubrey's cabin was located. Haley had purchased land on either side of it. However, he could not convince Aubrey to sell even though the money was desperately needed. This cabin and land were all he had left. It was his only link to his parents and his past."

Jonathan Drake continued. "Haley put a lot of pressure on him. He even made threats but Aubrey would not be moved. Haley was furious. He needed Aubrey's property for a resort he was planning on Shadow Lake."

Molly thought of the property on the lake Barry Elkins had visited.

It was Jones' land.

She wondered why it had been fenced off.

Drake got to his feet. Molly could hear his joints cracking. He walked unsteadily to the window and looked out over the lake.

"Lucas Haley was a bully. He could not stand to have anything in his way, but Aubrey was stubborn."

"There was a fire, wasn't there?" Molly remembered her eleventh grade English teacher telling them the story.

"Yes, and after that Aubrey disappeared. The general consensus around Sunset was he died in the fire, but no one could say for certain. They did not find a body in the ashes."

He walked back to the chair and sat down, his eyes filled with anger.

"You think Lucas Haley set the fire," she said.

Drake nodded. As if to underscore this, a knot in one of the logs popped and propelled a spark into the fireplace screen.

"The irony is that a few years after he died, Aubrey Colgate Jones was rediscovered by a new generation. His work was released again in 1967 and has remained in print ever since. Today, he is considered an American literary icon and one of the finest poets this country has ever produced."

A strong gust of wind off the lake made the window glass shiver. Molly could see the clouds were much closer now; bad weather would be here before the end of the day.

"I understand you're his literary executor," Molly said.

"That is correct. It came as a surprise, but shortly before he died Aubrey went to see a lawyer and drafted a will which left everything to me. Sadly, I was his only friend. He also left me his original notebooks of poetry and his property on the lake."

"Those are the notebooks on display in the library?"

Drake nodded. "Yes, in the room dedicated to his memory."

"His poetry must have made a lot of money through the years."

"It is enough to endow a foundation in his name. We support literary causes, awards, and scholarships. It is all in a trust I administer with an advisory panel from the University of Michigan – the Jones' Foundation for the Humanities."

Molly was familiar with the name. The foundation had donated a large amount to the library project and she'd seen it credited for supporting specials on PBS.

"Our latest endeavor has been rebuilding Aubrey's cabin. We plan to make it available as a writers' retreat."

Now she understood why the property was fenced off. It was a construction site.

"You must really miss him," she said.

"Yes. I regret I was not able to see him before he died."

"Why was that?"

"I became ill that summer and was confined to bed. My housekeeper told me Aubrey had come by several days before the fire. Apparently, he was quite agitated. He was desperate to see me. Unfortunately I was too ill for visitors."

While all this was intriguing, Molly knew she had to get the interview back on track. She glanced nervously at the approaching storm.

"And you told this to Dr. Elkins when he visited?"

"Yes, with his credentials and academic background I thought it would be of value for him to have a first-hand account from someone who knew Aubrey." His brow wrinkled at the recollection.

"What is it?" she asked.

"Well, he was polite enough, but he took very few notes. To be honest, it seemed like he was just listening out of courtesy. He did not ask for more details. It was only when I was telling him about Aubrey's final days that he raised any questions."

"What kind of questions?"

"He wanted to know details about Aubrey's mood. He was particularly interested in why Aubrey wanted to see me just before he disappeared."

Molly wondered about it herself. "Any idea why?"

"I have thought about this for almost fifty years. I suspect he may have been working on a new series of poems. One particular evening after consuming a large amount of alcohol, Aubrey said he wished he had written an epic poem such as 'The Leaves of Grass', a work which would be remembered forever. Perhaps he had found the inspiration to write it. Sadly, we shall never know. It would have been burned in the fire along with him."

"And you told this to Dr. Elkins as well?"

"Oh yes, but I think he already knew."

"What makes you think that?"

"I do not really know. He did not react in the way one would expect. He was deliberately unemotional. A new book of poetry would be a major discovery. I assume Dr. Elkins would have wanted to make that the cornerstone of the biography he was planning to write."

"How do you think he would have learned about it?"

"Well, that is puzzling. I believe most of the people who knew Aubrey are gone. The only person I can think of is Barbara Harre. Sadly, however, she is not capable of recalling much from that time, if anything at all."

"How did Barbara know him?"

"She hired Aubrey to do odd jobs around the library. He would unpack shipments of books, wash windows, cut the grass, and shovel the walks in winter. That sort of thing. I think she hired him out of pity. He was not very good at manual labor and quite often injured himself. When I read his notebooks there were several pages badly obscured by blood stains.

"I did suggest that Dr. Elkins talk to Julia. Perhaps her mother had passed along some recollections of Aubrey to her which she might remember."

The room had grown darker, the shadows gathering around them. Molly glanced at her watch; it was almost four. The storm had finally arrived, not with large drifting flakes but as hard sleet propelled by a bitter wind that lashed at the windows and howled across the roof.

It was time to go, before the roads became impassable. Standing up, Molly apologized to Drake for taking up so much of his time. He rose and walked her to the door.

"Do you think it was random?" he asked. "The murder, I mean?"

Molly shrugged.

"It might have been but there is strong evidence that Dr. Elkins was ambushed."

"Ambushed?" Drake looked confused. "That does not make a lot of sense."

"No, it doesn't," she agreed. "But it still looks that way."

"Well, it is a sad loss. Dr. Elkins was a dedicated scholar."

Drake opened the door, shivering as a blast of cold air and a swirl of snow filled the entryway. Thanking him for his time, she shook his hand. Molly pushed against the wind as she walked toward her car. Drake stood in the doorway watching as she took the ice scraper from the back seat, brushed snow off the Blazer, and climbed in. In the dimness Molly saw Drake had a strange, faraway look. Something about it unnerved her.

~

Molly was frustrated. So far, every piece of evidence seemed to lead nowhere. She had just wasted half the afternoon listening to a story which, although interesting, had no bearing on the case.

Am I slipping?

The old Molly would have cut to the chase with a witness like Drake, gotten the details of Elkins' visit, and been out the door in twenty minutes. Instead, she'd indulged the old man in his loneliness and let him wax nostalgic at her expense. Maybe she wasn't ready for a murder investigation so soon after returning. Molly wondered if it was time to hand in her badge and move beyond Sunset.

She pushed the thought from her mind and remembered Drake's strange expression as she was leaving. He was hiding something. She had the feeling his story had been partially a smoke screen to bog her down with useless details. Drake had been crafty and manipulated their conversation. He'd only revealed what he wanted her to know.

She liked Jonathan Drake but the next time they met she would definitely pry a lot deeper. He was keeping secrets and she was determined to learn what they were.

FIFTEEN

After leaving Drake, Molly called Barney Pyke at the Marina and caught him just as he was closing up. She asked him to move her Zodiac into one of the covered slips for the night. Next she stopped at Glen's Supermarket to pick up a bucket of fried chicken and a small container of coleslaw from the prepared foods counter. As an afterthought she added a six pack of Wolverine beer.

The storm intensified as she drove home.

I'll need to get the snow blower out in the morning.

The wind whipped snow across the highway cutting her view to no more than twenty feet. Molly slowed the SUV and crawled along the highway praying there wasn't an eighteen wheeler barreling along behind her. The wiper blades strained against the weight of the snow as it froze, causing the blades to make a smeary mess of the windshield. If it wasn't for the GPS she would've had no idea whether or not she was even on the road. Molly was relieved when her turn off appeared on the map.

~

Molly didn't intend to think about the case that evening. She just wanted to have dinner and maybe watch something on TV. However, she was restless after she ate and kept coming back to Drake's story. Settling down in the living room with her third Wolverine, she reviewed her notes of the Drake interview.

Something in his story of Jones' stubborn resistance to Lucas Haley struck a sympathetic chord within her. She had similar feelings when it came to pride of place. It's why she'd returned to this house, the one she'd shared with Steve. She felt a sharp pang of regret.

Reminders of Steve were everywhere. This had been his home before it became theirs. It still resonated with their love. She remembered his awful wallpaper. It featured hunting dogs and men with shotguns shooting at flocks of ducks. Steve's only sense of décor was a massive entertainment system and a couch that smelled like someone's butt.

She had never lived in a home like this. While growing up, she'd been crammed into a tiny drab house with her brothers and parents. After leaving Sunset she'd basically lived out of a suitcase in a series of cookie cutter apartments, places that had about as much personality as a cheap motel room.

With Steve she had dared to put down roots and was surprised at just how much joy it brought her. Of course that had been in the innocent days of new love. That had been the time before the doubt and suspicion had started to take hold, followed by the inevitable recrimination and pain. She felt herself pulled into the spiral of grief once again. Her breathing increased. It came in sharp painful gasps.

Memories are a bitch.

They were overwhelming and plunged her into a much darker place. Antidepressants fixed that problem but left her feeling detached, which became a problem in itself. She'd weaned herself off them and learned to control her anxiety with relaxation exercises.

Molly closed her eyes, driving the memories and pain from her mind by focusing on each breath. A sense of balance returned and her breathing gradually slowed.

Her notebook had fallen onto the floor and she decided to leave it there. *No more thinking about the case tonight.*

She finished the rest of the beer and set the bottle on the kitchen counter. Feeling a little woozy she gripped the edges of the counter. As she leaned over the sink, she looked out the kitchen window into the back yard. Snow was piling up. The powerful spotlights mounted to the back of the house normally illuminated the path all the way to the dock. However, in the thick blowing snow the light barely penetrated as far as the oak twenty feet away. Beyond that was a darkness alive with the snow dancing inside it.

She shivered at the thought and turned from the window. She walked unsteadily down the hall to her bedroom. Later, she lay in bed reading but the mad dog growl of the wind against the eves kept her from concentrating. The beer finally did its job and she fell into a fitful sleep.

~

Molly woke up screaming. She was on the floor. She didn't remember falling but could feel an ache in her left hip where it had slammed into the hardwood. She crawled into the corner. She raised the Beretta and aimed it at the bedroom doorway. Somewhere deep in the darkness of the house was a soft whirring.

The compressor on the refrigerator?

No. Something was out of place. It tore her from sleep. Fear was strangling her. She couldn't breathe. A weight was crushing down on her chest.

Am I having a coronary?

She tried to recall the other symptoms of a heart attack. The only one she could remember was sharp pains shooting up and down the arm. She didn't have any radiating pain so it must be anxiety.

The nightmare that woke her was fading. She could only remember shards of it, like a shattered mirror reflecting back her guilt and fear in the darkness. She was now left with a single remnant of the nightmare – in the glow of the moon's blue light an ice coated hand reached through the splintered surface of the frozen lake.

Molly's mouth was bone dry. She desperately wanted a glass of water from the bathroom. However, she could not shake the feeling there was something just beyond her bedroom door. She reached over with a shaking hand and tugged the duvet from the bed. She wrapped it around herself and gripped her Beretta tightly in both hands. But she knew her gun would not stop whatever was coming.

SIXTEEN

The storm had let up sometime before dawn. Late season snow wasn't unusual in this part of Michigan. However this had been a particularly brutal spring. The weather would tease with a stretch of warm sunny days and thoughts would turn hopefully toward putting away winter clothes and taking off snow tires. Then it would slam with a fierce blizzard which would shut down the schools and clog the highways. Around here no one trusted spring had truly arrived until after Memorial Day.

Molly fired up the snow blower and cleared the long driveway. The county road had already been ploughed.

~

The flashing voicemail light on her phone greeted Molly when she arrived at the station. She set down the coffee and freshly baked Danish she'd picked up at the North End Market. She sighed as she debated whether or not to enjoy her breakfast before diving right into her day.

The first message was from Richard Elkins wondering if she could give him an update on the timing of the inquest. His voice had a more authoritarian tone. The initial numbness and shock over his brother's death was obviously wearing off. He was sounding more like a corporate lawyer again.

The second message was from Kurt Harbou at the crime lab.

"Hey, Molly. Some snow, right? Anyway, I've got a couple of things that might interest you. Lloyd was able to crack the password on the Elkins' PC."

Lloyd was Lloyd Wilson who worked at the Radio Shack on Main Street and was an experienced hacker. Kurt called on him from time to time to crack passwords or help recover data from damaged hard drives.

"And he accessed the flash drive from Elkins' pocket. Apparently the water didn't affect it at all. Lloyd says you can put one of these things through a washing machine and the data will still be secure. Anyway, I'll be around all morning if you wanna to take a look."

The final message was from Simon McKean, a customer service manager with AT&T. He had received a request from Bell Canada to provide Elkins' cell phone records since entering the U.S. McKean had sent them to her in a PDF file.

Molly logged onto her computer and opened Outlook. She scanned her emails until she found McKean's message and PDF attachment. She printed a copy of the call records.

As she headed toward the printer to get the document, Kenton Sharpe waved her into his office. He asked for an update on the case, which surprised her because he usually wasn't that interested in what went on in the department. She took him through her investigation to date, giving it a positive spin and not giving a hint she was at a dead end. Things 'were promising' and she had 'good leads to follow up'.

This seemed to make Sharpe happy.

"I had a call from Palmer March this morning," he said.

Molly felt a lurch in her gut. Palmer March could be trouble. He was Senator Jake Haley's nephew and his Chief of Staff. Palmer was also Brian Haley's cousin.

"He had a concern about the way you handled his cousin the other night at the Villager. Brian claims you assaulted him."

"Brian was drunk and stumbled into me," she said.

"He sees it differently. He says you kicked him hard in the groin."

"Respectfully, Kenton, Brian Haley is a lying little shit and Palmer knows it. Paul was right there. Just ask him."

"I did and he confirms Haley was pretty drunk and made a lot of threatening remarks. He isn't sure what happened after that. He just saw Haley on the ground grabbing his balls in pain."

Thanks for the backup, Paul.

"So what are you saying, Kenton?" she challenged.

Sharpe thought about it for a few seconds then backed off. He hated any kind of confrontation.

"Let's just focus on the murder for now and not get sidetracked. The Haleys don't have anything to do with this investigation. Palmer has a full load right now. He doesn't need anything else."

Palmer's "full load", Molly knew, was due to the fact his uncle was in the hospital down in Traverse City. The Senator was in the late stages of acute lymphoblastic leukemia and wasn't expected to last much longer. Palmer was now in the unenviable position of having to assume his uncle's responsibilities, which included being nursemaid to his spoiled brat of a cousin.

Molly raged inside.

Fucking politics.

At least Booster made it clear which side he came down on. Sharpe, on the other hand, was like a bed of kelp moving whichever way the current flowed. Molly knew she would get no back up from either of them. She was on her own.

~

Back at her desk Molly scanned the cell phone report. She made notes on the calls Elkins had made and received since arriving in town. There were none after midnight on Sunday. That meant his Blackberry had fallen out of his pocket when he was dumped into the channel.

The records showed some data usage which meant he was getting emails or text messages. She hoped his computer held copies of the emails. Text messages, she knew from experience, were more difficult to retrieve and would require AT&T to do a data search.

The only call received on the day Elkins died had come in at 10:30 in the evening. It was a local number. She called the phone company and requested the location. The call had originated from the one remaining phone booth in downtown Sunset. It was located in Simmons Square, a block over from Main Street.

She wondered if it was worth getting Kurt to dust it for prints. Probably not, the phone would have been used hundreds of times. Even in this age of cellular communication there were still many people who preferred to use a land line even if it meant standing out in the cold and spending fifty cents.

The fact the call had come from a pay phone aroused Molly's interest. It meant whoever had used the phone didn't want to be traced. She wondered if the killer had been arranging a meeting for later that night.

But why? What would lure Elkins to a meeting in the middle of the night and in a strange town?

She put a big circle around 'phone booth' in her notes. If her suspicion was correct, it wasn't a random killing but a deliberate ambush. But where did it lead?

She put it aside for now. It was time to go and see what Kurt had discovered.

~

"The murder scene was definitely under the bridge."

Kurt held up a slide. She could see a tiny gray fragment held in place under a thin strip of glass.

"This is a fleck of paint from the railing. Luckily his parka had a nickel-plated zipper and this got snagged in the teeth. This ties him to the walkway under the bridge."

"That's great work, Kurt," she said as he put the slide back into the evidence envelope.

Elkins' laptop sat on the bench. It was a top-of-the-line HP with a seventeen inch screen and all the latest digital bells and whistles. Molly saw smudges of fingerprint powder on the keyboard.

"The only prints on here match Elkins. Lloyd removed the password and I cloned the contents onto an external hard drive so you can take it with you."

Kurt tapped the touch pad and the screen came to life. He stood back while Molly sat down in front of the laptop. The standard Windows background had not been customized.

Molly opened Outlook. Unlike hers, Elkins' inbox was clear of old messages. There was a series of folders and subfolders along the left side of the screen. She scrolled down until she reached one labeled 'Sunset'. There was a confirmation email from Expedia for the room at the Great North. He had made the reservation last week. Molly wondered if it was a spur of the moment trip or if he was a procrastinator.

She closed the folder and continued scrolling down. Nothing stood out. She was going to have to look through each folder and there were a lot of them.

Looks like it's gonna be a late night.

Molly reached the bottom of the list and scrolled back up. Near the top she saw a folder marked 'ACJ' and opened it. There was a long list of correspondence between Elkins and a woman named Anne Perkins. At the bottom of the first email the signature line identified Perkins as 'Executive Publisher, Harold and Son Publishing, New York'. Molly copied down Perkins' phone number. The message referred to a document that had been faxed to him. She read a few of the other messages. She noted the same kind of guarded language was used in each of them.

"Looks like you've got your work cut for you," Kurt said leaning over Molly's shoulder. "There's about 480 gigs on there. That's a lot of stuff."

When she got back to the office she would give Elkins' computer a more thorough going over. It would be an odious job. She had a thought and smiled. Instead of doing it all herself she would have Booster do the bulk of the work.

He should enjoy that.

"Okay if I take it with me?" Molly asked.

"Sure. Just sign the card for me, will you."

Kurt was annoyingly methodical. It was what made him an exceptional evidence technician.

Molly signed the card and handed it back to him. She shut down Windows and folded up the laptop. Molly asked Kurt about the laptop case.

"Sorry, I haven't gotten to it yet."

She tucked the laptop under her arm and Kurt handed her a USB key.

"I made a copy of his flash drive for you."

~

Molly called Anne Perkins, the publisher in New York. Perkins wasn't in so Molly left her name and number and requested a call back. She spent the rest of the afternoon looking at documents on the laptop. Elkins was well organized which made it simple to find things. There were files of lecture notes, class schedules, course outlines, minutes of faculty meetings, and book outlines. There was nothing unexpected until she came upon a hidden file of porn. It was nothing kinky, just old fashioned man-on-woman sex. Elkins seemed to have a preference for photos of couples doing it doggie style.

While she went through the computer she noticed Booster was trying his best to avoid her. Molly hadn't given him the good news yet – the computer files were about to become his responsibility. She would enjoy telling him.

She closed the file and wondered if Booster would find the porn as easily as she had. She smiled at the thought. He was a bit of a prude and a devout Christian. It would be fun to see him discover this hidden treasure.

By 5:00 Perkins still hadn't returned her call. Molly glanced across the office and noticed Booster preparing to leave for the day. She called him over and handed him the laptop with instructions to prepare a detailed list of all the contents.

"This is urgent. I need it before noon tomorrow." She smiled. "There are several hundred folders and maybe a thousand individual files."

He remained passive. He would not give Molly the pleasure of seeing his dismay. He knew it would take him a good part of the night to complete the inventory.

"I appreciate your support," she told him keeping the sarcasm out of her voice.

Molly tucked the case file into her bag and walked over to the marina to retrieve her Zodiac. Booster was left sitting at his desk. He stared at the screen of Elkins' laptop contemplating the enormous task ahead of him.

~

The sun had come out around noon and a good part of the snow from the night before had melted. Walking through the remaining slush was a little tricky as Molly made her way to Oleson's to pick up a few things for dinner. Hank Summerville came up to her while she waited in line.

"So, Molly, what's the latest?" he asked.

A dozen pair of ears swiveled in her direction.

Oh, the joy of living in a small town.

"Sorry, Hank. Can't tell you anything."

She imagined a sigh of collective disappointment rippling through the crowd.

Hank lowered his voice in concern. "But it's no one from around here is it?"

"I'm not ruling anything out right now."

Molly paid for her purchases and left the store satisfied she had done her part to frustrate the town's rumor mill.

To salvation denied
And fraught with heaven's domain
To fall into ice and fire
And thereafter remain.

~ Aubrey Colgate Jones

SEVENTEEN

Molly had always loved poetry. She appreciated its economy. A great poem is like a crime. The poet, like a perpetrator, offers clues for the reader to discover the larger truth within. The reward is a deeper insight.

It had been years since Molly had read any poetry and she found Jones' poems too grim for her taste. He painted the world as both desolate and chaotic. Molly could feel the pain of his words and that was a little too close to reality for her. However, she couldn't deny he had a power in his poetry. Reading it was like walking through a field after a battle. All around there was blood and carnage. Smoke still rose from the bodies and trees were shattered and twisted. This wasn't pleasant bedtime reading.

She set the book down and thoughtfully sipped a beer. She vowed not to pick it up again; it was too upsetting. The images painted by his words were indelible in her mind. Molly didn't need any more horror in there.

She returned to her case notes and reviewed them. Again, she felt frustrated at her lack of progress. While Sunset represented many years of heartbreak, it was still her home and she had vowed to protect its citizens. She detested the idea a murderer was loose in her town.

Maybe Booster would find something on Elkins' PC. He might be a sneaky son of a bitch but he was also thorough.

Must be his evangelical heart.

Thinking it over she realized she did empathized with Paul. It must have been difficult for him to go back to regular police work when she'd returned. It made sense that he resented her. Molly resolved she would work on repairing their relationship before it got any more frayed and hostile. Paul had once been a valuable ally and friend. She needed to restore that.

Kenton Sharpe was to blame, not Paul. Sharpe must have worked some sort of evil voodoo on him.

What had he promised Paul in addition to her job?

Perhaps he'd dangled the possibility that Paul would take over as chief of police. She couldn't see Sharpe beating Arnie Voxx in a race for sheriff but stranger things had happened. If Sharpe did win the election Booster would be the logical person to succeed him. Now that she'd returned the town council would probably back her for the job.

No wonder Paul Booster resented her so much.

~

On her way in the following morning Molly stopped to pick up a Danish. She got an extra one for Paul. It was a small gesture but there was no harm in beginning to repair the gap between them.

Molly found Paul's detailed report in the middle of her desk. He'd prepared an executive summary of the laptop's contents. After a quick glance she could see he hadn't found anything significant. She smiled when she saw his brief note about 'pictures of a pornographic nature'.

Yes, he was meticulous.

Paul had worked late into the night but was already at his desk doing paperwork. She handed him the bag with the pastry.

"Thanks for the thorough job."

Paul smiled at the compliment and took a bite of the Danish.

"It looks like there wasn't much there," Molly said.

He nodded in agreement.

"Why don't you grab a coffee and we'll go into the conference room and map out our progress so far," Molly offered.

~

Molly transferred information onto a large white board in the conference room. In the center she wrote Elkins' name. She wrote 'Persons he had contact with in Sunset' and drew a line. Under this heading she made a list – Peggy the hotel desk clerk, Hank and his staff at The Villager, Julia Harre, and Jonathan Drake. As an afterthought she added Tony Huffner's name with a question mark beside it. It was a short list, only seven names. One of them might be the murderer. Or it could be someone else still out there in the shadows.

As she wrote she narrated. "Elkins gets a call at 10:30 on Sunday night from a phone booth downtown and arrives under the bridge at approximately midnight. The murderer was waiting for him."

Molly saw Paul frown.

"What is it?" she asked.

"I keep coming back to the murder weapon. Fishing line? It doesn't make sense. There's a good chance it might have broken. I would have used a length of rope or maybe a short piece of chain. Even a necktie would have made a more dependable weapon."

Booster added with a note of regret, "I lost a five pound bass last summer on a twenty pound line."

"Okay, that's a good point. Why use fishing line?"

"Well, it's easy to conceal," he offered. "And light. Elkins likely wasn't even aware it was around his neck until he began to choke."

"Dr. Kolmenn said it would have almost instantly stopped blood flowing to the brain and Elkins would have blacked out pretty fast."

Paul looked at the white board again.

"Making him easier to control, no screaming or fighting back," she added.

"Yeah, he was a pretty big guy. He would've put a good fight," Booster noted leaning forward.

"Except," Molly said, "according to the tox report he had 10 milligrams of Zaleplon in his blood at TOD."

"That's some kind of sleeping pill, right?"

She nodded.

"If he woke up with that in his system he'd have been pretty groggy."

"So it made sense for the killer to use fishing line then. Elkins wouldn't have been able to put up much of a fight."

"Yup," she said grimly and added Zaleplon to the white board.

"Fishing line is also easy to get. Everyone sells it. I could canvas some of the shops."

Molly put a question mark next to fishing line. She wrote 'Motive' next to Elkins' name and underlined it. She added a list of options starting with the most common – robbery.

"I think we can rule it out. His wallet wasn't touched and he was still wearing his watch. Anyway, he was lured there," Paul said.

"We assume he was lured there. Maybe he had something else that was valuable to the killer," she pointed out.

"It could have been random. Maybe it was a serial killing."

The Sunset Strangler? It had a poetic ring to it.

She shook her head.

"It doesn't feel like serial murder. Normally serial killers are proud of their work and put it on display. Elkins was on his way to a watery grave. I don't think he was ever meant to be discovered. It was just dumb luck that Tony Huffner was at the end of the channel and spotted him."

Was it dumb luck?

Molly glanced at Huffner's name at the bottom of the list.

'Well, I think we have to take a good look at Huffner. I don't buy that he was down there just walking by. It just doesn't sound right," Paul said.

Molly nodded and underlined Tony Huffner's name.

"Yeah, there's definitely something wrong with his story," she said. "Still, I don't figure Tony for murder. He's a little wild but he's a decent kid."

Tony Huffner might make bad choices, such as choosing friends like Brian Haley but he had seemed genuinely upset about finding the body.

No, there was something else going on with Tony Huffner.

Molly wrote 'Aubrey Colgate Jones' on the board.

"There was a pretty detailed outline for a book about Jones on the PC," Paul said.

"He was planning to do some research at the library and he interviewed Jonathan Drake."

"We had to study some of his stuff in high school. I didn't like it much. His poems were practically obscene. My mother once complained to the school board about teaching filth like that. Of course, they wouldn't do anything about it because he was an important literary figure," Paul said.

Molly detected a note of sarcasm in his voice.

"Mom called him a vile seducer. When I asked her what she meant she wouldn't say any more about it."

A vile seducer?

She remembered her father's dismissal of Jones as a 'heathen fornicator'.

Molly imagined this was the fundamentalist view of a free spirit, especially in a town like Sunset. Small towns have narrow minds and long memories.

They both stared at the board in silence for a few minutes. Paul shook his head in frustration. She felt the same way. Most acts of violence they investigated were just stupid. A wife grabs a shotgun and blasts her philandering hubby or a drug dealer has a Buck knife planted in his chest like a fashion accessory.

This was different. It had been carefully planned and executed. There was so little to go on.

She shook her head and smiled grimly.

"If it was easy then we wouldn't be necessary," Molly said. "Anyway, we have things to follow up on. Something will shake out."

Paul looked dubious and said nothing. He just nodded.

It better happen soon.

Molly turned the white board to the wall signaling the conference was over.

She agreed with Paul that he should ask around about fishing line purchases at the local tackle shops.

Nothing tangible was likely to come from it but you never know.

She decided to talk to Tony Huffner again. This time she would find out the real reason he was down at the mouth of the channel.

~

Molly stopped at her desk to pick up new voice mail messages. There was only one – Anne Perkins, the publisher.

Perkins had a thin voice undercut with a no nonsense tone.

"I apologize for not returning your call sooner. I just got back from a book fair in London. I'll be in my office most of the day."

Molly called her immediately.

"Sorry, I am seriously jet lagged." Perkins sounded drained. "How can I help the Sunset police department?"

Molly explained about Elkins' murder and gave Perkins some of the details.

"Your name came up when we were reviewing Dr. Elkins' emails. You and he had been corresponding recently."

There was a brief silence as Perkins processed the news.

"How well did you know Dr. Elkins?" Molly asked.

"I've never met him in person. He was referred to me by a colleague who suggested Dr. Elkins could help us with something."

"Yes, I noticed in your email you refer to a 'document' without being specific."

There was a longer silence this time.

"This is quite sensitive," Perkins began. "Could I request the press not be made aware of what I'm going to tell you?"

"Okay, you've got my attention. But we don't have a huge press corps up here," Molly joked.

"Just over a month ago I received an anonymous letter stating I might be interested in the enclosed page. If I was, the sender assured me they had a complete manuscript to offer. The copy was of a handwritten page and appeared to be genuine."

Molly jumped in. "It was an unknown work by Aubrey Colgate Jones."

"That's right." Perkins was surprised. "The sender bragged it was several hundred pages in length."

Molly worked hard to keep the excitement out of her voice. "And you asked Dr. Elkins to help you verify it?"

"Yes. I contacted him and sent a fax of the page. He was skeptical until he saw it and then he became quite excited. He believed it was real but wanted to go to Sunset to compare it to samples of Jones handwriting in your library. We paid for his time and expenses but I believe he would've done it for the glory of discovering a long lost work of literature. To an academic like Dr. Elkins a discovery like this would have made him preeminent in his field."

"How much would it be worth?"

"In terms of dollars, I don't know," Perkins said. "Poetry is literature's poor cousin but Jones' continues to sell well, especially in the academic market. A find like this would definitely be worth a good deal of money."

"Did you speak to Dr. Elkins after he'd arrived in Sunset?" Molly asked.

"No. I was in London for the week. Though I did give him my cell number in case he came up with anything."

"Could you describe the letter and envelope it came in?"

"Certainly. Hold on a moment while I get them."

Perkins came back on the line. "The envelope is a standard number ten with no return address."

"What about the postmark?" Molly asked.

"I can't read it. It's smeared."

Molly knew the chances of a DNA sample were slim. The modern self-sticking envelopes and stamps eliminated any possibility of saliva traces.

"Would it be possible for you to overnight the original envelope and its contents to me? The department will pay any expenses."

"That won't be a problem," Perkins replied. "We'll make just make a scan of them for our files first."

"Please handle them as little as possible. They may contain trace evidence which might help us solve Dr. Elkins' murder."

Although knowing it was unlikely Molly hoped this was true.

"I need something from you in return," Perkins said.

"You want me to let you know if we recover the manuscript."

"It would mean a great deal to us if we could acquire it."

"I'm sure it would," Molly replied. "Can you send me a scan of the manuscript page right away so we can verify the handwriting?"

"No problem. Give me your email address."

Molly thanked Perkins and promised to keep in touch.

An hour later it arrived in her email inbox and she printed it out.

The page was written by hand on unlined paper. The number ninety seven was circled in the upper right hand corner. Molly tried to remember the handwriting in the notebook from the glass case in the library. She thought it looked similar.

She called Kurt Harbou and described the page. She asked him to check if it was among Elkins' things.

"There's nothing like that so far. I'm still drying out his notebook. Once it's finished I'll take a look in case he folded it and stuck it between the pages."

"What about his pants or jacket pockets?" Molly asked.

"Nope," Kurt replied. "Sorry, Molly, there's nothing."

Interesting.

Elkins had arrived with a copy of the manuscript page to use for comparison but it had disappeared.

Did the killer take it?

Molly saw possibilities opening up. What if Elkins had located the manuscript? To the right person it would have been worth killing him over.

She called Julia Harre at the library to let her know she was coming over. She also put in a call to Jonathan Drake. The housekeeper informed her

Drake had gone down to Traverse City for a doctor's appointment and wouldn't be returning until later that afternoon.

She wondered if he knew about the existence of the manuscript. When she thought about who would profit the most from its publication, Drake was on top of her list.

EIGHTEEN

Julia was waiting for her in the Jones' Room of the library.

Molly showed her the copy of the manuscript page. She watched Julia carefully for any flash of recognition. Julia caught her breath. Her hand began to shake.

"It certainly is in his style," she said, "and the handwriting is similar."

Julia opened the display case with a small brass key and carefully lifted out one of Jones' original notebooks. She set it on the glass and put the page down next to it. She moved it until a capital 'S' lined up with one in the notebook.

She pointed to the original. "He wrote this in the mid-twenties." Her eyes shifted back to the page Molly had given her. "I'm not an expert but I assume people's handwriting does change slightly over time, particularly as they grow older." Julia looked at Molly in awe. "I think these were written by the same person."

Julia looked around and dropped her voice. "Where did you get this?" she asked.

"You've never seen it before?"

"Of course not," Julia replied.

"And he handwrote all his manuscripts?"

"He only typed the final draft. A lot of writers worked like that back then. Everything was done in longhand. I remember my mother telling me he would use one of the library typewriters when he couldn't afford ribbons and paper."

Julia picked up the manuscript page. Her hand still had a slight tremor.

"Years ago she told me she believed Jones had been writing poetry again. She thought he'd found new inspiration."

"Julia, is it possible to talk to your mom? She's one of the few people left who knew Jones."

Julia shook her head. "She won't be able to help. Aubrey Colgate Jones died fifty years ago and in her condition she's barely able to remember what she had for lunch."

"But if she could recall anything at all it might help," Molly said. "I think there might be a connection between this and Elkins death."

"She's worse these days." There was a catch in Julia's voice. "Asking her about the past will just confuse her."

"Are some days better than others?"

"You mean are there days when she recognizes me?" Julia's eyes filled with tears. "The other day she thought I was one of the nurses. She started screaming at me, convinced I was going to hurt her."

Julia began to sob. Molly put an arm around her in an awkward attempt at comfort. Intimacy had always been difficult. Except with Steve. That had been easy.

Sensing her discomfort Julia stepped back and dried her eyes.

"Sorry," she smiled apologetically.

"That's okay," Molly said.

"I never had a chance to tell you how sorry I was about Steve. I thought we'd run into each other at some point but you left town." Julia averted her eyes. "I didn't think you were ever coming back. I felt like I'd let you down."

"You didn't let me down, Julia. I chose to be alone."

Molly took the manuscript page from Julia and studied it for a moment. *Time to move on.*

"Dr. Elkins didn't show you this page when he was here."

"No," Julia said with a frown. "This is the first time I've seen it."

"Is there a chance it could have come from your archives?"

"No. All that material was catalogued years ago. It would have been big news if we had found something like this."

"What about his letters or journals? Maybe Jones might have mentioned it in one of those?"

"We don't own Jones' journals. They're part of the collection at the University of Michigan," Julia said regretfully. "We had a student from Brown up here three summers ago. He indexed and annotated all the correspondence as part of his thesis. I read his manuscript after it was finished. There was no reference to anything like this."

Molly asked for the student's name and Julia promised to find it in her files.

As she was leaving Molly had a thought.

"What about your mom? She was close to Jones. Do you think he might have left a manuscript with her?"

Julia paused.

"There was a break-in at Mom's house last year. It was after she went into chronic care. I went by to pick up some of her things and discovered someone had smashed in a back window."

"What did they steal?" Molly asked.

"Nothing really valuable or expensive. Just an old TV and some costume jewelry. The investigating officer thought it was probably a junkie looking for things that could be sold quickly. You know, for drugs." Julia looked perplexed. "You don't think someone was looking for the manuscript there, do you?"

"It's not likely, but I'll take a look at the robbery report to see if there was anything out of the ordinary." Another thought occurred to Molly. "Do you happen to know who catalogued the Jones collection when it first arrived?"

Julia shook her head. "That was over fifty years ago, Molly. Our records don't go that far back."

"Julia, I know this is painful for you but I have a job to do. If there's any change in your mom's condition or if she has a good day I need you to call me. It's important I talk to her."

Julia looked strained. "If she has a good day … "

After Molly had gone Julia touched one of the pages of the notebook. She could feel the past stirring. It ran through her finger like an electric current, connecting her to the pain and torment that had surrounded Aubrey Colgate Jones. His legacy was a curse. She had a strong desire to take all his notebooks to the reading room and throw them into the fireplace. Instead, she replaced the notebook in the case and lowered the protective glass.

~

Palmer March was getting out of a gray Mercedes. He waved to Molly as she came down the front steps of the library.

"Molly," he called and walked over to her. "I'm glad I have the chance to speak to you."

She wondered briefly if it was chance. Palmer March wasn't the type of person to leave anything to chance. She had the distinct feeling this meeting was deliberate.

Palmer had been a grade ahead of Molly in high school but light years away in social standing. His father came from old money; his mother from new. However, there was nothing pretentious about Palmer March. He'd always treated all the kids at school, including her, with genuine respect and warmth.

Unlike his much younger cousin Brian, who believed privilege shone out his butt, Palmer had taken his family responsibilities seriously. Supporting and protecting his uncle had been his singular focus. Much of the Senator's success was due to Palmer's skillful diplomacy behind the scenes. With his uncle's illness and serious prognosis, Molly knew it was only a matter of time before he stepped forward to fill the Senator's seat.

He shook her hand; his grip firm and assured. Palmer moved with the confident smoothness of what he was – the power behind the throne as Senator Haley's chief of staff.

"I'm so glad to see you back in Sunset," he said. "This town needs you."

The Senator's sympathy card and a personal note of condolence from Palmer had been among the first she had received after Steve's death.

"How's the Senator doing?" she asked.

Palmer smiled grimly. "The treatments are taking a lot out of him. I wish I had his strength."

"And your cousin? He's feeling better?"

"What do you mean?" Palmer seemed genuinely puzzled.

"You complained to Chief Sharpe about how I handled Brian the other night."

Palmer shook his head. "I haven't talked to Sharpe in weeks. Did something happen with Brian?"

Damn it. That's why Sharpe let it go so easily.

"Just the usual," Molly said.

Palmer looked frustrated at the thought of his cousin. "Sorry, Molly. Brian's having a hard time dealing with his father's illness."

Molly doubted this. Brian Haley didn't care about anyone except himself.

"Just so I'm clear, Sharpe said I complained about something you did to Brian?"

Molly shook her head. "I'll deal with it, Palmer. Don't worry."

"You're sure? I can call Sharpe if you like."

"No, I'll handle it," she said. "What did you want to see me about?"

"I just wanted to say hi and welcome you back. Like I said, Sunset needs you."

"Well, most of Sunset anyway … "

He smiled. "That's only politics."

"Well, you'd know all about that," Molly said returning his smile.

"Politics isn't all bad. Uncle Jake has done a lot for this state. Hopefully he made things better."

Molly had no argument there. Senator Jake Haley was one of the good guys. He was driven by what he felt would be best for the people of Michigan. The voters recognized his commitment and supported him in election after election. As a result he was hated by the political hacks who thought they ran Sunset County. In their eyes, he was a maverick they couldn't control. But he didn't need their support and he certainly didn't need their money.

However, when Jake Haley became ill they saw it as an opportunity. They had their own man in the wings ready to run for Jake's seat. Dalton Tucker was a bombastic former town councilor who weighed about the same as a baby hippo. Tucker tried to portray himself as an everyman despite the fact his father owned a very successful company that printed bumper stickers and the family had millions. Maybe it was the influence of the family business but Tucker positioned himself with simplistic statements. He talked about "getting rid of the gravy train" and "respect for the taxpayer". In reality, he just wanted to bust unions and lower taxes for the rich. Dalton Tucker wouldn't be happy until, in the words of one of his heroes, "government was small enough to drown in a bathtub".

The slogan he was using this time proclaimed he was the man to take Sunset County "into the future". Molly thought he sounded like a screaming raccoon. Lately he'd begun to drop 'when I get to Lansing' into some of his speeches. She was certain many voters saw this for what it was – raw opportunism.

The prevalent view was that if Jake Haley died Tucker would try to ride his coffin all the way to the state house. However, he wasn't patient enough to wait until then and had started making speeches that were seen as trashing Haley's legacy. Even the political hacks who supported him had demanded he tone it down. Molly wondered if he was smart enough to take their advice. Somehow she didn't think so. Tucker never took advice from anyone, friend or foe.

Because of the Senator's declining health and Tucker's opportunistic politicking, a group of concerned citizens had lobbied the Governor. They wanted him to appoint Palmer March to succeed his uncle in the event he was no longer able to serve. Palmer represented continuity and would be an excellent choice.

Right now Palmer appeared dispirited. He wasn't thinking of his own political future; his only concern was his uncle.

"Please give the Senator my best."

"I certainly will, Molly."

Molly watched Palmer disappear into the library. It was no accident, their meeting like this, no matter how innocent he made it sound. He was a busy man.

What is Palmer March doing at the library at this time of day?

NINETEEN

When Molly got back to the office she decided to delay confronting Kenton Sharpe about her conversation with Palmer March. This was just more of his bullshit designed to throw her off her game. However, there was always the possibility that Palmer had lied to her.

But why?

She thought back to Jonathan Drake's story about what happened between Jones and Palmer's grandfather. But that had been fifty years ago and was history now.

She was also concerned that Booster had not defended her. He'd seen the entire incident with Brian Hayley.

Hell, he was partially the cause of it.

She felt the warmer feelings she had been having toward Paul Booster slither away. She could not trust him to protect her back. He'd obviously let his bitterness toward her cloud his better sense.

Well, two can play at that game.

She would find Booster another special task. She considered picking fly shit out of pepper as a possibility but dismissed it as too interesting. No, she would find something really mind numbing for Booster to do.

He would never consider double crossing her again.

She put revenge scenarios aside and spent an hour updating the case binder. There was precious little to add. She needed to talk to Drake and he still hadn't returned her call.

Was he trying to avoid her?

At 5:30, after spending almost an hour killing time on the internet, she decided that was enough for one day. She felt dead ended. The day had started out with promise, but had fizzled out. She locked the case binder in her desk and went over to the Villager to grab a bite.

~

The Villager was packed as usual. Hank had moved the stage back to allow him to squeeze in a few more tables in the back. He guided Molly to one.

"Busy tonight," she said.

Hank nodded. He appeared preoccupied.

"Everything okay?" she asked him.

"Jennie's out sick," he responded with a frown.

Since his wife had died a few years before, his daughter had been the entire focus of Hank's life.

He's a regular mother hen.

Hank excused himself and hurried back to the kitchen. A harried looking Desirée came over to take her order.

"God, I hate pizza night," Desirée muttered.

Molly grimaced. She'd forgotten it was pizza night. She liked everything on the menu except the pizza. It was awful – thick, greasy, and smothered in way too many toppings. However, contrary to her opinion, people loved it. It was by far the most popular special the Villager offered. Hank had stopped it the previous year after there had been a fight at the door between two overly zealous pizza enthusiasts. Obviously you couldn't keep a mediocre thing down. From the size of the crowd tonight, it had returned with a vengeance.

"Any chance I can get a burger, no bun, with a salad on the side?" Molly asked Desirée. She also ordered a pint of Wolverine.

Desirée took her order and hurried off.

"Tables seem to be at a premium here tonight."

Richard Elkins looked down at her. He had both hands on the back of the empty chair across from her as if to claim it. She invited him to sit down.

"I was going to call you," Molly said.

She took a copy of the manuscript page from her bag and passed it across the table. He examined it for a few minutes.

"What's this?" he asked.

"It's the reason your brother came up here," she replied.

Elkins took another look and shook his head. "It's not familiar. I'm certain I've never seen it before."

"It was sent anonymously about a month ago to a publisher in New York. The publisher asked your brother to confirm it was the real thing – a lost poem by Aubrey Colgate Jones."

Elkins handed it back to her. "Sorry, but my brother was the expert on modern literature. Biography and history are more to my taste."

Molly gave him a condensed version of the significance of the poem.

"It doesn't make any sense," he said. "The reason my brother was killed was over a poem?"

"It's a possibility."

Desirée brought Molly's dinner. She smiled at Elkins and handed him a menu.

"I think I'll have the pizza special and a pint of Guinness." His tone was dismissive and he didn't make eye contact or smile at Desirée.

So that's how high-powered lawyers treat the help back in Toronto.

Desirée's mouth grew tight but she managed to retain her temper and smiled. "Of course, Sir, right away."

Molly was reminded of Gilbert and Sullivan. A waitress' lot, like a policeman's, 'is not a happy one'.

After Desirée left Elkins said, "It looks like the coroner is going to release Barry in the morning. I spoke to Delta and I can take him on a flight tomorrow."

"We've finished with his car," Molly said. "What would you like to do with it?"

"Interested in a late model Toyota?" he replied. "I'll contract someone in Toronto to come back and pick it up in a few days. Unless there's someone local who could drive it there for me."

"No one I'd trust," Molly smiled.

He didn't return her smile and tapped the table.

"Other than this manuscript page, have you discovered anything else?" he asked impatiently.

Molly hesitated. As the closest relative he was entitled to an update. Although reluctant to reveal how little progress had been made so far, she gave him a brief summary. She could tell he wasn't satisfied.

"Basically, you know nothing," Elkins snapped. "I'm not surprised."

He glared at her for a second. Molly wanted to respond but held her tongue.

He has every right to take it personally.

He didn't, however, have the right to take it out on her. The silence between them grew uncomfortable. She looked down at her hamburger which was getting cold. She didn't dare take a bite in case it set him off again.

The tension between them was broken when Desirée arrived with Elkins' dinner.

The pizza was on a large pedestal tray which Desirée placed in the center of the table. She also set down a pint of Guinness in front of him. Elkins separated a slice from the pie and put it on his plate. He was one of those people who ate their pizza with a knife and fork, carefully cutting it into bite sized pieces.

"Not performing tonight?" Molly asked Desirée.

She shook her head. "Not on pizza night. Hank needs all hands on deck."

Desirée looked toward the front of the restaurant. Molly followed her gaze and saw Brian Haley leaning against the bar. He locked eyes with Molly and lifted his glass in a mock salute. He drained the beer and set the glass down on the bar with a loud smack. Standing beside him, Tony Huffner looked away in embarrassment.

As Desirée moved on to the next table, Molly broke eye contact with Haley. It was better not to provoke him.

Elkins had already finished four slices and declared, "This is the best pizza I have eaten outside of Naples." He finished his Guinness and moved the pizza tray aside.

"I guess you'll be happy to go home," Molly said with a smile.

"Yes, I have several cases that need my attention. My clients are only patient to a point."

Elkins hesitated and sighed. "I must apologize. I'm not normally like this. I'm exhausted and under a lot of stress. This whole thing has been overwhelming. However, that's no excuse for my rudeness. I know you're doing everything you can to find my brother's killer. If there's anything I can do to help please let me know."

He passed over a business card. "Here are my office and home numbers and my personal email address. Please stay in touch and keep me updated on your progress."

She promised she would.

He put a fifty dollar bill on the table. "Let me pay for dinner."

Molly looked down at the bill, "That's way too much."

"I'd like to leave the difference as a tip. I have enough insight to realize the waitress was insulted by my attitude. Hopefully, this will make up for some of my rudeness."

Molly decided to cut him some slack. After all, he had been through a lot. She shook his hand and he left. She gathered up her things and followed a minute later, leaving the money on the table for Desirée.

As she walked past him, Brian Haley shot up his middle finger defiantly. Tony Huffner took Haley's elbow and Haley shook him off. Molly slipped her bag over her shoulder to free both hands. In the background Hank watched, ready to intervene.

Molly resisted the urge to get into it with Haley and shouldered past him on her way out the door. Haley swivelled and watched her leave. His balls still ached from where she'd kneed them the night before. It was agony to sit on anything but a soft cushion. He vowed he would make her pay for the pain and humiliation.

~

Back at the hotel Richard Elkins called his wife Elaine. Toronto was far away and he was feeling the distance. He just wanted to be done with this dreadful little town.

He and Elaine had been married for over twenty years. They kept nothing from each other. He told her about his frustration with the investigation. He also confessed his rudeness to the waitress. Elaine had seen it before, usually when he was stressed or fatigued.

"Oh, you showed them old Snobby Dick." she said sarcastically.

'Snobby Dick' was the nickname she gave when they were first married. It was after an incident where he embarrassed her by snubbing a sales clerk. That was a side of him she worked hard to correct. Part of it, she knew, was as a result of the company he kept – powerful men who believed they were part of a superior class. Richard wasn't really like them. He was a kind person who lapsed into thoughtlessness when he was preoccupied.

They spent the rest of the call discussing the renovations being done on their daughter's room and her choice of color. When he saw the swatches taped to the wall, he had objected. Richard hated the green his daughter Carrie had chosen.

"It isn't my taste either but we asked her to take responsibility for choosing the color and we can't overrule her."

"Even though it makes me sick to look at it?"

"Even if it looks like vomit," Elaine replied.

"Which it does," he said with a chuckle.

They both laughed and he walked over to the refrigerator. He took out a bottle of Guinness and popped the cap, eyeing the left-over pizza on the counter. The grease was starting to stain the outside of its carton.

"God, I wish you were both here."

"I know. It must be tough. We all loved Barry," Elaine said. "Carrie keeps breaking down in tears."

Something outside caught his attention as he glanced toward the window. There was a red glow. He looked out and almost dropped the phone.

"Jesus!" he shouted. "I have to go!"

Elaine stood three hundred miles away in their living room staring at the phone in alarm.

What the hell just happened?

She knew instinctively that something was wrong. She stood holding the phone and feeling helpless.

"Richard," she whispered fearfully.

~

Elkins ran down a flight of stairs to the main floor and turned into a semi-darkened corridor leading to the hotel's parking lot. He hadn't taken the time to put on his coat and boots.

A patch of ice in front of the door saved his life. Melting snow from the roof had pooled there in the afternoon, freezing into a slick several inches wide when the temperature dropped again. Elkins didn't see the ice because he was focused on the flames shooting out the shattered windows of his rental car.

He also didn't see the hooded figure standing next to the door with a hammer raised high.

Elkins foot hit the ice. He twisted and turned his head to the left. Instead of striking the side of his head and shattering it like an eggshell, the hammer hit him in forehead.

Staggered by the blow, Elkins threw his hands up defensively. He landed on his back. The attacker loomed over him raising the hammer for another strike. There was a brilliant flash and the attacker turned away.

Elkins was consumed in a nauseating wave of pain. The sound of running feet and alarmed voices were the last thing he heard before he was swallowed into darkness.

The attacker, momentarily pinned by the glare of a car's high beams, broke and ran from the parking lot.

TWENTY

It was after 10:00 when Molly got back from town.

Too early to go to bed.

She thought about her dinner with Elkins. She felt badly that she had nothing for him. No wonder he was upset. He was frustrated that his brother's murder was in the hands of a Mickey Mouse police force.

Would he call Kenton Sharpe and complain about the investigation?

That's all she needed. Sharpe had it in for her already. A complaint about her capabilities as an investigator would give him the excuse he needed.

The BlackBerry's buzz startled her from her thoughts.

Where the hell is it?

It buzzed again.

The coffee table.

She saw the screen's glow leaking out from under a page of the case file. She grabbed the phone.

Booster — what the hell did he want?

"Yes," she said.

"Molly, it looks like we've got another one."

"Okay, pick me up at the town dock in fifteen."

"I'm outside," Booster replied. He punctuated this by bathing the interior walls with flashing red and blue lights from the roof array.

~

Booster passed her a cup of 7/Eleven coffee after she climbed into the passenger seat. Molly sipped it, tasting just the right amount of cream and sugar. She thanked him.

Well, he might be a sneaky prick but at least he knows how I like my coffee.

He quickly explained what had happened to Richard Elkins at the hotel.

"Hospital or scene?" Booster asked, shifting the squad car into reverse.

"Scene," she responded and drank more of the coffee.

~

The Sunset Volunteer Fire Department had extinguished the blaze by the time they arrived. One of the deputies had secured the scene with yellow tape. Molly saw a silver Chrysler 300 with Wisconsin plates parked at an odd angle. Its headlights illuminated the hotel's side entrance. A couple in their mid-forties stood next to a deputy.

They looked frightened.

The Andersons were from Green Bay. They had taken the ferry from the Wisconsin side of Lake Michigan across to Ludington late that afternoon. They were their way to her sister's cabin in the Upper Peninsula and decided to stop in Sunset for the night. It had been pure chance they had pulled into the parking lot when they did.

Luckily Mr. Anderson had had the presence of mind to stop the car and keep the attacker illuminated in his headlights.

"Over there," Anderson said and pointed to the other end of the parking lot after Molly asked him which way the attacker had gone. There was a low fence separating the hotel from the bank next door. Molly wondered if there might be security cameras back there. There was a drive through ATM so it was likely they would have CCTV coverage.

"Do you have any idea of his height or build?" Molly asked.

Anderson shook his head.

"He was, you know, average. He had on one of those hooded sweatshirts so I couldn't see much. He ran like hell though. Lucky thing we showed up when we did. He would have bashed that guy's brains in."

"That guy" was Richard Elkins and EMS was reporting he was in serious condition. Molly thanked Anderson and walked over to where Kurt Harbou was on his hands and knees working the scene. Molly wondered if the guy ever slept. She thought the same thing about Booster.

"No social life, Kurt?" she asked.

"Not when you guys keep bringing me all this work," he replied getting to his feet.

She passed him her coffee. It was still warm. He took it, blew across the surface, and gulped it down.

"Christ, are you trying to give me diabetes," he exclaimed looking at the bottom of the cup. "Way too much sugar, Molly. That stuff's poison."

She stared at him impatiently. "So? Anything?"

"Maybe a partial shoe print."

Kurt pointed to a spot next to the door and she saw the vague outline in the mud. "I can get a good cast from that."

From the location of the footprint, Elkins wouldn't have seen the attacker when he came through the door.

"Well that's something," she said. "We know the attacker wore shoes."

"Yeah and with any luck I can match it on the footwear database."

"Footwear database?" Molly shook her head. "You crime scene guys have such interesting tools to work with."

"You should see our condom imprint catalogue," Kurt joked. "Now, let me get back to work."

She walked to Booster who was busy taking a formal statement from the Andersons.

"I'm going to the hospital," she said taking the keys for his cruiser. "After you finish up here see if you can pick up any kind of trail." She pointed toward the bank. "We need to take a look at the surveillance footage from their cameras."

~

When she entered the emergency room a few minutes later Molly was surprised at how busy it was.

A group of anxious parents stood close to the admitting desk. Four high school students had been in a crash on Highway 31. The kids were returning from a movie in Petoskey and a drunk had crossed the center line and slammed into them head on. Other seats in the waiting room were taken up with a variety of hapless looking souls with ailments either real or imagined.

Dr. Kevin Myers was on call that night. He greeted Molly as she walked into the treatment area.

"Your guy is really lucky," Myers told her.

"He probably doesn't think so."

Myers pointed to several x-rays on the wall-mounted light box. "He got hit here," he said tapping a dark spot half an inch over the right eye on the nearest one.

Molly nodded. "We think he slipped on some ice by the door."

"He lucked out," Myers said. "If you have to be hit anywhere on the skull, the forehead is the best spot. The bone is thicker there."

"So how's he doing?" Molly asked.

"He's stable. There's a small fracture local to the area of the blow. I don't see much in the way of bleeding but the neuro resident is going to stop by in the morning and take a look. Right now he's unconscious and I think we'll leave him that way.

"We'll wake him in the morning. With any luck he'll just have a bad headache and a large lump for a week or so."

Just then Arnie Voxx entered, trailed by a couple of his deputies. He looked weary. He'd been investigating the drunken driving crash.

Molly greeted him and he drew her aside.

"Looks like your victims are coming in matched pairs these days," he said.

Molly smiled grimly. "He was lucky. The attacker was getting ready to smash his head in with a hammer. But you're right; it's a weird coincidence that someone went after both of them."

"I don't believe in weird coincidences," Arnie said.

"Neither do I." Molly asked, "You know anyone in Toronto?"

"Maybe. A couple of years ago the Toronto police picked up a fraud artist who skipped town after kiting a bunch of checks. I went there to handle the extradition but the paper work wasn't ready so I had to wait around a couple of extra days.

"The guy handling the case was a detective named Blake Reynolds and he turned out to be a pretty helpful. He took me around the city and showed me the sights. Anyway, we got to be friends and he came up last summer with his wife and stayed with us for a week. I could give him a call."

"I'd appreciate it, Arnie. These guys appear legit but I think we need to take a closer look."

"I'll call Blake in the morning. I'm sure he'll help us out."

Arnie turned toward one of treatment rooms.

"You have to excuse me now. I've got a drunk to book."

"Are the kids going to be okay?" she asked.

Arnie nodded, "Yeah, I think so. They weren't going too fast and the airbags took a lot of the impact."

Fucking drunks.

Molly asked Myers to call if there was any change in Elkins' condition. Walking back through the waiting room she saw the parents looking relieved at the good news they had just received.

Crap, I have to notify Elkins' family.

She took out the business card he'd given her and dialed his home number.

Elaine Elkins answered on the first ring. Molly introduced herself.

"What's going on?" Elaine's voice was filled with panic. "I was talking to Richard and he yelled something and hung up on me. I called him back and he didn't answer."

"Richard is going to be okay, Mrs. Elkins. He was attacked outside his hotel this evening and received a blow to the head," Molly said calmly.

"Attacked? How?"

"With a blunt instrument," Molly said. "But that's not important right now. His injuries are serious but not life-threatening. He's in the hospital and I just spoke to his doctor. He's confident your husband is going to be fine and will likely be released within the next few days."

"Thank God," Elaine sighed softly.

"Right now we're doing everything we can to find his attacker."

"This has something to do with Barry's death, doesn't it?"

"That's one possibility we're looking into," Molly said. "Can you think of any reason why anyone would want to hurt them?"

There was silence.

"You're asking if they were involved in anything illegal, aren't you?"

"Yes, I am, Mrs. Elkins. Right now the only leads I have point to your husband and brother-in-law. The only thing that makes sense is they were involved in something dangerous or criminal."

Elaine started to sob. Molly regretted her bluntness. There was a good chance that even if Richard and Barry Elkins were up to something, Elaine would know nothing about it.

She softened her tone. "You said you were talking to him when he was interrupted. Did he mention anything which might help us?"

"We just talked about family stuff," Elaine sniffled. "Barry's death hit him hard."

"I understand," Molly said gently. "You've had a shock. I'll call back tomorrow and we can talk more then."

"No. I'm going to come up there. I'll be on the first flight in the morning."

Molly was impressed by the resolve in Elaine's voice. It had a take charge quality.

"Thank you for calling," Elaine said. "I'll see you tomorrow."

She hung up.

Molly sensed this was a strong woman. She wondered if Elaine had the same hard edge as her husband. She had the impression Elaine Elkins wasn't a woman who would stand passively by while those she loved were threatened.

If that was true Richard was a lucky man. He had certainly been lucky tonight. If he hadn't slipped when he did he might have been sharing a slab in the morgue with his brother.

TWENTY ONE

After leaving the hospital she had been too keyed up to sleep. Molly went back to the office to write up her report. When she arrived she took a look at the night's incident log to see if anything needed her attention. It was the usual litany of brawling drunks, break-ins, and vandalism.

Another normal night in Sunset.

Molly spent the next hour putting her report together. When it was finished she leaned back and read it. In the space of twenty four hours things had gone from confusing to downright enigmatic. Her eyes burned from staring at the computer screen and her neck muscles had knotted up. She took a couple of Advil to try and knock out the headache that was beginning to form.

The office was quiet, not surprising at this hour of the morning. There was a single patrol unit during the overnight hours and she heard occasional bursts of radio chatter from the dispatcher's cubicle near the front door.

Molly walked to the conference room and turned the white board around. She added Richard Elkins' name next to his brother's. She stared at the two names and the surrounding information.

Was there a pattern?

If there was, it wasn't obvious to her. The only thing she saw was that they had both been lured – Barry with the manuscript page and phone call; Richard by his brother's death and the burning car.

She wrote 'lure' on the board and stepped back. She thought about it for a second.

Lure?

Fishing line?

Did it have something to do with fishing?

What the hell did fishing have to do with this?

110

There had once been a thriving commercial fishing industry here. That was gone now she reflected sadly. Sunset still attracted a lot of sport fishermen but this wasn't fishing season.

She exhaled the breath she'd been holding and rubbed the side of her face.

I need to get some sleep.

She thought of her empty house on the lake.

Shadow Lake.

The lake had been appropriately named. It certainly had its shadows. She felt a tingle of fear about what those shadows hid.

Molly folded her arms on the conference table. She rested her head on them and after a few minutes drifted into a semi-sleep. Jumbled thoughts came in and out of focus, mingling dreams with reality. At one point she was certain someone had been standing in the doorway watching her.

A couple of hours later she felt surprisingly refreshed but stiff. Molly stood up and stretched, glancing at the clock. It was nearly 6:00.

God, I'm famished.

~

The August Diner was almost empty when Molly dropped in at 6:30 to have breakfast. Costas put a cup of coffee down on the counter before she had time to sit. She ordered the breakfast special – three scrambled eggs, a short stack, bacon, sausage, home fries, and rye toast.

"Worked up an appetite this morning, Molly?" Costas said cheerfully as his cook threw bacon strips on the flattop.

Ah, the glorious smell of bacon frying.

The fry cook was an artist. Molly watched in awe as he cracked eggs on the grill and moved his spatula like a pallet knife, cutting the yokes into the whites to create the perfect creamy texture. He dropped a thin slice of butter on top of the mound of eggs and flipped them onto a plate along with the rest of her food.

Costas had timed it so the rye toast popped just as Molly's breakfast was put on the plate. With great ceremony he set it in front of her and stepped back.

"Oh my … " Molly exclaimed at the mountain of food. She devoured the entire breakfast in ten minutes.

~

Molly spent most of the day on her other paperwork and transcribing notes she would need for an upcoming court appearance. She worked through lunch still full from her huge breakfast.

Turning her thoughts back to the murder Molly called the Great North. Elaine Elkins hadn't checked in. Next she called the hospital. Elaine was there and Richard was still unconscious. Molly thought about going over to talk to her but decided it wasn't necessary right now.

~

She drove over to Jonathan Drake's. The housekeeper told her he hadn't returned from Traverse City. Molly thought that was odd considering he'd just gone down there for a doctor's appointment.

Is the housekeeper lying?

Or had Drake lied to the housekeeper?

If so, where is he?

~

It was time to have another talk with Tony Huffner. Molly called Booster and explained how she wanted to handle it. He sounded sullen again.

So much for kissing and making up.

~

At 3:25 Molly pulled into the parking lot at Glen's Market. Tony Huffner was working the 7:30 to 3:30 shift. According to the DMV Huffner drove a 1998 Nissan. It was next to the market's loading dock. She parked nearby and waited.

She was hungry again.

Molly toyed with the idea of going into the market to get a donut but when she glanced at the dashboard clock she saw it was 3:29. Huffner did not strike her as a keener. He was the kind of guy who would be out the door on right on the dot.

Sure enough Huffner came down the metal stairs at exactly 3:30. He stuck a cigarette in his mouth and paused by his car to light it. Molly stepped from the Blazer.

He looked puzzled, maybe even a bit panicked. The element of surprise was the best approach with a witness like Tony Huffner. Ambush him and don't give him time to prepare.

Huffner tried to brush past her. "I'm kind of in a hurry."

"In that case I won't take up too much of your time," Molly said.

She blocked his way and made it clear leaving wasn't an option.

"Do you remember the man I was with at The Villager last night?" she asked

He looked puzzled. She couldn't tell if it was real or an act.

"Nah, I didn't notice."

"He was the brother of the man who was murdered. The man you found."

Huffner frowned at the memory. It was obvious she didn't need to remind him.

"He was attacked outside the Great North around 11:30 last night. Someone set his car on fire to lure him outside and then whacked him on the head with a hammer."

"Holy shit!" Huffner grimaced.

"You were out with Brian Haley last night," she said.

"We got thrown out of the Villager. Hank told us not to come back until we could act "respectful". We went to the Blue Moon and had some more beers."

"What time did you boys finish up?" she asked.

"They cut us off around 11:00. I got home around 11:30."

"Did you guys split up after leaving The Moon?"

"Yeah, I think Brian was picking up Desirée."

"So he dropped you off?"

"No, I walked home from downtown."

"So you didn't see Brian after 11:00."

"Yeah, I guess that's about right."

She made him wait while she wrote down the details in her notebook.

Make him squirm a little.

She looked up and locked eyes with him.

"I have a hard time believing your story about the other night."

Molly made a show of flipping through her notes. "You told me you'd been drinking and were taking a short cut home."

"That's right. I did."

"Were you alone?" she asked.

Molly let the question hang in the air between them. His eyes flicked away for a second.

Gotcha!

"I brought a six pack down there to drink."

"By yourself?" Molly gave him a disbelieving look. "I didn't see any empties around when I got there"

"I threw them in the channel.

"Cans or bottles?"

"Bottles."

"And you drank all of them by yourself?"

He nodded and again his eyes flicked away.

"You're what – six foot and one eighty nine?

"Six one and one eighty five," he replied.

"If you drank six beers in that short period of time you'd either be falling down drunk or passed out. You looked pretty sober to me."

"I can hold my booze well."

"Maybe, but I think you're bullshitting," Molly said. "Tell me what you were really up to."

She could see him formulating the lie.

"It was like I told you. I was having some beers," he said sullenly. "Now I really have to go. My dad's expecting me to help him."

"With what?"

He paused and then said. "The toilet's fucked up. We have to fix the ball thing in the tank. It won't stop running."

Too much detail.

"Isn't your dad on duty this afternoon?"

"He's taking the afternoon off so we can get it fixed."

She doubted it. Coast Guard commanders like Tony's father don't take too many afternoons off – especially for something as mundane as fixing a toilet.

"Why not just call a plumber?"

Tony ignored the question. "I was alone like I told you. Drinking beer."

He opened the Nissan's door and slid into the driver's seat.

Before he had a chance to close the door Molly leaned in.

"I think you're holding something back, Tony," she said in a low voice. "We're talking about a murder here. Think about it. Because the next time we talk it's going to be at the station – and it's not going to be friendly."

She let him shut the door and Huffner drove away.

Let him stew on that for a while.

~

As Tony Huffner turned onto the highway Paul Booster watched him from the parking lot across the street. Booster was driving his own car; a late model Malibu. He waited for Tony to pass and then pulled out and followed him. Booster stayed a good distance behind the Nissan as Tony headed through town.

A couple of hours earlier Molly had briefed Booster on her strategy. She was going to catch Tony by surprise and rattle his cage. Then Booster would tail Huffner and see where he headed.

Booster had a pretty good idea Molly already knew the answer. This was just another menial assignment.

I should be running this thing. She's the one who deserves to be sitting on her ass going through hundreds of computer files and wasting the last hour waiting on Tony Huffner.

I was the one Chief Sharpe asked to fill the gap when Molly took off. I stepped up to the plate and assumed her responsibilities. I earned the Chief's confidence and respect.

While she was away he'd done a darn good job. And what did he get when she came back after all those months? He couldn't say it; it would be unchristian of him.

Booster was a born again Christian. He didn't drink, smoke, or swear. His religious views carried over into his police responsibilities. He saw his work as a type of lay ministry where he could help the weak and make sure the sinful were punished.

Damnation! Molly Parsons had not even taken a law enforcement course before joining the sheriff's department. I spent three years in college getting my criminal justice diploma!

Booster acknowledged Molly had a keen sense of curiosity which made her a natural investigator. She had to know all the answers, learn all the facts, and put it all together seamlessly to make a case. However, he could see she was struggling now. She was off her game, not showing her usual arrogant confidence.

He figured her husband's death had taken a lot more out of her than she was willing to admit.

She's an emotional wreck, just going through the motions.

Even so, it was obvious she still had a great sense of awareness and had picked up on his machinations. Trying to undermine her was a stupid move on his part.

And now she's making me pay for it.

~

The Nissan turned onto Beach Road north of town. There was only one residence out there – the Haley estate.

Huffner stopped in front of a pair of ornate iron gates. He leaned out his car window and pressed the intercom button.

Booster saw the gates swing open and watched as Huffner disappear from view.

The Senator's estate was huge. It covered a half an acre of prime Lake Michigan shoreline. Built of local limestone, the main house had over twenty rooms. Booster had been inside once, for a reception. The high vaulted ceilings reminded him of a church. An entire wall of glass in the living room provided a breath-taking view of the lake.

A cement pier jutted out into Lake Michigan. Beside it was a large stone boathouse which had enough docking space for three thirty five foot cabin cruisers plus their twenty eight foot vintage wooden Chris Craft. Booster had admired it last summer during the Fourth of July sail-past in the harbor.

Across from the big house was a two story garage with space for six cars. The apartment upstairs is where Brian Haley lived. Booster wondered, not for the first time, why Haley had been banished from the main house.

Haley came around the corner of the garage and slapped Huffner on the back in greeting. Booster watched as they talked. Haley stiffened and then grew more animated and aggressive. He poked Huffner in the chest. Huffner backed off. Haley got right back in his face screaming so loudly that Booster, a hundred yards away, could almost make out what he was saying.

What got him so pissed?

Booster considered intervening after Haley smashed a fist into Huffner's face sending him crashing to the pavement. Haley towered over him kicking.

Enough!

Booster put his car in gear.

Haley stopped kicking and glared down at his pal. He shook a finger at him and made some kind of threat.

Booster shifted back into neutral and waited to see how it would play out.

Haley gave Huffner one last half-hearted kick and stormed off toward the dock. Huffner got up slowly, wiping blood from his face as he watched Haley go. His expression was a mixture of anger and despair. Finally, Tony Huffner walked back to his car.

Paul Booster turned his vehicle around and headed back toward the highway. He'd seen enough to make him curious.

What were those two up to and what had Tony told Haley to make him so angry?

The bleached bones sing
O'er the desert sands,
Telling tales of doomed kings
and lost caravans.

~ Aubrey Colgate Jones

TWENTY TWO

August 1960

Aubrey Colgate Jones heard the crunch of tires on gravel.

Drake is early.

Smiling, he walked around the corner of the cabin to greet his visitor.

It wasn't Jonathan Drake.

Aubrey watched a stranger climb from a large Chrysler sedan. He was a tall man in his mid-thirties and moved with the self-assurance of someone who had the world by the balls. His black dress pants were sharply creased and his white shirt stiff with starch. Despite the heat, a blood red tie was tightly knotted around his neck. He grabbed a snap-brimmed hat from the front seat and placed it on confidently on his head.

"Can I help you?" Aubrey asked.

"I certainly hope so." The voice was soft, as if soothing a baby.

The stranger extended a hand. "I'm Lucas Haley." He said it like it was supposed to mean something.

Aubrey shook the offered hand and instantly felt wary.

Haley strode past him for a few feet and then stopped to admire the cabin.

"Build this yourself?" he asked, his eyes still on it.

Aubrey stayed a couple of steps behind him, not wanting to get any closer. A sense of uneasiness started to seep into his gut.

"My father did."

Haley's gaze moved beyond the cabin to the lake. "I'll get right to the point." He turned with a smile and looked at Aubrey. "I'd like to make you an offer for your cabin and land."

"Sorry," Aubrey said, "My property is not for sale."

119

"I'll pay a good price for it. I've already made deals with a couple of your neighbors and they were pretty happy with the money I offered them."

"Well that may be, but I'm not interested in selling – at any price."

His smile was wider, less genuine. He dipped his head toward Aubrey, his eyes disappearing into the shadow cast by the hat's brim.

"At any price?" A coldness crept into Haley's voice. "I believe everything has its price. It's just a matter of discovering what it is."

Aubrey looked toward the cabin and shook his head.

"I can appreciate this place has sentimental value for you," Haley said. "I'd be willing to sweeten my offer a little. Say a fifteen percent premium over what I paid your neighbors. How does $8,500 sound to you?"

"That's a lot of money, but I'm still not interested in selling."

"Think it over," Haley said as he handed Aubrey a business card. "You might change your mind."

Aubrey glanced down at the card. 'L. Haley Property Development Inc.'

"I suggest you speak to some of your neighbors. They'll tell you what a good deal they got from me." Haley's voice became slightly cooler. "When you're ready, give me a call."

"I don't plan on changing my mind," Aubrey said as he put the card in his shirt pocket to be polite.

I'll throw it in the fire later.

"Well then have a good day, Sir." He turned and strode back to his car.

Aubrey watched him drive away. The uneasy feeling lingered long after the car disappeared from view. He took the business card from his pocket and looked at it again. Despite the heat of the day, it felt cold and clammy – just like the hand of the man who had given it to him.

Aubrey Colgate Jones walked toward the lake hoping the sunshine would melt the cold knot of dread which had formed inside him.

Trouble is on its way.

TWENTY THREE

Back at the station later that afternoon Booster gave Molly a thorough description of the scene he'd witnessed between Brian Haley and Tony Huffner.

"Too bad we don't know what they were arguing about," she said after he finished.

"With Haley's temper, it could have been anything," Booster said. "Stupid and mean is always a bad combination."

"Yeah," Molly agreed, "and when you bundle in his sense of entitlement and power who knows what he's capable of."

Maybe even murder.

"You think they had anything to do with it?" Booster asked.

"Hard to say. Haley … maybe, but Tony has more of a conscience," she replied. "They're up to something but I don't think it has anything to do with Elkins' death."

Molly was exhausted. It was now 5:30 in the afternoon and it she was running on very little sleep. Her concentration was waning but she resisted the temptation to close her eyes.

"Why don't you write this up and leave it on my desk," Molly said stifling a yawn.

"You okay, Molly?" Booster asked.

"I'm fine. Just a little tired."

Booster nodded and walked back to his desk.

Brian Haley.

She had nothing that could tie him in any way to the investigation; just a strong feeling there was a connection. Haley was dangerous, and not just because of his explosive temper.

Somehow the crimes of his grandfather are reaching from the past and entwining this case.

Molly knew she had to talk to Brian Haley but not when she was this tired. She would leave it until tomorrow.

Time to go home and get some sleep.

~

On her way home Molly called Arnie Voxx to sound him out about the best way to interrogate Haley.

"The Senator and Palmer are decent enough people but if you go after Brian without a solid reason they'll circle the wagons to protect the family name," Arnie said. "The way things are right now, Sharpe would have a shit fit if you stirred up anything with the Haleys."

She considered this. Arnie was right about the politics; there would be blowback. One complaint from the Haleys could get her pulled off the case.

Or worse.

"Molly? You still there?" Arnie asked.

"Yeah. Sorry, Arnie," Molly replied. "I don't know what to do. I'm at an impasse here. Everything in this case leads me nowhere."

"Don't worry. It'll come together," Arnie assured her. "Let's take a look at where the Elkins brothers lead us. Who knows, maybe horny old Professor Elkins tried to put the moves on Desirée and Haley lost it."

"I doubt that."

"You never know. Maybe it was some sort of twofer," he joked. "You know, that twins thing, like that old movie with Jeremy Irons."

She remembered it vaguely – Dead Ringers. Steve had rented it years ago and they both found it pretty creepy.

Especially when one twin tried to pass himself off as the other to seduce his brother's girlfriend.

"Somehow I think Desirée would have better sense than that."

"If she had any sense at all she wouldn't be going out with Haley in the first place."

Good point. Desirée was intelligent as well as pretty. Why would she be interested in a shithead like Brian Haley?

"Thanks, Arnie."

"Get some sleep, Molly. It'll come together. You're too good for it not to."

They disconnected and she looked at the clock on the dash. It was almost 6:00. Molly needed to talk with Desirée to confirm Brian's whereabouts on both evenings. If she was lucky she might have a chance to talk to her before the dinner rush.

Molly turned the Blazer around and headed back into town.

Sleep – and the terrors it held – could wait.

~

The Villager was quiet except for a couple of the regular seat-warmers at the bar arguing about the Tigers' chances for the new season.

Everyone's an optimist on opening day.

Hank Summerville had moved a few tables to the side to clear a space for dancing. On the stage Desirée sat on a stool tuning her guitar. She smiled as Molly approached.

Molly kept it light and friendly. "I really enjoyed your playing the other night. You did a great version of 'Long Black Veil'."

"Thanks." Desirée smiled and set the guitar in its stand. "I'll get you a menu."

Molly held up a hand. "No, that's alright. I just want to have a quick word with you."

Desirée's eyes narrowed.

"I'm following up on a couple of things and I hope you can help," Molly said.

Desirée relaxed. "Sure, if I can."

"Let's sit over here," Molly said and gestured to a table against the back wall.

She sat across from Desirée and flipped open her notebook. Desirée tapped a plastic guitar pick on the table softly as if trying to keep a beat in her head.

"You and Brian Haley are involved."

"Yeah, I guess you could call it that," Desirée replied. "We like each other."

"That doesn't sound too serious."

"Well it's fine for now but I don't see us spending our whole lives together."

They shared a smile.

"I talked to Tony Huffner this afternoon and he says you and Brian got together last night."

"Yes, we did."

"What time was that?" Molly asked.

"I don't know exactly. I finished up around 11:30 and then went home to have a shower. Brian came by sometime around 12:30 I think. Or maybe it was a bit earlier."

"How did he appear when he arrived?"

"You mean was he in a panic and covered in blood or something like that?" Desirée joked. "He was a little drunk and wanted to go out to his place. I refused because I didn't want to drive with him in that condition."

"So he stayed over then?"

"For most of the night. We had a little argument and he left around 5:00."

"Argument? Anything serious?" Molly asked.

Desirée shook her head and sighed. "Just the usual – his drinking too much."

She was covering up abuse. Molly could tell. She'd seen it many times before.

"He didn't get physical did he?"

"If you're asking if he hit me, no, nothing like that."

"You would say something if he abused you," Molly said.

Desirée shook her head. "I can take care of myself. I've been doing it since I was sixteen."

Molly let the topic drop. It was hitting too close to home.

"Do you remember anything else that might helpful in our investigation of Dr. Elkins' murder?"

"Like I told you the other day, he came in, ordered dinner, and that was all."

"He didn't make a pass at you or anything?"

Desirée laughed. "What? You think he put the moves on me and my insanely jealous boyfriend tossed him into the channel in a murderous rage?"

"Where was Brian the night of the murder? Was he with you?"

Desirée hesitated. "No. He was doing something else that night. He didn't tell me."

"And you didn't see him at all on Sunday evening?"

"No, I didn't. Look, he has a mean temper and he can throw his weight around but Brian isn't capable of murder. He just isn't."

Molly saw tears forming in Desirée's eyes. She regretted upsetting her however it had been productive. She'd established Brian Haley was out and about the night of the murder and didn't have a clear alibi.

"Sorry, I didn't mean to upset you."

Desirée nodded. "I have to get back to work."

"Thanks for your time," Molly said.

Desirée stood and started to turn away.

"Don't let things get out of control," Molly cautioned. "If he ever touches you let me know … because it won't stop. I guarantee it."

"I'll be okay," she said over her shoulder.

Across the room Molly saw Hank looking at her strangely. At the door, as she was leaving, he asked, "Everything okay, Molly?"

"Yes, Hank," she snapped, "everything's fine."

She immediately regretted her words. here was no reason to talk to Hank like that. He was just concerned about Desirée.

"Sorry, Hank, it's been a long day," she said with a smile and left the restaurant.

As she drove Molly thought back on her conversation with Desirée. In a small town like Sunset Brian Haley was bound to learn about it and that would mean trouble.

Fuck it.

TWENTY FOUR

Molly was trapped under the ice. Drowning. She frantically searched for a way out the frigid water before it leached her remaining strength. There was nothing left in her lungs.

I need to breathe.

She couldn't. She was too deep. It would mean certain death.

She was in the grip of uncontrollable panic.

Find the hole! Find the hole!

Desperately, she searched. Her eyes couldn't focus. There was a stab of pain in her chest. She could no longer fight the overwhelming desire to take a breath. She opened her mouth and felt icy snakes flood down her throat.

Oh, God ... I'm dying.

Molly couldn't catch her breath. She was hyperventilating, covered in sweat, huddled in a corner of her bedroom with the duvet wrapped around her once again. She buried her face in its soft folds and continued to gasp for air. Crazy slivers of the dream flashed in the swirling darkness surrounding her.

She desperately tried to focus on her relaxation exercise.

Just breathe ... slowly ... just breathe ...

After a few moments her body began to relax.

She felt around on the floor until her fingers found the Beretta a few inches away. She clutched it to her chest, her sacred totem of defence against the darkness.

Welcome to my nightmare. So much for a good night's sleep.

Adrenalin continued to flood through her body making her head pound and heart race.

There's always the pills.

They were sitting in their translucent orange vial tucked behind the tampons in the medicine cabinet. She wouldn't take them anymore. She didn't like the feeling of being cocooned in their narcotic embrace.

I'll work it out on my own without drugs or therapy.

What could she really tell a therapist?

Not the truth, that's for sure.

Coming back to Sunset had been a bad idea. It had made sense at first. She wanted to prove she was strong enough to confront the past. Instead it had become a nightly circus of fear and despair. Each morning she felt worse, more dragged out from fighting the demons and foggier from the building fatigue.

The Beretta was heavy. Over two pounds fully loaded. She put it down on the floor. Arnie had urged her to get a lighter weapon, a Glock or a Sig Sauer, but she took comfort in the formidable bulk of the gun. It was a talisman. She'd carried it for a long time. She knew it and was comfortable with it.

She feared the night when she would stop pointing it at the darkness and turn it on herself.

That night might not be too far off.

The gun would be her final comfort. It would be her release from fear and fatigue.

Molly got up and placed the gun on her bedside table. She put on her robe. It was 4:30 a.m.

Time to start another day.

TWENTY FIVE

Molly guided the Zodiac across the plate glass surface of the lake. It was a beautiful day, the first true day of spring. She could hear the bright sound of bird songs from the shore. A scent wafted toward her. Geosmin – the breath of the earth, produced by tiny organisms in the soil as it began to warm when the sun's rays penetrated the frost. It signalled the ground was nearly ready for planting. Molly always felt this fragrance was a declaration of life.

What a glorious morning.

Her gloomy mood had lifted and she allowed herself to feel a little hope – for now.

She walked from the dock to the station. It was quiet when she arrived. Only one person was around, a deputy filling out an arrest report on a DUI.

She picked up her phone messages. Jonathan Drake had finally returned her call. He apologized for not getting back to her sooner. His trip to Traverse City had taken longer than he had expected. He did not elaborate as to why but invited her to drop by before lunch.

The second message was from Kurt Harbou. He'd done a complete review of all the evidence in both cases. She wondered if he'd found any similarities between the two attacks. Molly decided to drop by the crime lab on her way to Drake's house.

Maybe Kurt had turned up something to add to the list of questions for Drake.

Hopefully this time her visit with Jonathan Drake wouldn't turn into a lengthy story telling session. It would be interesting to see how he would react to the news about the manuscript.

~

Molly had known Kurt Harbou for seven years. She saw past his intimidating size and recognized the sensitive person underneath. However, he could still surprise her. When she entered his lab she found him finishing up his breakfast — a bowl of some healthy looking grain cereal which he ate with chopsticks.

"Hey, Molly. Had breakfast yet?" He held up the bowl.

"No, just some coffee."

"You mean that sugary poison you like."

She grimaced as he poured a cup of tea that smelled suspiciously like Herbal Essences shampoo.

He set the bowl down and picked up one of the autopsy photos of Barry Elkin. It was a close up of his throat. She could see the faint blue line under the chin where he'd been strangled. Kurt pointed to it.

"I had the crime lab in Grayling take a closer look at the ligature marks. There's a guy there who knows a lot about death by fishing line."

"There's an expert on death by fishing line," Molly chuckled.

"Well, it happens more often than I ever imagined," he grinned. "Accidents mostly. Divers and swimmers get entangled in it and drown."

Kurt referred to the report on his desk. "From the width of the ligature on the victim's throat my guy thinks the line was a heavy one. The heavier lines are popular for deep sea fishing. Up here it's used for musky and pike but even that's pretty rare." Kurt flipped a page on the report. "He's pretty certain the line is fluorocarbon, which is denser but also more transparent."

"Anything else?" Molly asked.

"Flour."

"Flour?"

"Yeah, a special type of industrial flour used in commercial baking. I found traces of it on Elkins' pants. It made a paste after mixing with the water and didn't all get washed away."

Molly thought of Tony Huffner. He worked at Glen's Market. They had in an in-store bakery. She often bought bread there.

"Could you match the flour if I get a sample?" Molly asked.

"I'm not sure. I might have to send it over to Grayling to have them take a look."

The State Police had a more sophisticated regional crime lab in Grayling just a few miles away. It was close but it also could take a while to get evidence examined there.

"That's it for our murder vic. With the exception of the flour, all the other trace fibers and dust were washed out by the water."

"Where on his pants did you find the flour?"

"Just below the right knee," Kurt tapped a spot on the back of his leg.

"Could it have gotten there when he was pushed over the railing?"

"I think so. He was a big guy and the attacker would have had to muscle him over," Kurt made a diving motion with his hand. "It was pure luck that it stayed there. It could have been easily washed away."

Yeah, lucky me.

"How about his brother?" she continued. "Anything on the attack?"

"A little," Kurt replied. "Kolmenn measured the wound on the forehead for me."

Molly had a vision of Ronnie Kolmenn climbing up on Richard Elkins' hospital bed with a step ladder, measuring tape in hand.

That must have been amusing for the staff.

"I was able to match the wound using my hammer database. I'm 99.9% certain it was a Stanley SteelMaster. It weighs a pound and would have done that kind of damage to his head. Kolmenn thinks another blow would have killed him."

Molly shuddered. She felt the beginning of a headache.

Time to talk to Richard Elkins again, if he's regained consciousness.

"The downside is that the SteelMaster is one of the most popular hammers in the country. It's sold everywhere so tracking down a specific purchase is going to be almost impossible. However, there were faint traces of rust in the wound so it's not a new one."

He opened a file and pulled out an eight by ten photograph of a shoe print.

"I have a positive match on this. It's a Van's Canvas Authentic sneaker. Size nine. Unfortunately, like the hammer, they're really popular. A lot of people wear them."

Kurt lifted his foot and showed her his blue sneaker. She could see it was a Van's.

"They wear like iron and are really comfortable," Kurt continued.

What type of shoe does Haley wear?

"How about the security camera footage?" Molly asked.

Kurt set an iPad on the table in front of them. On the screen was a freeze frame of the parking lot of the hotel. From the angle Molly guessed the camera was located somewhere high over the side door, maybe eight or nine feet over the entrance.

There's a blind spot next to the door.

Kurt touched the screen and the footage started to roll. The time code on the bottom displayed the date, time, and frame number. Kurt had cued it to a few seconds before Richard Elkins came through the side door. Molly could see the car burning across the lot.

"Was there a shot of the assailant setting the fire?" she asked.

Kurt shook his head. "It was too dark. The camera doesn't have night vision."

Elkins ran into the frame and slipped on the ice. His body twisted as he fell. There was another quick movement. He hit the ground on his back and looked up at his attacker. A hooded figure moved out of the darkness and raised a hammer.

Kurt froze the image. He used a pen to point to the hand holding the hammer. "Looks like a leather glove."

Molly started making a list of spots where the hammer and gloves might have been tossed. The lake was the first place that came to mind.

Bundle them up with a couple of big rocks and throw them in the water.

She had requested that a State Police dive team check the channel for the missing BlackBerry. She would ask them to look for the gloves and hammer at the same time.

Kurt restarted the video. There was a sudden blaze of light. The attacker hesitated and then ran out of the frame.

"I found a few tiny traces of the vic's blood at the far end of the parking lot," he commented. "It must have come from the hammer."

Kurt reached past her and started a second video clip. "This is from the camera covering the parking lot behind the bank."

The hooded figure ran through the lot and out of the camera's range. Kurt wound the footage back a few seconds and froze the attacker on the screen.

"He's really moving," Molly said.

"Yeah," Kurt agreed. "I did a calculation on the range the camera covered and the number of seconds it took for him to go from one side to the other. He's not quite an Olympic sprinter but definitely good track and field material."

"What about his height?" Molly asked.

"Well, I don't have a good reference point but I would estimate he's between five eight and six one. I uploaded a copy of both clips to Grayling to see if they can enhance them. The lighting's shitty but they may be able to find something we couldn't."

She looked down at the figure frozen on the screen. The video pointed to someone in great physical shape. She began to eliminate suspects.

That didn't make the list much shorter.

Molly stifled a yawn. It wasn't even lunch yet and she was already exhausted. The lack of sleep was starting to wear her down.

Those damn dreams.

She shuddered as she remembered the helpless feeling from the night before – the feeling of drowning. It was what Steve had experienced. Old emotions rushed in.

She turned away from Kurt to hide her pain.

Steve.

TWENTY SIX

The day Steve came into her life started with Molly on a park bench trying to look like a tourist. The bench was in Founder's Park in downtown Sunset. She was watching the Blue Moon Bar on Main Street, waiting for Derek Foldes to come out. She'd been tracking him for three days as he made his way up I-75.

Derek Foldes was your proverbial scumbag low-life. He'd become Molly's responsibility when he'd failed to show up in court to stand trial on a charge of armed assault. This displeased Billy Sanderson, the Detroit bail bondsmen who'd posted $100,000 on Derek Foldes' behalf to guarantee he would appear in court. So he called on his favorite bounty hunter – Molly – to go after Foldes and bring him back.

Molly had never intended to become a bounty hunter. She'd been working on her degree in library sciences at Wayne State but had a hard time making ends meet. She'd dropped out for a semester to make enough money to continue her education. Since she wasn't looking for a career she found temp work suited her best.

~

The temp agency had sent her to Beaman and Company. They knew they could depend on Molly to take on the most challenging assignments with the most difficult and demanding clients. Beaman and Company was their worst. The last five temps sent there had requested different assignments within the first week. The most recent one left after only one day. Molly was their last chance. If she couldn't make it work the agency would have to give up on them.

The company had been started early in the 1990s by former Detroit detective Dan Beaman. They were bounty hunters who went after bail skips

– dangerous scum of the earth who would stop at nothing to avoid going to jail.

Their offices were off Mount Elliott near the cemetery in the heart of one of Detroit's worst neighborhoods. The cinderblock building was surrounded by an eight foot fence topped with razor wire. It was painted bright white in defiance of the neighborhood's graffiti taggers. The front entrance was a single steel door with a security camera mounted overhead. It looked more like a bunker than a place of business. A neatly lettered sign on the door told visitors 'If you don't have business here, fuck off'.

Up to this point Molly had worked mostly in accounting or law firms where the atmosphere was sedate and reserved. Entering Beaman's was like stepping into a commodities trading pit. There were dozens of voices shouting at once. The atmosphere was somewhere between mayhem and utter chaos.

A security guard sat where a receptionist normally would. He watched a bank of monitors displaying different views of the building's exterior. The guard didn't look up or acknowledge her in any way. From the back of the building came a metallic banging sound and an endless stream of profanity.

"Hope you don't offend easily," said a voice from behind her.

Molly felt a hand on her shoulder and turned to face one of the largest men she'd ever seen. Dan Beaman was huge, over six foot five and almost three feet across from shoulder to shoulder. She introduced herself and explained she was from the temp agency. She handed him her resume so he could see her qualifications. He didn't bother to look at it. Without a word he started walking quickly down a corridor, motioning for her to follow.

Beaman stopped outside an office and shouted, "When's Dearborn PD picking him up?"

"I don't know," a man's voice replied from inside. "They said in an hour and that was three hours ago."

There was another blast of profanity from the back.

"Well he's upsetting the decorum of the office," Beaman snorted.

Dominick Velezarb, Beaman's second in command, came out of the office. Beaman pointed to Molly.

"This is Molly. She's here to help you guys get your paperwork finished. Molly, this is Dominick."

In stark contrast to Beaman's massive bulk Velezarb appeared emaciated. He'd put in twenty with the FBI before taking early retirement so he could do some 'real detective work'. He was dressed like a homeless person in ripped stained clothing. He also smelled like he'd been living on the streets for a while. Molly assumed he must have just come back from an undercover assignment. Later she learned this was how he normally dressed, and worse, how he usually smelled.

Molly turned to see Beaman already half way down the corridor.

She shouted after him, "Can anyone in this zoo tell me what the fuck I am supposed to be doing?"

Beaman stopped dead in his tracks then turned in surprise. He stared at her for a few seconds before remembering her resume in his hand. He quickly scanned the document.

"Library Sciences?" he muttered shaking his head. "Well, Molly, this ain't a library. But with a mouth like that I can see you'll fit right in here."

He stared at her for another moment. "You're smart enough to figure out what you need to do."

And she was.

~

It took Molly a week to clean up the backlog of paperwork. From the volume it was obvious Beaman and Company was overwhelmed with work. The recession had knocked Detroit on its ass. The auto industry – the traditional industrial backbone of the city – teetered on the verge of bankruptcy and thousands were out of work. As a result, crime flourished. So did bail bondsmen. In this dire economy it was a good time to be a bounty hunter.

Dan Beaman had been a Detroit cop for over twenty years and his connections within the department stretched all the way up to the commissioner's office. This gave him an inside edge – and there was plenty of business because the bondsmen knew he got results.

A couple of weeks later Beaman called her into his office. It was the first time they'd talked when he wasn't moving at full tilt.

He looked at her sternly. "The boys are complaining you're busting their balls to get your job done."

Molly started to protest and he stopped her with a wave of a massive hand.

"I think it's great. I love tenacity and you have gallons of it."

Molly was pretty sure tenacity didn't come in gallons.

I'll have to check next time I'm in Home Depot.

"Dom thinks the only way to get you out of our hair is to put you out on the street."

"Look, Dan, I need this job … " she began.

"Nah, that's not what I meant. He thinks you should go out with him and learn the ropes. We both think you'd be good at this."

Molly was stunned.

"Of course it's a lot more dangerous than working in a library but we'd teach you how to protect yourself." He opened his jacket to reveal a large pistol in a nylon shoulder rig. "You can ride along with Dom to see if you like it. If you do then we can talk."

That night Molly and Dominick Velezarb hit the streets to track down a low life and she was hooked. She didn't just like it, she loved it.

~

Six months later Molly was a licensed bail enforcement agent. After she got her license Beaman arranged for her to get advanced weapons training at a private range near Troy. Upon completion of her training, the range master, another former Detroit cop, had helped her pick out a pistol – a Smith & Wesson .357 magnum with a six inch barrel.

When she returned to the office from the range that day Beaman looked disapprovingly at the .357. He passed her an oak box.

"A little gift for all the hard work," he said with a smile.

The box contained a Beretta M9, identical to Beaman's own gun. Molly hefted it. The weight was a lot more than the .357.

"Sorry, Dan, my bag is heavy enough as it is."

"Look, when you have to draw a gun I want you to show the assholes you're serious. Your .357 only holds six rounds and with some of these morons that's only enough to get their attention. The M9 holds seventeen and it takes two seconds to reload. That gives you a real edge in a fight."

He passed her a nylon shoulder holster. "Keep the .357 in your bag but wear the M9. Don't be afraid to use it if you have to. There's plenty more scumbags in the sea."

Molly took off her jacket, adjusted the shoulder holster until it was comfortable, and then slipped the Beretta into it.

It had stayed with her ever since.

~

Two years later veteran bounty hunter Molly Parsons found herself sitting on a park bench thinking about the strange turns her life had taken.

The latest had led her back to Sunset – waiting for Derek Foldes who was drinking boilermakers in the Blue Moon.

Ever since she'd begun to follow him she was certain Foldes was up to something big. Instead of taking Foldes down when she'd first located him she decided to trail him and see where he'd lead her. According to the intelligence she had on him, he was a known associate of another one of her skips, Mel Howard. She'd been after Howard for the past seven months but he'd always managed to elude her. She was betting Foldes would hook up with Howard at some point.

When she'd arrived in town the evening before, Molly checked in with the Sunset County Sheriff's Department. As a courtesy she provided them with the details of her investigation and who she was tracking.

"You say you're originally from up here?" Arnie Voxx asked once she'd finished briefing him. "Are you one of Jacob Parsons' kids?"

"Yes," Molly frowned. Her memories of Sunset weren't fond. She thought of the weathered gray house on the edge of town and the shack next to it her father had called a church.

Arnie remembered her father. He'd been a sullen bastard who sucked the joy right out of life. He also remembered a pretty little girl with bright green eyes.

This lady bounty hunter had the same color eyes. He tried to reconcile his memory of that girl with this self-assured young woman standing in his office.

Arnie had always wondered what happened to the Parsons family. He had an uncomfortable feeling that whatever it was had not been good.

~

Steve Fraser stopped at the water fountain in the park and took a drink. He'd been out for a run and had stripped off his sweat-soaked tee shirt. Molly glanced at the buff young man as he wiped his mouth with the back of his hand. He was obviously in great shape.

He had a neatly trimmed beard. His blond hair was long, a little bit out of fashion but still attractive. However, it was his eyes which held her attention. They were a dark gray; their pupils open and inviting. Steve had an easy smile which he flashed at her when he saw her looking at him.

She turned her focus back to the bar across the street.

"Don't I know you?" His voice was soft with just a touch of huskiness that made her tingle.

She remembered him.

Steve Fraser.

Steve had been a couple of grades ahead of her. The self-confidence she'd spent years accumulating disappeared. She felt herself becoming a shy awkward high school junior once again.

"You're Molly Parsons, aren't you?"

She looked away, keeping her gaze fixed on the front door of the bar.

Small towns were cruel places. As the gray little daughter of the crackpot minister living on the edge of town Molly was an outsider. Perceptions were formed early and followed a person like an unwanted shadow. They lingered far into the future.

Her fellow students had broken into cliques corresponding with their parents' social status and income levels. Most of the kids had an occasional kind word or smile for her. It was just a small group who'd treated her badly. Although she tried to fade into the background their snickers and snarky comments followed her through the corridors. She was never certain which was worse, the nasty remarks or the pity. Both made her withdraw deeper into herself.

As soon as could, Molly had escaped from Sunset. She'd been successful at putting it all behind her – until now when fate had brought her back.

Steve sat down on the bench beside her. She remembered him as one of the students who always had an encouraging smile for her.

"Wow, I can't believe it's you." He left the 'you look so different' part unsaid.

She resisted looking at him. "Steve, it's nice to see you but I'm working right now."

He followed her gaze to the front door of the Blue Moon.

"I think you're just blowing me off," he laughed.

Derek Foldes stepped out of the bar and blinked in the strong sunlight. Molly stiffened. Steve followed her gaze and saw Foldes.

"Oh, you're with him," Steve said, disappointment clear in his voice.

"Not exactly," she whispered.

Foldes stood waiting in front of the bar. He swayed a bit. Even though he'd had a lot to drink he didn't let his guard down. He looked around warily.

Molly turned to Steve and took his hand. "Keep talking to me like we're together," she said in a low voice.

Steve was confused but did as she requested. "So what have you been doing since high school?"

She smiled as if he'd just suggested a romantic dinner out. "I track down scumbags like him for a living," she said lightly.

Steve, much to his credit, resisted the temptation to look over at Foldes. "Like your boyfriend over there?"

"Yeah, he's one of them. I'm waiting for another one to show up."

A fifteen year old Pontiac turned onto Main Street and rattled to a halt in front of Foldes. Molly took Steve's other hand and glanced at the car before kissing him on the lips. She caught a glimpse of the driver as he leaned out to speak to Foldes. A barbed wire tattoo circled his neck. Her pulse picked up speed. It was Mel Howard.

A twofer.

She leaned away from Steve still smiling. "I want you to walk away casually. Okay?"

He started to protest but stopped when she slipped a gun from her bag.

Across the street Howard got out of the car. He left it running and walked to the rear. He pounded a fist on the trunk lid as he twisted a key in the lock. The lid popped open and he lifted out a shotgun.

On the sidewalk, Foldes took out a large pistol and they headed toward the bank on the corner.

"Oh shit," Molly exclaimed.

She pushed up from the bench, keeping the Beretta at her side where it would be less visible.

"Get down," she hissed as she passed Steve. His eyes were wide with alarm.

As Molly strode across the park she dialed the sheriff's office on her cell phone. When the emergency operator answered she gave the details and hung up.

Molly tried to appear casual as she strolled across the street. She leaned through the driver's window of the Pontiac. It smelled foul – a mixture of body odor and cigarettes. She turned off the ignition and pocketed the key.

The doorway of a nearby store gave Molly an excellent view of the bank. She moved into position and put the bank's door in the pistol's front sight. A few seconds later muffled shouting told her the robbery was underway.

Derek Foldes burst from the bank with a duffle bag slung over his shoulder. Behind him Mel Howard backed out covering their escape with the shotgun. They ran to the car and Molly tracked them with the Beretta.

"Fuck," Howard screamed in frustration when he discovered the car wasn't running and the keys weren't in the ignition.

Molly put a round through the Pontiac's back window, spraying Howard and Foldes with glass. Howard dropped to his knees and raised the shotgun. Foldes released the bag and struggled to pull out his revolver.

"Give it up boys," she called.

"Fuck you!"

Howard fired a blast from the shotgun in her direction. Pellets smacked into the bricks all around her. She felt a sting in her leg and put a bullet into the car's body panel above his head. He rose and aimed the shotgun at the doorway. She leveled the front site of the Beretta on his chest. They locked eyes.

Two police cars screamed into view, one from each end of Main Street. They screeched to a halt blocking any escape routes. Arnie Voxx jumped from one and took cover. A pair of deputies leaped from the other.

Molly looked at Howard. His eyes flicked nervously from one side to the other.

She could tell he was thinking about it, weighing his odds.

Don't do it asshole.

Her finger tightened on the trigger.

The air compressed. It was just the two of them. His mouth constricted and he broke eye contact with Molly. Slowly he lowered the shotgun and set it down on the pavement. With a scowl he laced his fingers behind his neck.

Foldes ... where the fuck was Foldes?

She'd forgotten him. She looked around in a panic and then relaxed. Derek Foldes was passed out on the ground.

TWENTY SEVEN

The evening of the big shoot out, after Foldes and Howard were secure in their cells, Molly was in The Villager at the invitation of Arnie Voxx. It was his way of saying thanks.

"I'm not sure I like my town being turned into Dodge City," Arnie said after the first round of beer arrived.

Molly had spent most of the afternoon at the sheriff's office giving her statement and helping them fill in their paperwork. She had also called Dan Beaman who was delighted to hear she'd not only captured two bail jumpers but had also prevented a bank robbery.

She touched the spot on her leg where the shotgun pellet had struck. A quick flip of the scalpel and a soft tink on the bottom of a steel tray had taken care of it. Luckily it hadn't required stitches. There wasn't much pain, only a dull throb like a hornet's sting. The doctor assured her it would go away in a day or two.

Beer would help take the edge off.

"They told me you'd be here." She looked up to see Steve Fraser standing next to their table.

"I thought I should give a witness statement or something." He sat down without being invited.

"No, I think we have all the witnesses we need," Molly said with a smile. "Right, Sheriff?"

"Actually, we do need Steve's statement," Arnie said to Molly. He looked at Steve and said, "Come by the office in the morning."

Steve started to rise and Arnie held up a hand. "We haven't ordered our dinner yet. Why don't you join us?" Arnie said. "As a matter of fact, you'd be doing me a favor if you could keep Molly here company. I still have a whack of paperwork to do."

Arnie got up before Molly could object.

"See you in the morning," he said and walked away quickly.

Steve sat back down and smiled. "Sorry, I didn't mean to interrupt," he said awkwardly. "You won't shoot me, will you?"

It was her turn to smile. She couldn't help it. He sounded as if he really meant it.

"Nope, I've bagged my quota today."

He laughed and she joined in. She could feel the day's tension draining away. His good-natured sense of humor relaxed her. Before she knew it they'd consumed huge dinners and sinful desserts.

"I can't believe it's really you," Steve said after their plates had been taken away.

She knew what he was thinking.

How did a wallflower from high school become Dirty Harry?

"I had such a crush on you … " he trailed off, embarrassed he'd said it out loud.

Molly looked at Steve in stunned silence.

I didn't think he even knew I existed.

She didn't know what to say but something in his eyes told her he was telling the truth.

He held up the empty wine bottle and smiled apologetically. "Sorry, too much vino I guess."

"You meant it, didn't you?"

He lowered the bottle and looked into her eyes. "Yeah, I wanted to ask you out but I was afraid."

"You don't strike me as someone who's shy."

"Not so much now but back then I was. I missed out on a lot of things."

This surprised her. That's not how she remembered Steve. He'd seemed confident and outgoing – part of the in crowd. From the look in his eyes she could see remnants of the same kind of pain she had lived with during her high school years.

Molly empathized with him. She'd missed out on a lot of things as well – like having friends and a normal home life.

"I always wondered where you went," he continued. "I hoped that someday we'd see each other again and things would be different."

Well, things certainly are different now.

His honesty and vulnerability attracted her. She thought about their fake kiss in the park and wondered what a real one would be like.

After dinner Steve walked her back to the hotel. The gulf of time between them had vanished. They held hands like a couple of teenagers on a first date. Even simple contact like this had always made Molly uncomfortable. That was one of the reasons why she was still a virgin. Now, with Steve, it felt natural. He had an impish sense of humor that put her at ease and she giggled like a schoolgirl at his silly jokes and funny faces.

They stood in awkward silence in the hotel parking lot. What was next? Would they part again, just friends who'd had a nice evening together? She didn't have time to think any further.

Steve pulled her into his arms and kissed her — for real this time. Warmth flushed through her body. His strength and tenderness made her feel safe. There was no urgent desire to his embrace. He just held her protectively in his arms.

Molly wanted to yield to him, to have him carry her off.

His eyes met hers. "Thanks for a really nice evening," he said. "Could we do it again?"

"I'd like that," Molly replied softly.

They exchanged phone numbers and promised they would get together soon.

Later in her hotel room Molly couldn't sleep. She kept going over the evening. Just thinking about Steve awoke something she had never felt before. She stared at the piece of paper with his phone number.

Take it slow. There'll be time for that later.

~

Molly didn't have to wait long for Steve's call. When she returned to Detroit there was a message from him inviting her up to his place on the lake for the Fourth of July.

The discipline of her job left little room for emotion. Consequently she'd buried her feelings under a layer of toughness over the years. It was one of the ways to survive in this profession. In the days leading up to her visit with Steve, however, she found thoughts about him intruding on her work. She felt distracted and a little disoriented.

"Your head's not in the game," Dan Beaman cautioned after he found her day dreaming at her desk.

Dammit, he's right.

The anticipation of seeing Steve and the implication of staying at his place were impacting her work.

She tried to define what she was feeling.

Is this just a retro schoolgirl crush?

There was another possibility and she found it terrifying.

Am I falling in love?

Molly immediately dismissed that idea and threw herself back into her work with a renewed energy. She blocked all thoughts of Steve and their forthcoming weekend from her mind.

Before she knew it July Fourth arrived.

~

Steve's home was beautiful. It sat on the lake directly across from Sunset. The house had belonged to his parents.

Molly smiled as she looked around.

This is a guy's place alright.

While it was neat, there wasn't a piece of furniture that didn't look at least twenty five years old.

There was a bit of awkwardness when she first came in and set her bag down near the door. After a brief hug Steve picked up the bag and led her to the guest room.

Molly looked around. "Where's your room?" she asked.

They looked at each other for a long moment, reading each other's thoughts as clearly as if they had spoken.

~

That night Molly and Steve made love for the first time on a chaise lounge down by the lake as Fourth of July fireworks exploded over Sunset. At first Molly was nervous but Steve was a gentle lover and took his time. Warmth flowed through her body as they slipped into a soft rhythm that carried her away. Afterward, she cuddled against him and he wrapped protective arms around her. They lay in silence together savoring feelings no words could express. For the first time in her life Molly felt truly safe.

Molly reached for Steve in the dark. She felt an irresistible desire to explore this new world he'd initiated her into. The last rumbles of the fireworks rolled across the lake as they made love again, more intensely this time, their quiet passion exploding into wild abandon.

They lay entwined, her head resting on his chest and listened to the soft lapping of the waves. Molly found herself telling Steve things she had never been able to express to anyone. She shared some of the pain of her early years. However, she still couldn't tell him about being an outsider, dreaming of a life she would never have.

Steve talked about losing his parents in an accident. They had been passengers in a float plane that went down in the lake three years earlier. Their bodies had never been found.

He'd inherited his father's commercial fishing business. Steve's tone brightened as he told her of his plans to expand the business. From the confidence in his voice she knew he would be successful.

They talked for most of the night, revealing things to each other that neither thought possible. His hand caressed her bare thigh and she found herself wanting him again with a longing that surprised her. They made love until dawn.

Their first night together was one she would hold close to her heart in the years to come.

~

In the months that followed Molly and Steve saw each other every weekend. They knew they were in love even before they declared it to each other. Steve proposed to Molly on New Year's Eve – a dream she never knew she had was coming true. With eyes full of tears she accepted.

However, Molly wasn't sure how they would make it work. She didn't know if she could leave the career she loved. There was no question of Steve leaving Sunset; he had a business to run.

But what about my life?

Molly was afraid she might end up resenting Steve if she moved to Sunset.

Damn it – why does it have to be Sunset?

A partial solution came a few weeks later when she received a call from Arnie Voxx. He offered his congratulations on her engagement. He also offered her a job as a deputy in his department. It wouldn't have the intensity of her current job but at least it would allow her to use her law enforcement skills.

When Molly told Steve about Arnie's offer she could see he was troubled. Steve wanted her to leave that life behind once they were married. Her stories about some of the cases she'd worked alarmed him. Every time they parted he begged her to be careful. Once she even noticed tears in his eyes as he held her in his trembling arms.

"I couldn't live if something happened to you."

Steve tried to persuade Molly to apply for a job at the library. She assured him the job with the sheriff's department was safe.

"This is Sunset. Nothing ever happens here."

Steve finally came to terms with Molly taking the job. She was right. Sunset was a quiet town. There was a slim chance of anything happening to her.

Six months later they were married.

For the first time in her life Molly was truly happy.

TWENTY EIGHT

Steve was still on her mind when Molly pulled up in front of Jonathan Drake's home. Thoughts of the past had overwhelmed her once again. Tears stung her eyes and she needed to spend a few minutes pulling herself together before she rang the doorbell.

~

Through the window in Drake's living room Molly watched the ferry a mile offshore as it headed toward Cedar Channel and the safety of the inner harbor. The lake was kicking up and she knew it would be rough out there for the passengers.

Handing her a glass of sparkling water Drake said, "I understand new information has been uncovered."

Who had talked to him?

"A page from a poem by Aubrey Colgate Jones has turned up," Molly told him. "It appears to be part of an unknown work."

Drake didn't react.

He already knows.

"What's your take on it?"

He took a small sip of water. "A manuscript such as that would represent a valuable literary treasure."

"Wouldn't its only value be to someone who could actually publish it?"

"Yes, that is true," he replied.

"And you're the literary executor so it would have to be with your permission," Molly said. "I thought literary works were in the public domain seventy years after an author's death."

"It could be over a hundred years old and it would not matter," Drake said sharply. "It has to be a published work. In this case, it would only fall into the public domain seventy years after it was first published."

Molly nodded. "So how could someone profit from having the manuscript if they can't publish it?"

"They would have to contact me."

"Has anyone offered it to you?"

He shook his head. "Unfortunately they have not."

"But you believe it exists."

"I believe Aubrey was working on something in the months before he died. He was happier than I had ever seen him."

"And the manuscript wasn't among the things he left you?"

"No."

"Was there anyone else he might have given the manuscript to?"

"Aubrey was quite close to Barbara Harre and her husband Donald. I know he trusted Barbara. Aubrey might have given it to her. Of course it will be difficult to confirm due to the nature of her illness."

Molly thought again of the librarian and how upset Julia had been when she'd asked about questioning her mother.

"And there's no one else you can think of?"

Drake shook his head slowly.

Molly could see he was lost in his thoughts, perhaps remembering a time before she was even born.

On the mantle a wooden Arts and Crafts style clock chimed three times. Molly closed her notebook and stood.

"Thanks again for your time, Mr. Drake," she said.

Jonathan Drake blinked and his eyes refocused on the present. He rose from his chair and walked to the door with Molly.

"Miss Parsons, I know your principle responsibility is to learn who killed Dr. Elkins. I cannot help but feel his murder and this manuscript are intertwined.

"Aubrey Colgate Jones died without knowing the impact he would have on American literature." His voice was choked with emotion as he continued, "That manuscript is his legacy. His words must live."

Knowing she could offer no comfort Molly left.

She thought about Drake as she slid behind the wheel. She felt uncomfortable about their interview. Again she wondered if he was manipulating her.

Is this all an act?

She remembered the blurred camera image of the attacker running away. It was obviously not Drake. There was no way it could be him.

However, he certainly could have hired someone to do his dirty work.

~

On her way back to the station Molly decided it was time to get the truth from Tony Huffner.

No more bullshit. I'm really gonna squeeze him now.

Molly had a strong suspicion Huffner would implicate Brian Haley. If he did, she would have a solid reason to bring Haley in for questioning.

She would have Paul Booster pick up Tony Huffner first thing in the morning. She wanted him alone in the interview room for at least half an hour before she arrived.

Let's make him sweat.

TWENTY NINE

The frozen lake sparkled in the moonlight. A fierce wind drove hard crystals of sleet across it. Something stirred deep in the frigid water and began to rise toward the surface. It was blocked by a barrier of ice. It smashed its fists against it in rage. The blows tore pieces of waxy flesh from its thin hands. The ice shattered under its assault. A fist punched through into the night air. It kept punching until the hole was big enough.

Skeletal hands, coated with a layer of frost, reached out through the jagged shards of broken ice. They clutched at the sides of the hole. The figure dragged itself free and stood up. Its sunken eyes burned with a hellish intensity as it shambled toward the silent, dark house on the shore.

~

Inside the house Molly woke to a scream of buffeting wind. The front door rattled and crashed open. The blizzard exploded into the living room. The door swung back and forth wildly, threatening to tear loose from its hinges. She jumped out of bed and felt the cold bite into her. She ran through the swirling snow into the living room. She knew what was coming. She had to shut the door to keep it out. She threw herself against the door trying to force it shut but the frigid wind sapped the last of her energy.

I can't do it.

She was knocked to the floor. Through tears she could see something coming out of the shadows. She didn't want to see it but it was too late. She watched in terror, unable to look away.

It filled the doorway, looking through her. She caught her breath.

Steve.

Released from its hiding place under the lake the corpse was swollen and bloated.

She tried to rise but a blast of wind threw her back onto the floor, pinning her there. The corpse stood glaring down at her. Its mouth opened. A deep roar of agony escaped from its throat. The sound mixed with the storm, crushing her in its cold embrace. The corpse reached for her. She screamed in terror.

When she stopped screaming it was silent again.

No howling wind.

No snow.

Molly huddled in the corner pointing the gun at the darkness beyond her bedroom door. It had been the most vivid dream yet. It wasn't fading as quickly as the others had. It was the image of Steve, her lovely Steve, which remained the longest.

He was lost to her forever.

THIRTY

Tony Huffner was suffering. The night before he and Brian Haley drank a bottle of vodka. Brian drank it straight but Tony had mixed his with orange juice. The sweetness had made him sick.

He woke up in his car in Glen's parking lot at 7:00 that morning when Deputy Paul Booster rapped on his window. He was freezing cold and had a massive headache. The sound of Booster's college ring tapping against the glass sent slivers of pain deep into Tony's head.

Booster reached in and dragged him from the car. He put Tony's hands behind his back, snapped on cuffs, and pushed him into the back of the cruiser. Tony was too weak and nauseous to resist.

~

Booster had left him handcuffed to the table. Tony really didn't give a shit. At least the interview room was quiet. All he wanted to do was lie down somewhere and die. He put his head on his arms and tried to go back to sleep.

Paul Booster thought Molly looked worse than usual when she arrived. There were dark blue circles under her eyes. She hadn't even tried to cover them up with makeup. Her voice had an unpleasant rasp, like she might be coming down with a cold. Booster wondered what kind of night she'd had. This wasn't the first morning she'd looked like this. In his opinion she wasn't fit for duty. He planned to mention it to Sharpe this morning.

I should be lead on this.

Molly used her thumb to pop the plastic lid off her jumbo take out coffee. Her hands had a slight tremor and the surface of the liquid quivered. She leaned on the back of a chair and stared at Tony Huffner through the one way glass.

"He looks like he's asleep," she said to Booster.

152

"Slept in his car last night. He's hung over."

Molly decided to change her approach with Tony. Instead of gradually wearing him down like she planned she'd go for a full-on assault.

Hopefully he'll fuck up and I'll have him.

She entered the interview room and slid into the chair across from Tony. He didn't stir. She slapped the table in front of him with both palms. Tony's head flew up at the loud bang. He looked like he was going to toss his cookies.

"Rise and shine," she shouted in his face.

He grabbed the sides of his head in agony.

"Tony, this is what happens when you bullshit me."

He fought back tears of despair.

Fuck him. One man was dead and another seriously injured.

"I told you the truth before," he whined.

Molly didn't relent. She wasn't putting up with his shit any longer.

"No, you didn't. And we both know it."

He tried to lower his head into his arms once again. She put a hand under his chin and pulled his face close. She fixed him with a stare.

"Now what were you and Brian up to out there on the lake?"

His eyes flicked up to the right.

"And before you start telling me another lie, think twice. I've got a cell in back all ready for you."

"For what?"

"A charge of drunk driving to begin with. Deputy Booster tells me he found you behind the wheel of your car this morning, passed out from drinking."

"Aw fuck that. I was asleep and my car keys were in my pocket."

"Maybe, but suspicion of DUI will get you a jail cell just the same. We can let a judge sort it out in a day or two."

She released his chin and his head lolled back and then tilted forward. Molly wondered if he was going to be sick and pushed her chair back with a screech. The sound drove daggers into Tony's brain.

Everything in the room rolled for a second and he felt his mouth filling with saliva. He fought back the nausea and took deep breaths. Finally the sick feeling abated and he dropped his head into his hands again.

"You want to hear what I think you were up to on Sunday night when Professor Elkins was killed?"

He shook his head slowly.

"You and your BFF Brian Haley were down at the mouth of the channel in that speedboat of his. Now, why would you be down there in the middle of the night? Well, maybe you were there because you knew the Coast Guard wouldn't be."

He tried to mask his surprise with a yawn.

"I was sitting down there on the rocks drinking beer like I told you," he whined. "I don't know where Brian was. Maybe out with his girlfriend."

"I spoke with Desirée and Brian wasn't with her that night."

She let that sink in for a few minutes before continuing.

"So why were you sitting down at the end of the channel in Brian's boat?"

Tony didn't raise his head.

"How did you know the Coast Guard wasn't around? Snooping around on your dad's computer? Found his patrol schedule?"

Tony looked up in stunned silence.

Oh shit.

He felt disembodied hands grip his skull. They squeezed harder and the urge to vomit rose in his throat again.

"Knowledge like that would be really valuable if you were making a high speed run to pick up something. Like a boat full of weed down from Canada. Or was it Ecstasy?"

"You can't prove anything," Tony protested.

"With the right warrants we can prove it all." Molly rose slowly and loomed over Tony. "What do you think we'll find when we do a drug residue test on Brian's boat?"

Tony, anxious and in considerable discomfort, kept his mouth shut.

Maybe he isn't as dumb as I thought. Time to throw him for a loop.

"What type of shoes do you wear?" she demanded.

"What?"

"Shoes. You know those things you put on your feet to keep them dry. What brand do you wear?"

Booster observed the interrogation from behind glass. He had to admit she was good. Although exhausted, Molly had become energized during the interrogation. He admired the way she pulled disjointed pieces together. The bit about the Coast Guard patrol schedule was really impressive.

Of course Tony would have access to information that would make him valuable to a scumbag like Haley.

"Your shoes," Molly repeated impatiently.

"Vans mostly but I've got a pair of Sketchers for work. They hold up really well."

"What were you wearing on the night you found the body?"

"I'm not sure. Probably my Vans."

Tony relaxed now that she'd stopped asking questions about speedboats, Coast Guard schedules, and drugs.

"What's with the shoes? You keep asking me about shoes?"

"Did you and Brian see Dr. Elkins on the walkway by the bridge?"

"I didn't see him down there."

"When you pulled the body from the channel how did you snag it?"

"I used the rescue pole near the dock."

"That's the one which was lying on the rocks, right?"

"Yeah, that's right."

"It has a loop at the end where a drowning person can reach through and hold on while you haul them in."

"Yeah … "

"How did you use it?" At Tony's confused look she added, "Did you slide it around his neck or what?"

"I snagged it around his leg and pulled his body in."

"Did you notice the small rip on the back of his parka?"

Tony looked puzzled.

"The crime tech said the rip is from a sharp object, like a boat pike. Did you use a pike to haul him in next to the boat?"

Booster had read Kurt's report. There was no mention of a tear in the victim's parka.

She's bluffing again.

"I told you," Tony said continuing to shake his head. "I used the rescue pole to drag him out of the channel."

"What size shoes do you wear?" Molly demanded.

"Size nine."

"Okay, Tony, why don't you tell it to me again from the top – all of it," Molly said as she pulled her chair back to the table.

Tony slumped down further.

155

"Let me get you started," she said. "You and Brian are out in his boat waiting for the Coast Guard to pass by so you can head out into the lake. One of you spots the body in the channel. Before Brian can stop you, you use the boat pike to snag it."

Tony shook his head back and forth.

"Brian doesn't have your sense of decency. He got mad because he wanted to let it drift on out into the lake. He doesn't care about people but you cared. You did the right thing. Brian must have been pretty pissed off at you, especially when you called 9-1-1. So he dropped you by the rocks and took off. Where did he go? Did he pick up the drugs without you?"

Tony looked at Molly.

"No, it didn't happen that way at all," he shouted in frustration. "I was on the rocks – alone. Brian wasn't there."

Molly sighed. "I'm going to get to the truth here, Tony. You're going down for obstruction of justice and anything else I can pile on."

Tony Huffner sat back in his chair and crossed his arms, signalling he wasn't going to budge.

Booster could see Molly was at an impasse. He watched her storm out of the interview room and slam the door behind her.

Well, Lady, what're you gonna do now?

~

Outside the interview room Molly paced impatiently.

"How long before he lawyers up?" Booster asked.

Molly's reply was interrupted by an angry John Huffner barreling down the hall trailed by Kenton Sharpe.

"So what's this all about, Molly?" he demanded stopping in front of her. "You pick up my son this morning and don't even let me know? I thought we were friends."

He was right. They were friends. She and John Huffner had even worked on a few cases together, mostly to do with drug smuggling which was rampant on this part of the coast. John had always struck her as a sad man. She knew he'd been a widower for a long time and had devoted his life to raising Tony. She hated that she was causing him pain by treating Tony like this. However, bigger things were at stake.

I wonder who tipped him off.

She looked at Booster and Sharpe before leading John further down the corridor. The soundproof door to the interview room was shut but she didn't want to take any chances.

"I'm sorry, John. I should have called you," she apologized. "But I think he's lying to us about Sunday night."

"Lying? Why? He did the right thing and called it in."

"We believe he was with Brian Haley in a boat not on the rocks like he told us."

"So what's the difference? Maybe he doesn't want to get Brian involved."

"We think it's more than that. We think they were out there doing something illegal."

Sharpe stepped between them. "I think we all need to go down to my office and discuss this," he suggested.

~

Once in Sharpe's office John Huffner refused to sit. Instead he stood and continued to glare at Molly.

"Now, what the hell are you talking about? What kind of illegal activity do you suspect them of?"

"I don't know for sure, John, but I suspect it was drug smuggling."

"That's not possible. These waters are heavily patrolled. If they'd been out on Sunday night one of my cutters would have spotted them."

"Not if they knew your patrol schedule," she said softly. "You keep a copy of it on your computer, don't you."

"Yes, I do but it's password protected."

"Come on, John, a twelve year old hacked the New York Stock Exchange website last week," Molly said.

Realization hit. John sat down and shook his head.

"When he was little I was his whole world. We hung together out all the time. Tony was my best buddy. When Sylvia passed he seemed to drift away from me. He found it hard to cope with the loss. God knows I was going through the same thing myself."

John looked over at Molly. His eyes were damp.

"So what do we do now?"

"John, as far as my investigation goes he hasn't committed a crime. I don't know for certain what they were doing out in the channel and I don't care. I just need to have him confirm he was there with Brian Haley so I have a good reason to go question him."

John understood the influence the Haley family wielded in Sunset. He looked at Kenton Sharpe. Sharpe would never allow her to mess with the Haleys without a really good reason.

"I'll talk to him," John said softly.

Molly led him back down the hall and opened the interview room door. Tony looked up with shock when he saw his father. John Huffner sat in the chair and stared at his son. Molly moved silently into a corner.

~

Forty five minutes later Molly had Tony's signed statement that he and Haley were in a boat at the mouth of the channel. She didn't ask what they were doing there at that time of night so Tony didn't have to admit to any criminal intent. It might come out in court later – it probably would – but for now Tony was in the clear.

Kenton Sharpe read Tony's statement twice. Molly enjoyed the way it made him squirm.

He frowned at her. "You don't suspect him, right? He's just a potential witness so there's no need for you to bring him in here."

Molly nodded and Sharpe continued, "Let's question him at his house."

She agreed. It would be better to conduct the interview at Brian Haley's home. He would feel more in control which would probably make him more arrogant. Arrogant people often made mistakes.

"Kenton, I'll talk to Palmer March first and give him a heads up. I'll even offer to let him sit in on the interview," Molly said. "All I need from Brian is his statement that he was there and if he saw anything which could help us."

Sharpe mulled this over.

"Okay. Talk to him," he said.

~

There was no answer at the Haley residence. Molly tried the private cell phone number Sharpe had given her for Palmer March. It went straight to voicemail and she left a brief message asking Palmer to give her a call.

She asked Booster to release Tony. She was confident he wouldn't warn Haley.

Molly thought again about Brian Haley and his brazen arrogance. She was looking forward to taking the smirk off his face.

Right now, however, Molly was going to talk with Desirée Platt to see if she knew what Brian was actually up to on Sunday night.

THIRTY ONE

Desirée Platt sat across from Molly at a small table in The Villager. It was getting close to the dinner rush and the restaurant was filling up quickly. Desirée shuffled in her seat.

"Tony Huffner says they were out in Brian's boat on Sunday night when he found the body," Molly said.

Desirée shook her head, "Well, like I told you before, I wasn't with him on Sunday night."

"How about earlier in the evening?"

"No." Desirée's voice had gone flat.

"You're sure?"

"Positive."

Molly could see Hank eyeing them from the bar. He was anxious to have Desirée get back to work. The place was getting crowded.

"Sorry, I didn't mean to interfere with your work," Molly apologized. "We can finish this later."

Desirée got up and walked back to the bar. She and Hank talked for a couple of minutes. Then she grabbed a pile of menus and headed toward a party of eight.

Brian Haley must have come through the kitchen. The regulars did that when they parked in the back. It saved walking around the block. Haley looked around. He spotted Molly and staggered toward her.

Drunk again.

"I hear you wanna question me," he slurred.

Haley swayed as he stood over her. Molly knew what he was capable of. She got up and faced him.

"You hear me, Bitch?" He held his fists at his side, barely containing his rage. "You got something to ask me?"

160

"I think you'd better go home." She spoke softly and calmly.

"You think I had something to do with killing that guy?" he shouted.

Before Molly could reply Tony Huffner stumbled in from the back. Blood was flowing from his nose. He moved quickly toward Haley.

"Brian, don't do it man," Tony yelled.

Haley turned on Tony. "You want more, you lying prick?"

"You need to leave now," Molly told him in a level voice. She had to get control of the situation before it escalated.

"Fuck you! You wanna ask me questions then go ahead, Bitch. You've had it in for me for a long time."

She refused to take his bait. It would be a lose-lose situation.

"I'll come out to the house in the morning after I've talked to your cousin."

"I don't need Palmer's permission to talk to you. I can fucking speak for myself."

Molly saw Hank move up behind Haley. Desirée stood beside Hank, alarm written all over her face.

She took Haley's arm. "Brian, please," Desirée pleaded.

He backhanded her. Desirée slammed against a table and slid to the floor. Hank leaped forward and pinned Haley's arms. He struggled to break free of Hank's iron grip.

"I don't care who you are – you're never coming in here again," Hank said in a low menacing voice.

Brian continued to struggle. The ex-marine was unmovable. He'd handled a lot of drunks in his time. Molly took a pair of handcuffs from her bag.

Desirée looked despondent. "No. Please," she begged.

"Sorry but he hurt you," Molly said coldly.

"I don't want him charged," Desirée cried.

Haley tried to kick Molly as she snapped the cuffs on his wrists. She took a canister of mace from her bag and aimed it at his face.

Desirée looked up Molly. "Please … "

Hank wrapped his arms around Haley again and held him tight.

"Let me go, you fucker," he screamed at Hank. Haley struggled until he realized he wasn't going to get anywhere. He glared at Molly.

Molly helped Desirée to her feet. A trickle of blood was coming from her nose. Molly took a napkin from the table and wiped away the worst of it.

"Hey Bitch, you ain't seen trouble yet," Haley muttered to Molly.

Molly turned on him with rage. "What's that supposed to mean? That you're above the law? That you can beat the shit out of anyone you choose to?"

He smiled at her defiantly. "We'll see."

A deputy arrived and led Haley out to the cruiser. Molly followed and looked down at him when he was seated in the back.

"We'll talk in the morning after you get back from court."

"Court? I'm not going to fucking court," he screamed defiantly. "And I'm not talking to you about anything."

Molly slammed to the door and the deputy drove off.

Desirée was still in tears when Molly went back inside.

"He didn't mean to do it," Desirée sobbed. "He was drunk."

"There will always be another excuse. 'He was drunk.' 'He wasn't himself.' 'He's been under a lot of pressure.' Then he'll promise that he'll never do it again. Believe me he's not going to change and he will do it again." Molly looked at her with sympathy. "I'm guessing this isn't the first time he's hit you."

"No, he's never laid a finger on me before. He won't do it again."

"Yes, he will. It's how he controls you. It has to end now." Molly softened her tone. "You think he loves you. Maybe he does. But he has to be stopped before he really hurts you."

Desirée nodded and wiped her tears.

"I'd like to take you to the hospital and have you checked out."

Desirée shook her head. "I just bumped my nose. It stopped bleeding already."

"Okay, then let me drive you home."

"But I haven't finished my shift yet."

Hank stepped forward. "Don't worry about that. You go with Molly. We'll be okay here." He smiled at Desirée. "I don't want you crying in the customers' beer. The regulars think I water it down enough as it is."

Desirée returned his smile and sniffled. "I'll get my things," she told Molly and walked toward the kitchen.

"I don't understand how anyone with her smarts could fall for a loser like Brian Haley," Hank said.

Domestic abuse was a sad and ugly part of her job. She'd seen it too many times. Molly remembered the battered wife who blamed herself for her husband's rages. And the more vivid memory of a woman who had been severely beaten. A coma had spared her the pain of seeing her toddler's body after a boyfriend had beaten the child to death.

It filled her with disgust. She wasn't sure what made her angrier – the abuser or the victim who couldn't let go of a toxic relationship. She wondered how many other times Desirée had been beaten.

Molly knew she wouldn't sleep that night. She would replay the scene of Haley and Desirée over and over in her head.

~

After dropping Desirée off at her apartment, Molly thought about going back to the station. Although it would be good to see Haley behind bars she didn't want to deal with any more of his crap right now. She would be at his arraignment in the morning. Hopefully Judge Pomm would order him held without bail.

Of course that wasn't going to happen. Palmer March would be there with a check book and a dozen reasons why his cousin didn't represent a threat to the community. Topping the list would be the unstated reason.

He's a Haley, part of Sunset's ruling class.

Molly decided to go home.

Standing in her kitchen she thought about having a beer. She poured herself a glass of water instead. She kept thinking about Haley's assault on Desirée.

What would he have done if I hadn't been there to stop him?

Molly felt the blow as if she'd been the one he'd struck. That morphed into something intensely personal.

A darker doorway opened.

THIRTY TWO

The first year and a half of Molly's new life with Steve had been bliss. She fell in love with his place by the lake and together they made it theirs. Now it was more than just new furnishings and a fresh coat of paint; it was the first place Molly had ever called home.

In the summer the lake buzzed with boats and jet-skis and in the winter snowmobiles raced across its surface. She loved it most in autumn when the tourists abandoned Sunset and the changing leaves cast their crimson reflection on the still waters.

It was here their love deepened. There had been an awkward period of adjustment where each of them had to come to terms with the other's quirks and foibles. But it had passed quickly as they settled into a new life together.

There were also challenges. A serious drop in fish stocks had left the commercial fishing industry suffering. The recession caused banks to tighten credit lines and that compounded the problem. Along with everyone else, Steve's business struggled.

In an effort to save his business, Steve sold a pair of his trawlers. They had been in his family since the 1950s. He also had to let employees go, including some who had worked with him for many years. It troubled him but it was what he needed to do to save his business.

Although Steve had tried to keep the worst of it from Molly she noticed small changes in him. He had a difficult time sleeping and was drinking more than usual. But the learning curve of her new job distracted Molly from paying closer attention to what was happening with Steve.

The job with the sheriff's department wasn't as boring as she'd expected. Her experience had been in tracking and apprehending criminals but that was only a small part of a deputy's job. She found the work was both exciting and heartbreaking. Best of all, in her two years as a deputy her gun had stayed in its holster.

Arnie Voxx was impressed with how quickly she learned. He began to assign her more difficult cases. She definitely had a talent for investigating. By methodically working through the evidence Molly would build a case difficult for the defence to challenge.

The darkness had arrived when she least expected it.

It was supposed to be a romantic evening. Molly was going to pick up steaks and a video at Oleson's on the way home from work and Steve would grill them. It had been an especially hard winter for Steve because of the business but it was showing signs of turning around. They felt this was a perfect time for a little celebration – a delicious meal, a nice bottle of wine, a good movie, and the promise of an intimate night together.

It didn't turn out that way.

Later she learned the buyer had cancelled the deal when he discovered the poor condition of the trawlers. This led to a cash flow problem at the bank. The manager wanted to see Steve about his line of credit. It had not gone well. They were demanding a larger monthly payment which Steve couldn't afford. Without a line of credit he would be forced into bankruptcy.

Molly was concerned when Steve didn't come home at the normal time. Her concern turned to alarm when he didn't answer his cell phone. She continued to try for three hours, her panic growing by the minute. She even called the office to see if there had been any accidents. She was relieved to learn there hadn't. Then another thought occurred to her when she recalled that Steve had taken their boat across the lake to town that morning.

The lake could be rough at the best of times and there had been a brisk wind blowing all day.

Oh God no.

With a sickening feeling she dialed the Coast Guard.

What she didn't know was Steve had turned off his phone before the meeting with the bank and forgotten or hadn't bothered to turn it on again. He'd gone straight to the Blue Moon Bar.

Molly was relieved when she finally heard the Zodiac out on the lake. Through the kitchen window she could see its running lights in the dark. She ran down to the lake in time to see Steve guiding the boat up to the dock.

Steve slipped climbing out of the Zodiac and fell on his back landing hard on the dock. Cursing, he got up and tied the bow line around the front cleat. She stood in the dark and watched. He staggered to the stern and tied it off

Molly had never seen him this drunk before. A little tipsy perhaps, like one night on their honeymoon when they had both had too much wine with dinner, but not like this. Not falling down drunk.

She stepped forward into the light. Steve noticed her and grimaced.

"That's right, I'm loaded," he said belligerently.

He stumbled toward the house, trying to avoid her.

"It's okay, Honey," Molly said.

"No. It's not," Steve yelled. "You're disappointed in me."

"No, I'm not," she said quietly to reassure him.

Molly tried to take his arm. He shook her off.

"Just leave me alone." His voice took on an ugly tone. "I don't need your help."

She reached out to him again. "Come on, let's go up to the house and I …"

Molly never got to finish the sentence. He smacked her in the face. She staggered backward from the blow. She was stunned. Steve stepped toward her, his face filled with rage. He raised his fists.

"Steve," she screamed.

He stopped. "Oh, Jesus," he cried.

He shook his head as if waking from a trance. He looked at Molly as if seeing her for the first time. She had tears in her eyes. He took her in his arms.

"I didn't mean it," he sobbed. "I'm so sorry."

She was silent as he continued to beg for forgiveness. She turned away from him and walked back to the house.

~

Steve told her about the meeting with the bank. He was going lose everything his father had built. He shared his feelings of shame and how frightened he was. He was overwhelmed and didn't know how to deal with the situation.

Later that night with Steve asleep beside her Molly convinced herself his violence had been an aberration. Steve was kind and gentle. He'd just reacted horribly under extreme pressure.

It won't happen again.

However, she couldn't block the vision of a battered child lying dead in its crib from her mind.

It won't happen again.

~

The next morning Molly dropped by the firing range to put in some practice and create an excuse for the small bruise Steve's ring had left on her cheek. When Arnie asked about it she said the Beretta's extractor had thrown a casing back in her face. He suggested she have the department's gunsmith take a look at it. She promised she would.

Throughout the day Molly kept going back to the night before – to Steve's raised fists and his face filled with rage.

It was just once.

Molly wanted to believe. She had to believe the ground beneath her feet had not shifted. This was still Steve, her loving husband, the man who made her happier than she'd ever been in her life. Nothing was going to change. The pain and terror of the previous evening would fade.

It won't happen again.

~

Molly arrived home that evening to find Steve grilling steaks. The table was still set from the dinner that hadn't happened the previous evening. He greeted her with his usual hug and kiss. After dinner they sat together on the couch and watched the comedy she'd rented. She loved the sound of Steve's laughter. It was boisterous, goofy, and contagious. As usual she found herself joining in.

Steve pulled her close. They finished watching the movie with her nestled in his arms. He kissed her gently on the lips and she responded passionately.

But in bed later that night Molly was unable to sleep.

It was just a one-time thing.

Lying beside Steve she wanted desperately to believe it would never happen again.

We'll be together – forever.

Oh mystery abides
In scented pines
Seldom seen
In darkness dines.

~ Aubrey Colgate Jones

THIRTY THREE

Palmer March watched Uncle Jake take his last breath. When it was over he dropped his head into his hands and sobbed. Although his uncle had been seriously ill for a long time, his death had taken Palmer by surprise. After a new round of chemo the Senator's condition had improved. The doctors were so encouraged by his response to the treatment they were certain he would be released within the next week. His uncle had always shown an amazing energy and vitality. Even in the grip of leukemia he woke up every morning determined not to surrender.

The Senator had been tired earlier that evening. Palmer put their legislative paperwork aside and suggested he get some rest. His uncle did not respond. His eyes were closed and for a few seconds Palmer thought he'd gone to sleep. But he wasn't breathing; he'd suffered a massive stroke.

Jake Haley died in the Traverse City Hospital at the same time as his son Brian was arrested in Sunset.

Palmer March was afraid of what lay ahead. He thought of his cousin and frowned. A good man like his uncle did not deserve a son like Brian. His out of control behavior was a continual source of anguish. Palmer resented the pain Brian had caused his father. He thought of his uncle at his weakest, after gruelling chemo sessions, asking for Brian with tears in his eyes. Palmer was always quick to make excuses for Brian but his uncle knew his only child was too self-centered to care and it broke his heart.

However, Jake Haley had an unshakeable faith that his son Brian would someday turn himself around. Until that day came Palmer March was legally in charge of the family fortune.

Palmer had to tell Brian of his father's death. This was one family responsibility Palmer was reluctant to assume. Brian was sure to challenge his authority over the family assets. There would be years of litigation and expense ahead as Brian wasted his limited resources trying to fight for control.

This is going to get nasty.

In the end Brian would lose. His father had made his wishes clear in a string of legal documents which gave Palmer complete control over the estate. This didn't mean Brian would end up with nothing. His father had established a trust fund for him which would pay a monthly allowance. He would also inherit a small house in town where he could live. Palmer no longer wanted his cousin living on the family estate. Brian would be comfortable if he lived within his means but Palmer knew he wouldn't. He would burn through the money as quickly as he got it.

~

It was after 3:00 a.m. when Palmer March returned from the hospital in Traverse City. He'd sat alone with his uncle's body for nearly an hour, thinking about what he needed to do next. Funeral arrangements and phone calls had to be made. The press had to be notified. He would call the Governor personally. The Governor would have to decide who would serve out his uncle's term. As the Senator's chief of staff, Palmer knew it would most likely be him.

The lights in the guest suite above the garage were off. This wasn't unusual. Brian was always out somewhere with his girlfriend or the Huffner kid. He dialed his cousin's cell phone but it went straight to voice mail. He swore under his breath. Now he was going to have to wait until Brian came home to tell him.

Lord knows when that will be.

Palmer was numb with sadness. He hesitated before he poured himself a drink from the small wet bar in his uncle's study. It felt strange. His uncle was the one who normally poured the drinks. This had been his uncle's sanctuary. Palmer looked around at the pictures and awards that lined the panelled walls. He'd lived in this house since he was fourteen. His uncle had taken him in after his mother's death. Now this was his study – along with the rest of the house.

He turned on the computer monitor and brought the estate's security cameras online. The screen was split into six sections. Each one covered a different approach to the house. Palmer sat in front of the monitor waiting for his cousin to return.

One hour and another drink later he saw Brian's Expedition stop at the front gates. They swung open and the vehicle disappeared from view and reappeared on the next screen which showed the parking area in front of the house. The SUV stopped and Palmer watched his cousin climb out.

Palmer finished the drink in a single gulp. He got up and pulled on his jacket.

I hope he isn't too drunk.

He opened the front door and was surprised to see Brian approaching the house. That was unusual. Normally he staggered up the stairs to his apartment over the garage. Palmer wondered if Brian had already heard about his father. From the strange expression on Brian's face he guessed he must have.

Who would have told him?

Brian stumbled drunkenly toward him. Palmer stepped out onto the front porch.

Brian was ten feet from his cousin when his face exploded in a glistening red spray.

Boom! Palmer dove for cover as the sound of a gunshot reverberated around the property. From behind a stone planter Palmer fished out his cell phone and dialled 9-1-1. He was barely coherent as he blurted out the details to the operator.

Palmer March looked at his cousin in horror. Brian Haley lay face down in a spreading pool of blood and brain matter.

THIRTY FOUR

Brian Haley's body still lay on the pavement where he'd fallen.

"Looks like a 30-30," Dr. Ronnie Kolmenn said. He kneeled over the body and probed the entrance wound in the back of the head.

Sheriff Arnie Voxx stood nearby watching the pathologist as he worked. It was bad. Even with the head facing down Arnie could see most of Haley's face was gone.

"This was the first." Kolmenn pointed to a spot on the back of Haley's jacket. There was a small entry wound ringed in blood. "It likely hit him as he got out of his car. Have Kurt check for blood trace from there to here."

Arnie was glad he'd secured the entire driveway area as a crime scene. He ordered the front gates locked and a deputy posted there. The press would come sniffing around soon. This was a big story. He pitied Palmer March and the innuendo he would have to endure. Reporters would jump on the most lurid scenario – father dies, son murdered, cousin inherits everything. It would all fall on Palmer and there was nothing Arnie could do about it.

Molly parked at the foot of the driveway and walked up to the house. Arnie watched her approach. She was furious.

Molly looked down at Brian Haley's body in disbelief.

"He shouldn't be here," she said bitterly.

"You're right. No one deserves this."

She shook her head. "He was supposed to be in jail. I arrested him for assault last night."

"Well, I guess someone gave him a 'get out of jail free' card then," Arnie said.

Molly knew who that someone was.

Kenton Sharpe was the only one who could have released him. She suspected Paul Booster called Sharpe as soon as Haley arrived at the station.

"Fuck," she exclaimed in frustration continuing to look at Haley's body.

Another promising lead gone – like his face.

The questions she had for Brian Haley would go unasked. He'd been an important lead in Elkins' murder. Now he was lying on the pavement with his brains leaking out because her boss chose to play political games.

Arnie could see her frustration. He was worried about her. Was she letting her emotions get in the way of her investigation?

"Look, Molly, if you think there's a tie between this and Elkins, I'd be willing to let you take the lead," he offered.

"Sorry, Arnie. I can't prove a link. In fact, I can't prove anything," she said softly.

"The offer stands. Right now you'd be doing me a favor. With all these cutbacks I'm having a hard time clearing our regular caseload."

She had a thought. "Let me talk to Sharpe about it. If we can find out who did this, it would be a real coup for him. He'll love the publicity. It would help him if he decides to run for Sheriff." Molly looked at Arnie, immediately regretting she'd said the last part.

"Let's deal with that when it comes," Arnie smiled reassuringly. "Right now, I could use your help."

There was a loud scream from the front gates. Molly could see Desirée down by the gates trying to break free from the deputy holding her.

Desirée. How had she gotten here so fast?

News travels quickly in a town like Sunset and bad news moves at light speed.

By the time Molly reached her Desirée had stopped struggling.

"Is it true?" she asked Molly tearfully.

She put an arm across Desirée's shoulders. "I'm sorry. Brian's dead." Desirée moaned and started to collapse. Molly reached out to support her.

"I want to see him."

"You can't go up there." Molly tightened her drip on Desirée. "It's a crime scene. You don't want to see it," she said softly.

Desirée deflated. Molly lowered her to the ground and knelt beside her. "Desirée, I'm sorry, but I need to ask you some questions. It's important."

Desirée looked toward the house. "I thought you had him in jail," she sniffed.

"We did. He was released."

"How did that happen?" she said in an accusing tone.

Molly shook her head. "I don't know."

"And then someone shot him," Desirée said bitterly. "He should never have been in jail in the first place."

"Sorry, but I saw what he did to you," Molly said. "I had no choice."

"Yes, you did. You didn't have to arrest him."

This wasn't an argument Molly wanted to have right now. Desirée wasn't thinking clearly.

"Brian made the wrong choice," Molly told her. "He was probably sorry about what he did to you."

Desirée nodded.

"I'll have someone drive you home," Molly said.

She spoke to the deputy at the gate and he radioed for a cruiser. Molly waited with Desirée until it arrived.

"Molly, promise me you'll get the bastard who did this. Please."

"I promise you, Desirée," she said. "I'll get him."

Molly put her into the cruiser and watched as she was driven away. She looked back at the house. She had to talk to Palmer March.

~

Palmer was still in shock. He'd seen two people close to him die in a single night. He picked up a fountain pen from the desk and stared at it as if he was trying to remember its purpose.

"Palmer, I'm so sorry," Molly said. She was sitting across from him.

"I was prepared for Uncle Jake. He'd been sick for a long time. I always hoped he would bounce back. I guess it just wore him down."

"Sheriff Voxx wanted me to ask you a few questions."

Palmer set the pen down. "Sorry, Molly. Please ask whatever you wish."

"You saw your cousin park in the driveway, right?" she asked.

"Yes, I saw him drive through the gates," Palmer indicated the computer monitor. "On the security feed."

"Does the system record the footage?"

Palmer shook his head. "The Senator didn't think it was necessary. I had a hard time persuading him to have the cameras installed in the first place."

"What did you do after you saw Brian come through the gate?

"I walked to the front door. I was going to meet him and tell him about his father."

"Do you have any idea where he'd been?"

"No, I thought he might've been with his girlfriend." A thought occurred to him. "Has anyone contacted her? She'll be heartbroken."

"I spoke to her a few minutes ago. She wanted to come up here but I sent her home."

Palmer nodded and continued, "I opened the door and Brian was walking up to the house. From the way he looked, I figured he'd already heard about his father."

"What do you mean by 'the way he looked'?"

"He had kind of a puzzled expression on his face. And he was staggering." Palmer squeezed his eyes shut trying to block out the image.

"Did he say anything?" Molly asked.

"Nothing, he … " Palmer's voice choked.

"Can you recall how loud the shot was?"

"I don't know. It wasn't too loud."

"And you didn't hear another shot before that?"

"No. Just the one."

Molly looked around the room. The house was built of quarried stone and expensive wood. The windows were triple glazed, designed to keep exterior sound to a minimum.

No wonder Palmer hadn't heard the first shot.

"Did you know Brian had been taken to jail last night?"

Surprised, Palmer shook his head.

"I arrested him for assault," Molly said.

"Assault?" He looked at her in disbelief. "Who?"

"I saw him hit Desirée and arrested him. He was supposed to spend the night in jail and be arraigned this morning."

"And you let him go?"

"Well, someone did," Molly said bitterly.

Palmer nodded. He was astute enough to understand the politics involved.

"My cousin caused a lot of grief for everyone he came in contact with. He didn't deserve any kind of preferential treatment," he said. "In fact, facing the consequences of his actions would have been a good thing."

Molly couldn't help but admire Palmer. He'd been through a lot but he was a decent guy. He took his position in the community as a responsibility and not just an entitlement.

Palmer's thoughts turned to practical matters. "The press hasn't been notified of Uncle Jake's death yet. I have to prepare a statement." He paused. "What should I say about Brian?"

"It would be best if you say he died under suspicious circumstances and leave it at that," she replied.

Palmer nodded, lost in thought once again.

Molly stood up. "We need to search Brian's room and the boat house. I can get a search warrant if you'd like."

"No, it's all right," he said looking up. "You have my permission to search the entire property if you think it will help."

"Thanks. We'll have a crime tech take a look," Molly said. "Did Brian mention a book or a manuscript or anything like that?"

"No," he said flatly. "I don't think he ever read a book outside of school. I'm sure he considered it a waste of time."

Molly thanked him and left. Palmer continued to stare down at the desktop. He was shattered.

~

Molly stood in the doorway and watched Kurt Harbou go over Brian Haley's room. She was surprised at how neat it was. Maybe the years spent in boarding school had instilled something in Brian. An oak bookcase by his bed was crammed. She noticed a matched set of Aubrey Colgate Jones' poetry on the top shelf next to works by Coleridge and Whitman.

Kurt held up a glass bong he'd pulled from under the bed. A tarry residue coated the steel bowl.

"Looks like he smoked a lot of weed, Mon," Kurt said in a piss-poor Jamaican accent. He indicated the space under the bed. "There's lots of grass under here. At least a pound, maybe more."

Too bad it didn't mellow him out. Maybe he wouldn't have been such an asshole.

She left Kurt on his hands and knees and went downstairs to the garage.

~

The odor of motor oil was faint. A mechanic's workbench and tool cabinet were against the back wall. An old Austin Healey was up on stands. Its wheels had been removed. The coating of dust on the body told Molly it had been there for a long time. It was British racing green. That brought back a memory from her childhood – of this sports car driving past her. It was the most beautiful thing she had ever seen. Its sleekness and powerful rumble had sparked a desire inside her. She wondered how much a classic Healey like this would cost today. She'd Google it when she got home.

Would Palmer consider selling it?

Another part of the garage was taken up with rows of file boxes stacked five high. Molly calculated there were at least a hundred of them. Like the Healey, the boxes were covered in a layer of dust. She took a closer look. Each box had a range of years written on its end. 'LGH' had been stenciled above the dates.

LGH – Lucas Graham Haley?

There had been a Haley building on Main Street near the bridge. The Senator had his constituency office there until he sold the building a couple of years ago. He must have had his father's papers moved here. It was probably deeds and legal papers, the kind of things the old man would have held onto.

She had a thought and looked at the dates. They were arranged in chronological order from the 1950s through the 1970s. She wondered if there was an inventory of the contents.

"The sum total of my grandfather's life," a voice said from behind her.

Molly turned with a start. Palmer had changed from his suit into jeans and an expensive sports shirt.

"Is there a list of what's in them?" she asked.

Palmer frowned. "There's at least a partial one. The Senator thought it would be a good job for Brian to create a spreadsheet for his grandfather's files. He started on it last year but, like everything else, he gave it up pretty quickly. I was actually going to hire someone to finish it up so we could put all this in storage."

Molly felt a twinge of excitement.

"When did he work on the inventory?"

Palmer thought for a moment. "Last winter. I remember he complained about how cold it was in here."

"Any idea how far he got before he gave up?" Molly asked.

"I'm not sure. He worked on it for a couple of months so he may have done quite a bit," he replied. "You could check his laptop."

Molly remembered seeing the computer on Brian's table upstairs.

"Thanks, I'll take a look."

Palmer stood with his back to the boxes.

"What's this all about, Molly?"

"I'm not one hundred percent sure. Once I've had a look at that inventory I'll know more."

"There are things in here that could embarrass my family," he said. "No doubt you've heard stories about my grandfather."

"I'm only interested in what's relevant to the case. I'll treat everything else with discretion."

"Thank you," Palmer said.

Molly's BlackBerry buzzed and she checked the screen. Kenton Sharpe. She let his call go to voicemail. She preferred to deal with him in person. She also drew a measure of satisfaction from blowing him off.

Let him wait.

THIRTY FIVE

March 18, 1963

Aubrey Colgate Jones stood by the window looking at the lake. His lover lay uncovered on the bed behind him. They had just finished making love.

She had come by after lunch. Aubrey hadn't been expecting her. He stepped onto the back porch and waved as she got out of her car. She had left her coat draped over the front seat and was carrying a white box. It held a peach pie from Wilson's Bakery.

Aubrey watched in fascination as she walked toward him, her body flowing smoothly. It was obvious she wasn't wearing anything under her dress.

As he leaned in to kiss her cheek she pressed herself against him. He put an arm around her waist and guided her through the kitchen door. She set the pie on the counter and turned to face him. She began to unbutton the front of her dress.

This was the moment. It had all been leading to this – the casual remarks, the half-hidden smiles, the casual brush of her hand against. Something had been growing between them. Now she had come to him.

She had moved into his arms and they made love until after dark.

At first it had been a frantic coupling, exploding with desire. Later they settled into an unhurried teasing and slow exploration of each other's bodies.

Propping herself up on one elbow she sighed softly and urged him to come back to bed. Cold air blew across her breasts and he could see goose pimples rise around her nipples. He felt the pull of desire and moved toward her.

Then he felt a stronger urge, something he thought had died. He was drawn to his desk. Their encounter had inspired him and he began to write. It was spiritual, the way the words flowed, arranging themselves in a precise order.

When he finished Aubrey sat looking at what he had written. He felt her behind him and heard a slight intake of breath.

"It's beautiful," she whispered.

She didn't need to tell him how she felt about his words. He could feel it. Draping her hands over his shoulders she began to stroke his chest. She kissed his earlobe and aroused him once more. He turned from the desk and took her in his arms. They made love again; softly, carefully. She let out a soft cry of pleasure a few minutes later as they climaxed together.

~

Aubrey woke near dawn to the sound of tires crunching on the gravel as she drove away. The sheets were still warm from her body and her fragrance lingered. Had he really heard her say she loved him? The thought disturbed him. He would have to break it off soon. Love would only complicate an already complicated situation.

Aubrey walked back to his desk and read what he had written the night before. He smiled. Sitting naked in the early light of dawn he picked up the pencil. He felt an overwhelming joy as the words poured from his soul.

THIRTY SIX

Molly stomped angrily into Kenton Sharpe's office. Paul Booster was sitting in a chair across from Sharpe looking smug. She'd had enough of Sharpe and his ruthless politicking. She also had her fill of Booster and his weasel ways.

"Why the fuck didn't you call me before you let Haley go?" she shouted at Sharpe.

He looked up at her in feigned shock. "Excuse me, Officer Parsons."

"You heard me. Because of you he walked straight into a bullet."

Sharpe's eyes narrowed and his nostrils flared. He was struggling to control his anger.

Booster shifted uncomfortably.

Sharpe stood up and leaned across his desk looking straight at her.

"How dare you question my authority?"

"Your authority – what, to let a violent drunk out of jail for no good reason?"

"I had a good reason. His father had died. I released him on his own recognisance. He wasn't going to run away."

Molly shook her head in frustration.

"I'm not convinced you should be back at work, Molly." He glanced at Booster. "Even your co-workers are concerned about you."

Molly turned to Booster in anger.

"Before you blame Officer Booster I think you should know he's already apprehended the killer."

"The killer," she said in confusion. "Who?"

"Anthony Huffner," Booster said softly.

"Tony Huffner? On what grounds?"

"On the grounds that we have an air tight case against him," Sharpe replied with cold certainty and sat down.

Molly sank into a chair.

"We have physical evidence tying him to the murders and the assault," Booster explained.

"What evidence?"

"We executed a search warrant on Huffner's home and seized the rifle used in the shooting and a pair of shoes which match the footprints from the scene," Booster replied calmly.

"It doesn't make any sense. Why would Huffner kill a total stranger and his best friend?"

Could I have been wrong about Tony? Is he capable of murder?

"We also found flour on his pants and a reel of heavy fishing line," Sharpe added.

Molly tried to digest all this.

"Kurt confirmed the shoes are a perfect match," Booster told her, "and the rifle had been fired recently. Dr. Kolmenn pulled the slug out of Haley's back. Kurt's doing a ballistics match right now but he's convinced Huffner's Marlin is the murder weapon."

"He also has no alibi for any of the crimes," Sharpe finished.

Molly slumped back in the chair. She felt a numbing weariness overcome her. It had been a long time since she'd slept.

"You look tired, Officer Parsons," Sharpe said condescendingly. "I think you need to get some rest. Let us handle things now."

His implication hovered in the room like an angry wasp.

Go home and think about your future.

Molly left the station and walked across town to the dock to get her Zodiac. She was stunned by the turn of events in the case. First she'd lost an important lead when Brian Haley was murdered and now Tony Huffner had been arrested. The evidence against him was overwhelming.

It doesn't make any sense.

But maybe that was the point. Murder was sometimes just a senseless thing.

Maybe her instincts were wrong. She'd trusted them for too many years and this time they had failed.

I failed.

Molly piloted the boat into the bay and headed for home. As she got farther from town her despair increased. It had been a rough couple of years. She thought the time away might help her heal. Maybe she had tried to take on too much too soon.

I should have stepped back and let Booster take the lead.

But the glory of solving a serious crime was just too tempting. She had something to prove – to show them she still had it. She'd failed, blinded by her own stubbornness and determination.

Booster's solution made sense. Tony and Brian were partners in a dope deal. They killed Elkins and had a falling out. It was simple and plausible.

Then he went home, put the rifle back in his closet, kicked off his Vans, and just waited for the law to show up?

If it had been the other way around and Brian was the one sitting in jail accused of Tony's murder it might make sense. She knew Tony. He was basically a decent person. He was the one who had called them to report the body in the first place.

No, there was someone else. Someone who knew what was hidden in the shadows. But right now her exhaustion was making it too difficult for her to think straight.

I need some rest.

Across the water she could see her home. She felt a shiver of fear. Tonight Steve would visit her again and there was nothing she could do to stop it. She thought about the pills in her medicine cabinet. They would help her sleep. The weight of her Beretta reminded her there was another alternative.

One way or another, tonight she was determined to get some sleep. After that she would find the real killer.

THIRTY SEVEN

What should have been the most wonderful day in their lives ended in horror.

Molly had a joyous surprise for Steve. What they had long been hoping for had finally happened. Throughout the day she'd run through various scenarios of the best way to tell him.

However, Steve had been late.

He'd had another meeting at the bank. The manager was concerned about continued missed payments and cut off the business's line of credit. Steve left the bank fearful of what the future would hold. He would have to shut down the plant and lay off the few remaining employees. It would mean shame and humiliation.

He couldn't face it.

When Molly discovered what had happened she raced to his office. The door was locked and it was dark inside. Desperately she drove to each bar in town to look for him. No one had seen him so, with mounting dread, she finally went home.

How had it gone so wrong?

Maybe if she'd taken more time before jumping in, if she'd gotten to know Steve just a little better, she might have seen the warning signs. However, she'd been blinded by love. She didn't realize that love could be dangerous. You fall in love and never expect it to end – but it does. For many it's the bittersweet parting of death and the shared love is carried on in the soul. With others love dies in bitterness and resentment; hatred drives it from the heart.

But sometimes feelings can be confused. The fear of losing love dominates everything. When logic tells you to leave, love holds you close.

This is the way it was with Steve. She was trapped by her irrational love for a man who had abused her.

Now it was too late.

The abuse had continued, usually after Steve had experienced some sort of setback with the business. The pattern was the same – get drunk, hit her, fall at her feet in remorse, and promise it would never happen again.

Until the next time.

Molly knew when Steve returned he would be filled with rage. She thought about the baby now growing inside her and feared what she might have to do.

~

Just after midnight she heard a car door slam outside. A couple of minutes later Steve pounded on the front door.

"Let me in," he demanded.

Molly stood frozen in fear. She could his silhouette against the frosted glass. He was hunched down.

He dropped his keys?

Even on his knees he continued slamming his fists into the door, making the frame rattle.

Molly started toward the door and stopped. Something told her not to go. This time it was different. She knew she couldn't leave him out there; it was freezing. But she couldn't let him in; he was out of control.

The tempo of his pounding increased in ferocity.

"Open the fucking door," he screamed in frustration. Steve slammed his body into it.

Enough!

She was a cop, an officer of the law. She needed to deal with this once and for all.

He doesn't love me. He only wants to make me feel his pain.

She'd let him control her; let him manipulate her into believing this was love.

He feels nothing inside.

Again she saw the dead child in its crib, nestled deep in its blankets as if it was trying to escape the blows. Molly cried from the pain of the image.

She had to protect their child – her child.

The banging at the front door stopped. A shadow passed the window.

The kitchen!

The glass door wasn't very strong. Molly heard the sound of it shattering.

Her hands were shaking as she punched the combination on the gun safe.

She pointed the large pistol at Steve. He stood swaying in the kitchen. He was covered in blood and surrounded by glass.

"What," he snarled, "you're going to shoot me?"

She centered the front sight on his chest. Her finger tightened on the trigger. This wasn't Steve. This was a monster who had invaded her home. It wanted to kill her.

Their eyes met. She could see the madness in his. Without warning he rushed toward her.

She stepped back. Too late. He slammed into her. The pistol flew from her grip and skittered across the floor. He reached for it. While he was distracted she slammed her knee into his groin. He shrieked in agony and punched her hard in the abdomen. She doubled over and fell to her knees, clutching herself.

He continued to writhe on the floor inches from her. She crawled away, the broken glass slicing into her palms and bare knees. She was weak and short of breath. Pain radiated from her abdomen. A series of sharp stabs felt like the jagged pieces of glass she was crawling over.

Snow, whipped by a demon wind, flew into the kitchen. She dragged herself up using the door frame for support. Behind her came a howl from Steve.

I have to hide.

She staggered out into the storm. The frigid wind cut through her thin cotton nightgown. Something warm tricked down the inside of her thighs as she stumbled toward the lake. Powerful cramping slowed her down. Tears froze on her cheeks.

She knew his blow had hurt the life growing inside her.

What if he finds the gun?

She knew he would use it on her.

She shivered violently in the intense cold, numbness creeping into her limbs. If she didn't find shelter soon she would die.

She could feel the ice as she stepped out onto the lake. It had been swept clean by the wind.

"Mollllllyyy!" his scream dragged out. He had externalized his rage and given it her name.

She didn't turn around. She knew he was coming after her.

Holding her belly, Molly stumbled farther out onto the lake. She wasn't making much progress. It was taking all her strength just to fight the buffeting wind.

She realized she'd made a mistake. There was nowhere to hide and even in darkness she would be easy to spot.

She could feel the vibration of his heavy boots through the ice.

The lake wasn't completely frozen. It was still too early in the season. Not far ahead there was thinner ice with open water beyond it. With each step forward she was increasing her risk of falling through. As if to emphasize this she heard an ominous crack. The ice shifted under her weight. She tensed then lost her balance and fell.

Steve came howling out of the dark. A length of steel pipe was raised above his head.

Molly screamed and tried to pull herself backward but he had almost reached her. He began to swing the pipe forward. She knew she was going to die.

Crack! The ice broke under Steve and he was gone.

The pipe flew through the air and slid to a stop beside Molly's right foot.

She crawled toward the jagged hole where shattered pieces of ice bobbed in the place where he'd been only a moment before. The ice creaked. It was too unstable to support her. She backed away carefully.

Steve's head broke the surface of the frigid water. The icy wind had turned his hair to glass. He desperately searched for a way out. His eyes, which had been filled with rage, were now wide in terror.

He was no longer a monster, just a man pathetically struggling against the grip of the lake. Panic set in as his sodden clothes and heavy boots dragged him down. His breath came in white puffs and she could see frost forming on the outside of his nose and around his eyes.

"Molly, please ... " he pleaded.

He grabbed at the edge of the hole and tried to drag himself out. The ice broke away.

The pipe.

She pushed it toward him. The pipe was only a few inches from his clutching fingers. They closed around it and he smiled weakly in relief. There was another loud crack and the ice tilted.

A stabbing pain ripped through Molly again. There was a gush of blood from between her legs. It was all gone now. Everything she'd believed in – Steve's love, their time together, the life they had conceived.

It was all gone in a single nauseating wave.

Their eyes locked. His were filled with a desperate pleading. She closed hers and let go of the steel pipe. Useless, it slid into the dark water. Steve watched it. He turned cold eyes on her as he comprehended what was going to happen.

"For God's sake, Molly, please," he begged. His voice was reduced to an exhausted whisper.

She slid back from the edge of the hole and watched as he struggled to pull himself free.

"No, Steve," she whispered. "Not this time."

Hypothermia stole the last of his strength.

He realized he was going to die, was going to be pulled down into the cold depths. He stared at her in resignation.

Molly would not save him because it was the only way she could save herself.

She wanted to scream at him, to tell him he'd destroyed their happiness – and he'd killed their baby. He killed it before he even knew it existed. She wanted to fill his final moments with all the pain she could inflict on him.

But she couldn't bring herself to do it.

She turned away. She couldn't watch him die.

When she looked back the hole was empty. There were only tiny fragments of ice floating on the surface of the water.

~

Molly somehow managed to get back to the house and call Arnie Voxx.

While they waited for the ambulance she told him in weak gasps how Steve had come home drunk and couldn't find his keys. He'd broken the back door trying to get in. In the process he'd injured himself. Steve had staggered onto the lake and had fallen through the ice. Molly tried to reach him but had slipped. She had landed hard on her belly and the fall had caused a miscarriage.

Her story left him with a few questions. However, he accepted what she told him. If he suspected it wasn't the whole truth, he never let on.

Later at home he and his wife Betty held each other in the dark and cried.

~

The following spring the State Police brought their dive team in to try to see if they could locate Steve's body. They searched for almost a week before concluding he'd been carried out into Lake Michigan by the current.

Steve was lost forever.

THIRTY EIGHT

Tony Huffner had been arraigned and was held over in the county lock-up.

The next morning Molly came to Arnie Voxx's office to ask a favor.

The D.A. was already hard at work building a case against Tony. While they were weak on motive, the physical evidence was overwhelming. They had established beyond a doubt that Tony's Marlin rifle had fired the shot that killed Brian Haley. His left shoe matched the print found at the scene of the assault in the hotel parking lot. The flour on his work pants was a perfect match to the traces on Barry Elkins' pants.

It didn't look good for Tony. But even with the strong physical evidence she was certain he was innocent.

"Sounds like wishful thinking to me," Arnie said.

"It just doesn't make sense," she replied impatiently.

"I heard you had it out with Kenton. The word is he's going to suspend you," Arnie warned her.

Son of a bitch. He'd do anything to stop me from making waves.

"We probably shouldn't be talking about the case at all," he said.

"Maybe we shouldn't. But really, Arnie, how does this feel to you?" she asked.

He thought about it for a moment. He'd known Tony since he was a little boy. Finally he shook his head.

"It feels wrong," he replied, "but the evidence says otherwise."

"Did your guy in Toronto turn up anything about either of the Elkins brothers?"

Arnie shook his head. "No, from everything he learned they were model citizens."

Molly put the manuscript page on the desk.

"This is the key. The manuscript. It was used to lure Elkins here." She tapped the page. "I don't think Tony is that conniving."

"Maybe. But you haven't found it yet."

"Not yet," she admitted.

He considered this. "So where do we go from here?"

"We have Haley's computer," she said. "I need to take a look at the documents on it."

"You're asking a lot," he smiled, "but anything to piss off Sharpe is alright with me."

He passed her an external hard drive. Molly slipped it into her purse and stood up. She was anxious to get to her computer to see what the files might reveal.

"Molly, walk around the edge for a while. Don't give Sharpe a reason to think you're trying to mess up his case." Arnie looked at her with concern. "Because I guarantee he'll hang you out to dry and there'll be nothing I can do. For now let him think he has got the right man in jail."

Arnie was a cagey old bastard who understood the jungle in which he roamed. He also had faith in her. She would be the instrument which would help him to cut Kenton Sharpe off at the knees.

"It's all political isn't it?" she chuckled bitterly.

"You bet," he replied.

~

Elizabeth Pierce had been director of the Sunset County Jail for the past eighteen years. At sixty three she had the kindly appearance of a doting grandmother. However, no one messed with her or her lock-up.

People who made that mistake saw a different side of Elizabeth Pierce. Anyone who acted up in her jail ended up spending a lot of time in solitary. And when the county tried to cut her budget a few years ago she was ruthless. Especially when she learned that some of the commissioners demanding the cuts were also accepting money from a corporation which wanted the contract to privatize the jail.

The weasels had argued it made sense to turn the jail over to a company. To counter this Elizabeth wielded statistics and projections with the deft expertise of a CEO. Her research showed private sector prisons actually ended up costing the taxpayers more and provided poorer service.

Off the record she also threatened to go to the press about illegal campaign contributions. Her budget remained intact.

"Kenton doesn't want anyone talking to Tony except his lawyer," Elizabeth said as she opened the door to a small room where a dejected Tony Huffner sat. "Especially you," she smiled.

Tony looked up in surprise as Molly entered. He was frightened.

"Take your time," Elizabeth said and left them alone.

"Have you spoken with a lawyer yet?" Molly asked.

"Not yet," he replied in a strained voice.

She looked around. The interview room was deliberately drab. It was painted an industrial green. A narrow slit window ran the length of the outside wall near the ceiling. It allowed in a tiny amount of light. The room smelled faintly of body odor, Pine Sol, and fear.

"I didn't kill him," Tony whined.

"Have you spoken to a lawyer?" she asked again.

"Dad hired a guy from Traverse City. He's supposed to come up this afternoon."

"Well officially I can take down everything you say and use it in evidence against you."

"Yeah, they told me that when they … " he choked up.

"But I'm not here officially," she said softly.

Tony looked at her in confusion.

"When we searched Brian's place we found a lot of dope. There was ten pounds hidden in the boathouse." She let this sink in. "I'm guessing you guys were out in the channel doing a run when you first saw the body."

He hesitated and then nodded.

"Brian has a contact up in Canada. He runs it down the coast in a trawler. We know the Coast Guard's schedule so we'd tell him when it was safe. Then we'd run out and pick it up.

"We were coming back in last Sunday night when I saw the body. I made Brian stop and he freaked out. I snagged it with a pike. He wanted me to let it go but I couldn't. It would have been wrong. No one would have ever found that guy again."

Molly shuddered thinking of a body lost out in the lake and the relatives never having closure.

"What were you planning to do with the drugs?"

"There's a guy down in Traverse City. He takes everything."

Molly shook her head.

"Why'd Brian do it?"

"He needed the money. His father was sick and he knew he wasn't gonna get a penny when he died. It was an easy way to make some cash."

"Do you think there's a chance one of the people he was dealing with might have killed him?"

Tony shook his head. "I don't think so. We were on good terms with them and they were paid up front. They're pretty cool guys really, just trying to make it in hard times."

Molly nodded. She stared intently at Tony.

"They tell you about the evidence they found in your closet?" she asked.

"Yeah, they said they matched my rifle and shoes to the crimes."

"How do you explain that?"

"I can't. Someone's trying to frame me."

"That sounds pretty farfetched," Molly pointed out.

He shook his head violently. "I don't always lock the door when I go out."

Like a lot of folks up here.

"My rifle isn't locked up or anything. I keep it in the back of my closet. I haven't used it since last fall. Same with the Vans. I got a new pair of Sketchers and I've been wearing them for the past few weeks."

Molly looked at him dubiously. "Someone snuck into your house, took your rifle and shoes, and when they were finished they put them back without you or your father knowing?"

"I know it sounds weird but that's how it must have happened," his voice went up two octaves.

"What about the manuscript?"

She watched him intently to gauge whether or not he was lying. He looked confused.

"What manuscript?"

He might not be lying but he's not telling the whole story.

She let silence, the ultimate truth serum, hang between them. He looked down at the table.

"Last month Brian told me he was on to a score which could bring big bucks."

"What kind of score?"

"He wouldn't say. I figured it was a big dope deal and he'd give me the details when he was ready."

She pounced.

"Brian liked to read didn't he?"

Tony was surprised by the question but nodded in agreement. "Yeah, he read a bunch of things at the same time."

"What kind of books did he like?"

"I think he liked books about people and history."

"What about poetry?"

"Yeah, he read poetry. He didn't want anyone to know. He was afraid they'd think he was a fag or something."

"Do you remember what he was reading recently?"

"A book about Teddy Roosevelt. It had his picture on the cover, you know with that big moustache and wearing an army hat."

"Anything else?"

Tony shook his head and then had another thought. "Oh, a couple of weeks ago I noticed one of those books by the guy who used to live here, the poet … Colgate toothpaste or something like that."

Molly felt a twinge of excitement.

"Aubrey Colgate Jones," she said softly.

"Yeah, him," Tony nodded. "We had to read his stuff in eleventh grade. It was really weird shit. Cool when you're stoned though."

Molly rose and knocked on the door for the guard. After a few moments it opened.

"I'm finished." She said to the guard.

"Please, you gotta help me," Tony began to blubber. "I didn't kill anyone."

Molly wondered how often someone had said that in this room.

She looked at Tony. He was nothing more than a scared kid. She wanted to comfort him, to tell him she believed him. Instead she just stared at him impassively.

He's safer here for now.

~

Back at her house Molly hooked up the disk drive Arnie had given her. It took a few minutes to find what she was looking for – the Excel spreadsheet Brian Haley had created of his grandfather's files.

Following a strong hunch she started at the end of the document. When she saw the dates it made sense.

She called Kurt Harbou and asked him to go out to the Haley garage. She gave him the numbers of the boxes she wanted him to take a look at.

THIRTY NINE

Shadow Lake, June 24, 1963

Aubrey Colgate Jones guided his sixteen foot cedar strip canoe across the glassy surface of the lake. He was wearing a pair of polarized aviator-style sunglasses to help cut the brilliant glare off the water. There were three cartons stacked in the bow of the canoe. He lived frugally and his groceries barely filled a single box. The other two were filled with bottles of Ballantine beer.

Aubrey wore a tan cotton work shirt which had once been part of a Marine Corps uniform before he removed the insignia and cut off the sleeves above the elbows. Summer had come early and his arms were already deeply tanned. His face and forehead were the color of stained oak with a touch of sunburn running down the ridge of his thin nose. He hadn't shaved for a few days and thick black stubble covered his cheeks and neck.

He was tall and thin; his belly flat and hips narrow – ironic considering the amount of beer he drank and most of his meals came from cans. He kept in shape by doing yard work around town and chopping wood at his cabin.

Since early May he had almost filled the wood shed next to the back door. Normally he didn't finish this chore until Thanksgiving. This year he had worked with an intensity he didn't understand. It had vibrated inside him scattering the accumulated rubble and freeing his spirit. For almost forty years he hadn't experienced anything this heady. It was like a dull film had been wiped away and the resulting clarity lifted him to new heights.

He stopped paddling and let the canoe drift.

He'd finished the manuscript in the early morning hours and stared at it until dawn spread its pink light across the lake. This was his finest work. It

196

was alive with the enthusiasm of youth and matured by the experience of sixty years.

Tiny waves slapped the sides of the canoe gently as he drifted. He was content. He'd not felt this way in many years. He certainly didn't feel it when he wrote lurid tales for pulp magazines. Writing junk like that had made him a whore – a man who sold small pieces of his soul to survive.

That was over now. He thought of the thick sheaf of papers on his desk. It was finished. Complete. All that remained was to type the final version from his handwritten copy.

He didn't have any typewriter ribbons or carbon paper, or even paper. It had been a hard couple of years and he had little money left to buy them. He would have to ask Barbara about using a typewriter at the library again.

A slight breeze rippled the water's surface. It rose up from Lake Michigan behind him. He shivered as it cooled the damp patches of sweat on the back of his shirt. He felt an unexplained sense of dread, as if someone had just walked over his grave.

Aubrey was still feeling anxious when he reached the shore. After he carried the boxes up to the cabin he returned and dragged the canoe out of the water onto the grass. He flipped it over so it wouldn't fill with rain in case there was a storm.

As he put the food into the refrigerator it started to buzz. He slapped the round compressor on top and it stopped. His dread intensified in the silence.

Something's wrong.

Particles of dust drifted through the air creating tiny bursts of brilliance in the intense sunlight.

What had disturbed them?

He left the rest of his groceries on the kitchen counter and moved through the cabin. There was no visible sign of an intruder but he couldn't escape the feeling his privacy had been violated.

He'd opened the windows to let in the fresh morning air before leaving for town. In spite of this there was still a faint ghost of winter's mustiness.

Aubrey felt a prickling of fear in his belly.

He went to his parents' bedroom. He used it as his office. It made him feel as if they were still there watching over him. He'd moved their furniture out and lined the walls with bookshelves. The only thing of theirs he'd kept was an old oak desk and this is where he did his writing. Its surface was undisturbed. There was no manuscript here. He felt stab of panic and then relief.

I wasn't working in here. It's on the porch.

With the arrival of warmer weather he'd moved a small table onto the screened porch off the bedroom. He'd finished the manuscript there and left it under the softball-sized piece of granite he used as a paperweight.

The tin can which held his pencils had been knocked over, its contents spilled onto the desk. A sheaf of paper fanned out across the rough pine floorboards where it had fallen.

However it was not what he saw that caused his despair; it was he did not see.

The manuscript is not there.

His stomach clutched. He felt lightheaded. It was almost surreal, that horrible realization that the focus of his life was gone. His eyes darted around the porch looking desperately for the manuscript.

Did I put it down somewhere?

He quickly searched the cabin.

Nothing.

Possibilities flooded through him.

He froze.

There was only one possibility, only one person ruthless enough to do this.

Lucas Haley.

Aubrey's hatred rose as he thought of Haley with his flashy suit and insincere knife slash of a smile. The bastard had purchased most of the nearby properties and was building those ridiculous vacation resorts. But Haley wasn't satisfied.

He wanted it all.

He coveted Aubrey's land.

Haley had tried every legal means to get him to sell and Aubrey had turned down every offer. It had become an obsession for Haley, as if this single piece was preventing him from completing his puzzle.

Haley stopped playing fair.

Last fall Aubrey nearly died after his well was poisoned. In February someone had shot out the cabin's back windows while he slept.

Haley wasn't subtle and his message was simple: sell or else.

Now Lucas Haley had stolen his manuscript. He wouldn't see it as Aubrey's life work. He would only see it as a bargaining chip. What Haley couldn't possess he would destroy. Aubrey had no doubt Haley would burn the manuscript if he didn't agree to sell.

The threat was implicit.

Aubrey's anger turned inward. He cursed his own vulnerability and lack of resources to stand up to a powerful man like Haley. His rage left him feeling impotent and alone. He imagined Lucas Haley laughing at him.

The fire of his rage burned brightly – then died. Helplessness filled the space left behind.

Aubrey Colgate Jones sank to the floor and let despair consume him.

FORTY

Kurt Harbou took two bottles of Wolverine from Molly's fridge. He snapped off the caps using an opener attached to the kitchen counter. He'd waited until full darkness before making the trip out to Molly's place. He didn't want to take a chance he might be seen.

He set a beer down in front of her and opened a red file folder.

"We found more marijuana in the boathouse. It weighed in at just under twenty pounds. From its high potency it's probably from a grow op up north," Kurt read.

Tony had been telling the truth about the Canadian supplier.

"Arnie passed the information along to the DEA and they're going to follow up."

Molly winced. This would definitely cause John Huffner grief when they found out the boys had used Coast Guard schedules. That would lead to questions about how well John's computer was secured. However, with Tony in jail this was the least of John's worries at the moment.

"When Sharpe found out about the quantity of drugs he jumped right in and attached it to the murder. It didn't take him long to hold a press conference."

Media whore.

"While all this was going on I managed to quietly slip the boxes from the garage," Kurt said and sipped his beer.

"And?" Molly asked. He had the maddening habit of letting information trickle out slowly.

"There was nothing in the first box. Just file folders full of deeds and property surveys, that kind of thing," Kurt said and then smiled. "However, box number two was more interesting."

"What did you find?"

"Well, it's actually what I didn't find. The first box was filled right to the top, crammed with files. But this one had a two inch gap at the top.

"The files were in chronological order. I removed each folder and tried to match it to the one above it. It was pretty easy. After years of being tightly packed there's usually a rusty staple mark or an imprint of a paperclip. About three quarters of the way down something had been removed."

"How can you be sure?" she asked, excitement rising.

"One of the folders had an impression of a cross on its underside. The folder below it had the same impression on its top side."

Kurt drew a cross in the air.

"Judging from the gap at the top whatever had been between them was thick. The marks on the other folders tell me it'd been tied up with strings.

"And those are a few of my favorite things … " he sang, mimicking 'The Sound of Music'.

So there is a manuscript.

The evidence seemed to confirm it.

Then doubt seeped back in.

It could be just contracts or deeds.

As if reading her thoughts, Kurt smiled.

"I also lifted some prints off the boxes and the folders. We have a fresh set of Brian's on both the lid and the top file. There's also another set of prints on the folders."

"Any matches?"

"They don't match Tony's."

There has to be one other person who knows about the manuscript.

She had been right – the manuscript was the key.

"My guy at the state lab got back to me again on the fishing line used to strangle Elkins. He says it doesn't match anything in his database. He's not sure that it is actually fishing line."

Not fishing line?

"That's all I've got." Kurt passed the folder to Molly. "Now, if you happen to have another beer … "

FORTY ONE

Richard Elkins was conscious and looking very unhappy when Molly walked into his hospital room the next morning. She'd been relieved to see a bored security guard sitting in the hall outside his door. If it had been a deputy she never would have been allowed in.

Richard was sitting in bed eating an Egg McMuffin. He had a large dressing in the middle of his forehead with a dark bruise radiating from under it.

His eyes narrowed when he saw her. "Well, Officer Parsons, I must admit I'm not having a fun time in your little town." He touched his forehead.

"It pays to be hard-headed," joked an elegant woman sitting in an armchair next to the bed.

Richard introduced Molly to his wife Elaine. Molly instantly liked this good natured woman. Elaine was clearly the ying to Richard Elkins' anal retentive yang.

"I, apparently, will be getting out of here today much to the relief of my travel insurance company. The cost of health care in this country is absurd."

Molly couldn't disagree with him.

"I am sorry for what's happened. Sunset is normally a wonderful place to visit, especially during the summer."

"I'm sure you're not here to represent the Chamber of Commerce, are you?" He took another bite of his sandwich.

"No, Sir," Molly admitted.

She flipped open her notebook and rifled through the pages.

"When we last spoke you mentioned you had power of attorney over your brother's estate."

Richard nodded and continued to chew.

"Did your brother have a will?"

"As far as I know."

"But you didn't draft it for him."

"No, Barry had his own attorney."

"But you had power of attorney."

"That's different. It's quite normal for someone in a family to have power of attorney in case the person is incapacitated."

"Are you also his executor?" Molly asked.

"From what I understand," he nodded.

"And your brother had an estate?"

"Oh yes. Barry owned a house and there would be life insurance and some residuals from his books."

"How much would you estimate he left?"

Richard considered this for a few moments. "Maybe two million give or take."

"Do you have any idea who would inherit his estate?"

"He probably left some of it to charity and something to my daughter. He always had a soft spot for her. I would imagine he made provision for us as well."

"I need to take a look at his will. Would that be possible?" she asked.

"I'll speak to Barry's lawyer and ask him to email me a copy."

Richard and Elaine looked at Molly expectantly.

"Will this help?" Richard asked.

"It could. Right now it's just a hunch but if it plays out the way I think it will, it could bring your brother's killer to justice."

"Good," he said.

Molly gave him her personal email address. She asked him to send the will directly to her and not to the address on her card. He lifted an eyebrow.

"Off the reservation?" he asked with a smile. "Your boss came by yesterday. He mentioned you were no longer handling the case."

"That's right," she nodded.

"He told me they had a suspect in custody." Elkins fixed her with an intense stare. "You don't believe they have the right person."

"I think whoever killed your brother and assaulted you is still out there."

"I wondered why they still kept a guard on the door," he said softly. "This is your police chief covering his ass in case he's wrong."

"Yeah, I think so," she said with new respect.

As Molly walked out of the room she saw Paul Booster coming down the hall. She quickly moved in the opposite direction but it was too late.

Son of a bitch – this is all I need.

FORTY TWO

Fifteen minutes later Kenton Sharpe called. He was furious and demanded she come to his office immediately.

Sharpe glared at Molly when she arrived. "Sit down," he commanded.

She ignored him and remained standing.

"You were told to stay away from the investigation," he shouted. "Wasn't I clear about that?"

Molly held her tongue and let him vent.

"We have a suspect in custody and as far as I am concerned the investigation is finished."

She felt strangely serene as he continued to yell. Her attitude only provoked him further.

"You had no right to go see Richard Elkins." Spittle shot from his mouth. "And Kurt Harbou gave you evidence last night."

How the hell did he know that? Is he having me watched?

At least he didn't mention her questioning Tony Huffner.

Thank you, Elizabeth.

"This case has been solved."

Sharpe slammed a fist on his desk. He was shaking with anger and his ears matched his cinnamon eyebrows. He took a deep breath and she knew he was going to start shouting again.

"You have the wrong person in custody," Molly said softly to force him to listen.

Although still filled with anger Sharpe responded in a lower voice, "We don't have the wrong person in custody. You just can't deal with the fact Deputy Booster solved the case."

She shook her head. "You can delude yourself all you want but a good defence attorney is going to tear it apart."

"No, he isn't," Sharpe said coldly.

"I'm afraid so. No eyewitnesses, no gunshot residue."

"You know as well as I do that's common with a rifle," Sharpe retorted.

"Anyone could have gotten into his closet and planted the evidence. You've got a case with way too many loose ends, something I suspect you've already heard from the D.A."

Sharpe started to protest but stopped.

Jackpot!

"I'm close," she told him. "I know I am."

"Let me make this perfectly clear, Officer Parsons. You are now officially under suspension. You will remain on full salary awaiting a disciplinary hearing. I will recommend you be terminated from the department. If you attempt in any way to continue your investigation you will be arrested for obstructing justice. Now leave this office immediately."

Kenton Sharpe sat back and glared at her, challenging Molly to say something he could use against her.

She checked her anger. There was nothing to gain right now and too much she could lose.

"Right," she said in a mocking tone and left the office.

As she walked through the station she could feel all eyes on her. She wondered if she had any support left in the department.

Probably not.

Paul Booster sat at his desk pretending to do paperwork.

He must really be enjoying this.

She resisted the urge to lash out at him.

Molly returned home to mull things over. There was no way she was going to stop, not when she was this close.

There was still a murderer walking free.

~

Molly saw headlights coming down her driveway just after 9:00. She got her Beretta and held it inside a folded copy of the Detroit Free Press.

There was a soft knock. She looked down at the paper as she walked to the door and chided herself for being so paranoid.

John Huffner and Arnie Voxx stood on the porch.

"Sorry to disturb you so late, Molly," Arnie apologized, "but we heard about what happened with Sharpe."

When they were seated and drinks had been poured Arnie got right to the point. "He's tied your hands on this case but he's an idiot who can't see past the political gain this will bring him."

"Tony didn't do it," John said, his voice filled with pain.

She could only imagine how he must be feeling.

"There's an awful lot of evidence which points to Tony but Sharpe isn't interested in taking a closer look," Molly said.

"I don't care. Tony didn't do any of the things they've accused him of."

"I know he didn't, John. Right now being in jail is the best place for him. He'll be safe until I can wrap this up. It won't be long. I promise." She added, "Now I need to speak to Arnie alone for a few minutes."

John Huffner went out to his truck to wait.

"So you're willing to risk going to jail?" Arnie asked.

"If that's what it takes. But I need you to keep Sharpe and Booster off my back until this is resolved."

"Well, I think I can help you there," Arnie grinned.

Molly briefed him on her next steps and asked him to check the National Criminal Database. She wrote a name on a piece of paper and handed it to him. He looked at it in surprise.

"You sure about this?"

"Yes," she replied.

"I'll take care of it personally."

He folded the paper and put it in the top pocket of his shirt.

"Arnie, I need the information no later tomorrow afternoon."

"You got it, Kiddo."

After he'd gone she warmed a glass of milk in the microwave. She was hoping for a good night's sleep but knew it was unlikely.

~

The dream was especially vivid.

Molly was out on the ice staring down at the hole. She knew she should run but was mesmerized by what was going to emerge from the water. She hoped it was Steve. Molly needed to tell him she was sorry and beg him to forgive her.

Chunks of shattered ice stirred.

Steve ...

The waxen corpse of Barry Elkins pulled itself from the water. He stood at the edge of the hole and stared at her malevolently. She wanted to say something, to make an excuse for not finding his killer, but she couldn't speak. Instead she backed away, her bare feet leaving blood stains on the ice. Snow swirled around her, momentarily obscuring her vision. When it cleared another figure stood in the darkness. Brian Haley stepped forward and smiled at her. His mouth opened impossibly wide and she could see perfect white teeth lined up like a row of tombstones.

His voice was a soft, sibilant hiss. "Bitch."

He took a step toward her and his face blew apart.

She was showered in a freezing red mist.

~

Molly woke to a trailing echo of thunder.

She wasn't huddled in the corner. There was no paralyzing fear this time.

What's different?

Pulling the duvet around her she lay in the dark thinking.

Why should I feel guilty? Why do I need his forgiveness?

It disgusted her. She had nothing to apologize for.

I was the victim.

Molly faced the truth. She could have rescued him with the pipe. She chose not to.

Steve had taken too much from her. He ripped away her self-respect. He robbed her of her sense of security. And finally the most unforgiveable of all – he'd stolen their precious unborn child.

He didn't deserve to live so she turned her back on him. She let him drown.

An image of Steve's final struggle flashed into her head.

She felt his terror as the lake pulled him down.

The frigid bite of the water as it closed over his head.

The searing pain as he burned up the last of his oxygen.

The horror as his mouth opened and liquid flooded his lungs.

And the final nothingness that death brought.

This was the poisonous guilt she had filled herself with, the residual toxic embrace of Steve.

Now she felt something else – a sense of liberation. The torture of Steve's death was over.

Molly no longer regretted what she'd done.

FORTY THREE

It was the codicil in Barry Elkins' will which confirmed it. What had started as a nagging suspicion now solidified into a sickening lump in Molly's belly.

His Last Will and Testament had arrived in an email that morning as promised. The bulk of the estate had gone to Richard, Elaine, and their daughter. There were provisions for literary charities and a sizable amount set aside for a scholarship fund in Barry's name. The codicil was for ten thousand dollars. However, it wasn't the amount that was important. What was important was the person it was going to.

Everyone has shadows.

~

After being released from the hospital Richard Elkins had returned to the hotel.

It took guts for him to go back there.

Molly phoned his room.

"Good afternoon, Miss Parsons." Richard's voice sounded stronger. "The police chief told me about your suspension. He said I wasn't to discuss anything with you."

Damn.

"So, how can I help you?" he asked with a chuckle.

"Thanks for sending me a copy of the will," she replied with relief.

"There were a few surprises in there," he said.

"Yes, there were," she agreed. "What can you tell me about it?"

He paused. "It was a long time ago and I thought my brother had resolved everything."

Resolved? That's an interesting way to put it.

"Apparently it wasn't," Molly observed.

"No, apparently not," he said softly. "You don't think there's any connection do you?"

"I'm not sure," she sighed.

A thought occurred to her. "There's one way to find out. Why don't we have dinner at The Villager tonight?"

There was a long silence before he replied. "All right."

"Let's meet there at 7:00," she suggested.

"Okay, we'll see you then."

Molly took out her notebook and looked up Palmer March's private number.

"You're taking a big chance calling me," Palmer said. "Kenton talked to me about you this morning."

"Palmer, I'm betting on the fact you don't believe Tony killed Brian any more than I do."

"I'm listening," he replied.

Molly explained what she wanted him to do.

When they hung up she wasn't certain Palmer was convinced but she was satisfied he would go along with her plan.

Twisted trees line twisted trails
Leading forever to the light
Past winter snows and summer gales
Out of shadow, into night.

~ Aubrey Colgate Jones

FORTY FOUR

Molly arrived at The Villager a little after 7:00. It was crowded as usual. She saw Hank Summerville by the bar. He was in deep conversation with Desirée. Molly was surprised to see her back at work so soon after Brian's death.

Richard and Elaine Elkins sat at a table near the back and Molly joined them. Desirée came over to take their order. There was a deep sadness in her eyes.

"You alright?" Molly asked.

Desirée shook her head. "But I need to keep busy right now."

After she left Molly explained what had happened with Brian.

"Poor thing," Elaine said.

Hank walked over to their table. "Surprised to see you're still here," he said to Richard. "I thought you would have had enough of Sunset."

Richard smiled grimly. "Not until my brother's killer is brought to justice."

"I hear Tony Huffner is being arraigned the day after tomorrow so you won't have too long to wait," Hank said. "He always struck me as a decent enough kid, except when he was with Brian Haley. I guess you just never know."

Richard nodded.

"You folks enjoy your dinner now," Hank said and moved on to greet the people at the next table. Molly watched him go.

Desirée arrived with a large tray which she sat down on a folding table. The pizza was on a raised metal pedestal. Molly had to admit it smelled good. Maybe she needed to give the pizza another try. She seemed to be the only person in town who didn't like it.

Next time.

The whitefish and fries she ordered were done to a crispy deep-fried perfection. She shook a good quantity of malt vinegar onto them. The thin crust of beer batter carried a hint of hops. The fresh cut potatoes had been double fried. They snapped as she bit into them but were creamy inside.

Elaine watched her in amusement. "I thought it was just us Canadians who liked vinegar on our fries."

"Up this way everyone eats them like this," she replied.

Molly saw Palmer March walked through the front door. He took a stool at the bar and ordered a drink as he waited for a table to become available. She made a big show of waving him over.

"Care to join us?" she asked him.

Palmer thanked her and sat down. She introduced Richard and Elaine. Molly looked around while they offered each other condolences on their respective losses. She caught Hank staring at them. He looked away.

Richard offered to share their pizza and Palmer accepted. They had a lot in common, including politics, and got into a deep discussion about the difference between Canadian and American conservatism. She and Elaine talked about recent films they had seen and favorite books. Elaine was well read and had a great sense of humor.

The crowd thinned out as the evening passed. By the time they ordered dessert and after dinner drinks The Villager was nearly empty.

~

Kenton Sharpe walked into The Villager around 9:00 and sat down at the bar. The bartender poured him a double shot of Bourbon. His eyes narrowed when he saw Molly and her dinner companions. He walked over to their table and politely greeted everyone.

He looked down at Molly. "Can I have a word with you?"

Sharpe led her to the bar.

"What the hell are you doing?" he hissed.

"I'm having dinner with my friends."

"We both know what you're up to," his voice rose slightly. "An eyewitness and a victim? Let's get real here, Molly."

"We haven't discussed the case at all. Ask them." She leaned toward him and snapped, "So I think you should just butt out of my private life, Chief Sharpe."

His lips grew thin as he fought to control his anger.

She regretted adding the last part as soon as she'd said it.

Before he could reply Molly headed him off. "And if you're about to give me that 'you'll never work in this town again' speech, you can forget it. I spoke to a lawyer this afternoon and he told me the allegations you're making are paper thin. He even said we can go after a settlement from the city for the way you've treated me."

Of course she hadn't spoken to a lawyer but Molly enjoyed watching Sharpe's reaction. And at the very least it would keep him off balance and buy her some breathing room.

Sharpe smacked a ten dollar bill on the bar and knocked back the rest of his drink.

As Molly returned to the table she could feel his glare. When she glanced back at the bar a few minutes later Sharpe was gone.

Palmer insisted on paying for dinner over the protests of the Elkinses.

Outside Richard and Elaine turned down Palmer's offer of a ride. They thanked him but said it was a nice evening to walk. Palmer wished them all a good night and drove off.

Molly walked with the Elkinses for a block along Main Street and then bid them good night as well. As soon as they parted she dashed across the street and through the park. She needed to get to the Zodiac quickly.

FORTY FIVE

It was quiet in the harbor. Molly kept the boat parallel to Main Street. Instead of the noisy outboard she was using an electric trolling motor which produced only a soft whirr. She prayed there was enough juice in the car battery powering it to get her to the other side of the channel.

She passed the ferry dock and glanced over to the bridge. Crime scene tape still fluttered in the wind from under its span. Molly tied up on the rocks less than a hundred feet from where Barry Elkins had died.

Just in time.

Molly could hear the echo of footsteps crossing the bridge above. She imagined Richard and Elaine walking hand-in-hand oblivious to the danger that lurked below.

A shadow detached from the darkness under the bridge. A figure in a hoodie sprinted for the stairs. Light glinted off something in its hand.

A pistol.

She slipped her Beretta out and moved forward. The hooded figure was half way up the stairs. Molly could hear the metallic clank of the Elkinses' footsteps as they came closer.

Now.

Molly moved forward into the light and squared the figure in her gun sight.

"Freeze," she shouted.

No response. It kept moving.

Brakes screeched on the bridge followed by pounding footsteps and shouting.

The figure froze, trying to decide what to do next.

"Drop your weapon now," Molly ordered.

Her index finger tightened on the trigger.

The figure moved up a step.

Molly exhaled slowly as she squeezed the trigger. The bullet hit the ironwork next to the figure.

It swung around and aimed at her.

"Don't do it, Desirée."

Desirée froze for a moment, gun extended. The hood fell back and Molly could see her face. Her eyes were void of emotion.

Desirée fired.

The shot ricocheted off the rocks behind Molly and she ducked.

Molly returned fire. Her shot sparked off the railing.

Desirée raced down the stairs with incredible speed.

Molly stepped out from behind the rocks and took aim.

Please don't make me do it.

Desirée charged toward her firing wildly.

The world was reduced to echoing blasts and blinding light.

Everything moved in slow motion.

Molly calmly squeezed the trigger. The large gun barked and Desirée staggered, her forward momentum interrupted by the bullet. At the same instant Molly felt a crushing blow to her chest. The force of impact threw her backward onto the damp pavement.

I'm shot.

Excruciating pain overwhelmed Molly as she desperately fought for breath.

A steady thud of footsteps came relentlessly toward her.

Molly was helpless to defend herself; her Beretta was gone.

Desirée stood over her, a large splatter of blood on her shoulder.

Molly looked up at the revolver Desirée aimed at her head. It was so close she could count the blunt tips of the bullets in the cylinder.

"You don't have to do this."

"Yes, I do," Desirée whispered with a smile and cocked the hammer.

There was a blinding light from the bridge above and a loud boom echoed up and down the channel.

Desirée spun, slamming against the railing. Her pistol flew out of her hand.

She looked up at the bridge in surprise and then at Molly.

"It's over," Molly groaned.

Desirée hesitated before staggering up the walkway toward the Zodiac. She pulled the mooring rope loose and flopped into the boat. It was caught by the current and carried toward Lake Michigan.

Molly heard the outboard cough and realized she'd left the key in the ignition. Desirée was hunched over the console.

She's going to get away.

Desirée's revolver was lying on the walkway a few feet from her. Molly dragged herself over to it and closed her hand around the grips.

Please, let there be bullets left.

She propped herself against the railing and rode out another wave of pain.

Molly looked straight into Desirée's eyes as the current brought the boat parallel to her.

Steadying the gun, Molly took aim at Desirée.

"Stop … give it up," Molly gasped, each breath clawed at her chest.

Desirée turned the key and the boat roared to life. She pushed the throttle forward.

Molly fired two quick shots.

The first shot tore into Desirée's shoulder and twisted her around so she was facing Molly. The second slammed into her chest, lifted her up, and threw her out of the Zodiac.

Desirée's body landed in the cold water with a splash.

Molly watched it sink into the darkness.

The empty boat raced off down the channel.

Molly dropped the pistol and lapsed into unconsciousness.

~

Arnie called for an ambulance as he held Molly close and begged her not to die.

Still holding his rifle Paul Booster looked sadly down into the channel where Desirée had disappeared and shook his head. It had been his shot that had stopped her from killing Molly.

Off in the darkness a siren screamed as an ambulance raced toward them.

Paul prayed it would get there in time.

FORTY SIX

"You were lucky," the doctor told Molly.

I sure as hell don't feel lucky.

The impact from Desirée's bullet had deformed the right side of her Kevlar vest. An inch to the left and no amount of protection would have saved her. The shock would have ruptured her heart.

Dr. Kevin Myers was inserting an IV line into the back of Molly's hand. She felt a sting as he slid the tube into place and taped it down. This was nothing compared to the intense pain that radiated from her chest. It felt like she'd been hit in the ribs with a Louisville Slugger.

Over Dr. Myers' shoulder she saw a concerned looking Arnie Voxx. It brought back memories of another night when he'd brought her here to Sunset General's emergency room.

"The bruise is big but it should be gone in a couple of weeks," Dr. Myers said as he finished with the IV line. "In the meantime it will hurt when you laugh."

Laughing was the furthest thing from her mind.

Molly thought of the moment when Desirée turned in shock to face her. It was her eyes. They had looked so dead. Just before the second bullet hit her they'd briefly come to life, giving Molly a glimpse of the girl's inner torment.

Whatever was in the IV started to take effect. The pain faded and Molly felt herself melting into unconsciousness.

~

A mixture of powerful narcotics aided by a sedative kept Molly drifting in and out consciousness. When she finally came to, the pain in her chest was reduced to a dull throb.

Dr. Myers wanted to keep her in for another day but Molly refused. There were still issues to resolve.

~

Molly's Zodiac had run out of gas a few miles offshore. The Coast Guard had located it and towed it back to the harbor. The State Police were sending their dive team to recover Desirée's body.

Molly hoped they would have more luck than they'd had with Steve.

A line from Gordon Lightfoot's 'Wreck of the Edmond Fitzgerald' popped into her head.

"The lake it is said never gives up her dead ... "

~

They agreed neutral ground was best.

The Villager had been closed after lunch for them to meet. Kenton Sharpe and Paul Booster were the first to arrive, followed by Arnie Voxx and Kurt Harbou. John Huffner came in and took a seat between Arnie and Sharpe.

Molly arrived last. She walked in stiffly and sat down carefully across from Sharpe.

He glared at her.

This isn't going to be pleasant.

"I want your badge right now," Sharpe ordered.

"Let's just take a minute here, Kenton," Arnie said in his best conciliatory tone.

Sharpe continued to glare at Molly. "You deliberately chose to disobey my direct orders and violated your suspension," he said. "Your badge. Now."

Molly reached down painfully and pulled the badge case from her bag. She slid it slowly across the table to Sharpe.

"You embarrassed our entire department," he muttered.

"How the hell did she do that, Kenton?" Arnie demanded. "By catching the real killer?"

John looked at her gratefully and then turned to Sharpe. "My boy would still be in jail."

"She endangered two innocent civilians," Sharpe protested.

"Elkins and his wife were never in any danger. We picked them up two blocks from the bridge and substituted our own people to act as decoys," Arnie replied, "including Deputy Booster here."

Sharpe gave Booster a reproachful look. Paul, extremely uncomfortable, shrank into his chair.

"Still, you took one hell of a chance."

"It was a calculated risk," Molly replied sharply with impatience.

Sharpe started to respond and Kurt held up a plastic vial containing a deformed piece of lead. Conflict made him uneasy; he needed to defuse it.

"We recovered the gun at the scene. It was an old Smith & Wesson .38 with five chambers loaded with wad cutters."

"The sixth chamber was empty," Molly said grimacing. It hurt when she talked.

"Yup," Kurt replied.

"So how did you figure out it was Desirée?" John asked.

"I followed the manuscript. The manuscript was always the key."

"It's that valuable?" John looked surprised.

Molly shook her head. "Desirée wasn't interested in money. She was interested in what the manuscript would bring her – Barry Elkins."

Molly felt another twinge and gripped the arms of her chair.

"I kept going back to Barry Elkins' murder and the way it was carried out. Strangulation means getting close to a person. It's an intimate act. You can whisper your victim's crimes in his ear."

"What crimes?" Sharpe demanded with skepticism.

"Abandoning a child to suffer a life of cruelty and abuse," Molly replied softly.

"Desirée was his child?" Arnie asked.

"Her real name was Sharon Lewis but, yes, she was Elkins' child by one of his students," Molly explained. "He'd arranged for her to have an abortion and thought it was taken care of. What he didn't know was the girl decided not to go ahead with it. She moved back to Nashville and that's where Desirée was born."

Molly had to pause; it was a struggle to talk.

"When I first started to take a serious look at Desirée I did a background check and it came back clean. But when I got a copy of Elkins' will I saw there was a provision for a Sharon Lewis. I guess somewhere along the line Elkins had discovered he was a daddy and decided to make amends."

Sharpe leaned back in his chair and scoffed, "This is all bullshit. You don't have a shred of evidence."

Molly ignored him. "By then Sharon, or Desirée if you prefer, had suffered years of abuse. Her mother had done a thorough job of poisoning her against her father and it really messed her up. She spent a good portion of her teen years as a street hooker and drug addict. Then she cleaned up and changed her name to escape her past. But she couldn't. She seemed to focus all the pain and problems in her life into hatred for the father she never knew. It consumed her to the point where she had to make him pay for all of it, real and imagined.

"When she discovered his obsession with Aubrey Colgate Jones she came up to Sunset. She figured she might be able to lure him here so she could kill him."

"Why didn't she just go to Toronto to do it?" Arnie wondered.

"She couldn't. Although her name was different she still had a criminal record. She couldn't get a passport, which you now need to cross the border."

Sharpe started to interrupt. Molly held up her hand to stop him.

"In her twisted mind Desirée was likely looking for a way to get something she could use as bait for Barry Elkins. She'd heard the stories about Lucas Haley and how everyone suspected him of killing Jones so she seduced his grandson."

"And Brian discovered the manuscript among his grandfather's stuff," Kurt said.

"He saw it as a way to make some money and she saw it as the opportunity she'd been waiting for. She sent a page to the publisher. She knew with Barry Elkins' reputation in literary circles he would be the person they would most likely ask to verify that the manuscript was genuine. It was the perfect way of getting him to come to Sunset," Molly said. "Years of festering rage came down to this single act of revenge."

"And no one would suspect her," Arnie said.

"I was certainly fooled like everyone else," Molly agreed. "Desirée was always in the background. The only time she attracted any attention to herself was when she played her music."

Molly glanced at the stage near the back.

"When Kurt mentioned his expert said he didn't believe it was fishing line I got to thinking about what else it might've been. Then I remembered seeing Desirée replace a string on her guitar – a nylon string – and it all fell into place. She used a guitar string to murder her father, playing him like an instrument."

She stopped and let this sink in.

"There was another thing that bothered me," Molly said. "When I first searched his room I found a bottle of Advil PM but the toxicology report noted there were traces of Zaleplon in his body. Why would he need the Advil if he had a prescription sleeping pill? It didn't make sense, especially when Zaleplon is banned from sale in Canada.

"That got me thinking about how it could've gotten into his system. Desirée waited on him that night so I figure she must have slipped it into his food. She wasn't taking any chances. He was a big guy but wouldn't be able to put up much of a fight if he was drugged."

"A burger and fried," Kurt quipped.

No one laughed.

"But why try to kill Elkins' brother?" John asked.

"She was crazy," Molly replied, "and he was an identical twin. Plus he'd treated her like dirt when she first waited on him.

"But this time she didn't have an opportunity to do much planning. However, she had enough foresight to steal a pair of shoes from Tony's closet and wear them on her little adventure. She likely stole the hammer from him as well."

She looked over at John. He nodded.

"She set Elkins' rental car on fire and when it drew him outside, she hit him. Luckily she was interrupted and had to run before finishing him off."

Discomfort made Molly stop.

The faces around her were rapt, waiting for the next revelation.

She drew in a ragged breath and continued. "I think she became completely unhinged when Brian hit her. She went back to Tony's place and stole the rifle from the back of his closet.

"When I talked to some folks down in Nashville they mentioned she was a hunter when she was younger. Apparently she was a better than average shot.

"Once she'd blown Brian's head off she returned the shoes and rifle to Tony's closet and played the grief-stricken girlfriend," Molly concluded.

Sharpe pushed his chair back with a loud scrape. "Well that's all very nice, Miss Marple, but you've solved your last case."

He put her badge in his pocket and stood up.

Arnie pointedly faced Sharpe. "Molly, that was damn fine police work. When you're feeling better you come see me and we'll have a job waiting for you. We can use an investigator with your skills. I think a lot of departments will be interested in you once the news gets around."

"News? What news?" Sharpe was flustered.

Arnie smiled cannily.

"Kenton, I hope you have your press release ready. Ours went out fifteen minutes ago. In fact, I believe Mr. and Mrs. Elkins are standing by right now to answer questions from the media. This should make a good lead for the 6:00 news."

Sharpe looked stricken and then anxious as he rapidly left the restaurant.

Arnie smiled.

Perhaps he isn't that good a politician after all.

Molly got up and walked slowly to the back of the room. She stopped in front of the small stage.

Hank Summerville came out of the kitchen and stood nearby. He was clearly shaken.

"She played us, Molly," he said sadly.

Molly stared at the microphone and empty guitar stand on the stage and nodded.

"Hank, could you lift that front riser for me?"

Hank flipped it over. A worn guitar case sat on the floor.

Molly pointed at it. "Bring it here, please."

Hank set the case down on the table next to where she stood. The others gathered around and Kurt passed Molly a pair of vinyl gloves. She opened the case and removed some handwritten music sheets and a spare set of strings.

A package wrapped in paper lay at the bottom of the guitar case.

Molly gently picked it up and undid the twine holding it together. She opened it carefully and saw a stack of yellowed pages. A thrill went through her as she read the first lines of Aubrey Colgate Jones' last manuscript.

"Kurt, you'll need to verify the age of the paper and the handwriting."

Molly passed him the package.

"No problem if I have a comparison sample," he whispered in awe, holding it like it was one of the Dead Sea Scrolls.

"We can get a sample from one of Jones' notebooks at the library," she replied. "We need to keep this quiet until it's verified. Then we can announce it to the press."

It would be a great story – full of treasure, lust, tragedy, and murder.

The media would eat it up.

~

Molly called Jonathan Drake. She explained that Aubrey Colgate Jones had indeed written one final work – a book length poem. There was silence when she finished, followed by the sound of soft sobbing.

"Thank you," Drake said, his voice strained with emotion. "When may I see it?"

Molly promised to deliver a copy after it had been examined by the lab.

FORTY SEVEN

Because of her injury Molly wasn't supposed to drive. She called Paul Booster and asked if he would take her to the library.

"We need to talk," she added.

They drove in uncomfortable silence. At the library, Molly requested he stay outside and wait for her.

She'd called ahead and Julia Harre was standing by the front entrance. It was late in the day and the library was almost empty. In the Aubrey Colgate Jones room, Julia once again unlocked the display case and lifted out one of the original notebooks.

Molly slid it into an evidence envelope and sealed it. She wrote the details on a label.

"So it's true, you found it," Julia said with excitement.

Molly nodded wearily.

"Remember when we spoke about Jones a few days ago. You said he died several years before you were born."

"That's right," Julia replied tentatively.

"I checked the county records and you were born six months after he died."

Julia stiffened and fussed with the lock on the display case.

"How long have you known?" Molly asked.

"A couple of years," Julia said quietly. "When Mom first got sick she told me something I don't think she meant to. At first I thought it was the Alzheimer's, however I couldn't stop thinking about it. The dates all lined up but I didn't have definitive proof until a couple of months ago."

"Definitive proof?"

"Jones was inept as a handyman, always hurting himself. He got blood stains on more than one of the notebooks. I snipped off a tiny sample and had a private lab use it for DNA comparison. Apparently the age of the DNA doesn't matter," Julia said. "They matched mine to his."

Large tears welled up in Julia's eyes.

"My father was a loving and kind man who worked hard and cared for me his whole life. Except now I know he wasn't my father after all. I tried to convince myself Mom must have loved Jones too and she'd made a terrible mistake." Julia broke down in tears. "I was that mistake.

"She's helpless now, Molly. She doesn't know me. She doesn't even know who she is anymore. She's in the shadows," Julia whispered.

Molly could only imagine the pain Julia was suffering. She regretted having to make her go through it.

"Do you know the rest?"

Molly nodded.

"It must have been horrible for her. She'd betrayed the man she loved for someone who didn't even care. He was obsessed with his writing and had no use for her – and certainly no room in his life for a baby. She must have been overwhelmed with guilt and remorse," Molly said. "I think she just snapped and killed him."

"During one of her lucid periods she told me what happened," Julia said. "She wanted me to know, wanted me to understand what she had done.

"She set his cabin on fire expecting him to come out but he didn't. He'd been swimming in the lake and ran right by her without even seeing her standing there. She was in a rage and wasn't thinking straight. She killed him with an axe."

Julia looked off through the window at the dying light of day, conjuring up the scene in her mind.

"She dragged him to an old well near the edge of the woods and pushed him in. Everyone just assumed he died in the fire."

In the main reading room the lights flashed once indicating the library was getting ready to close for the day.

"And for all these years they thought it was Lucas Haley who'd killed him," Molly said softly.

They looked at each other in silence.

"So what happens now?" Julia asked.

Molly remembered the kind woman who had provided her with much needed sanctuary when she was a child

That woman is gone now.
"I think we'll just leave your mother in the shadows."

FORTY EIGHT

Paul Booster shifted uncomfortably in the seat as they drove away from the library.

Molly was exhausted. It had been a long day and she ached all over.

Paul looked at her.

"Molly, I just wanted to say that I'm sorry about how things went," he said. "For what it's worth, Sharpe is wrong."

She nodded wearily.

"I can't believe how you put it all together," he continued. "She was the last person I would have suspected."

"How long were you involved with her?" Molly asked.

Paul took his foot off the gas and let the car drift to the side of the road. Gripping the steering wheel, he stared straight ahead.

"She needed someone to talk to." His lower lip started to quiver.

"Yeah, well she was a suspect in a murder investigation."

"How was I supposed to know that?"

"By using your head." she snapped. "Or was it too far up Sharpe's ass."

"That isn't fair."

"No. You know what isn't fair? Someone I thought I could trust turning on me. You let your resentment poison your better judgement, Paul. And in the end it made you look like a fool."

She softened her tone. "You're a good cop, Paul, but you've still got a lot to learn about people. Investigation 101 tells us to consider everyone who had contact with a victim as a potential suspect. Instead you got involved with her and she manipulated you."

"You don't understand," he said. "I liked her. She was sensitive and intelligent."

"And she murdered two men in cold blood," she retorted. "Take a look at her last boyfriend. It didn't work out so well for him. He's on a slab in the morgue."

Paul started to protest and she cut him off. "Think about the anonymous tip you got about Huffner. You didn't even question who made the call. It was from Desirée."

"No way!" he said in denial. "It was a man's voice."

"Think, Paul. Who else could it have been? She was a singer. She had a great vocal range. I bet she could hit those low notes really well."

He shook his head still not wanting to believe it, even though he knew it was true.

"She figured you wouldn't stop to think about it," Molly continued. "You were so anxious to make the collar you threw logic out the window."

Paul slumped back in the seat.

"Shit." He dragged out the word.

Molly smiled. This was the first time she'd heard him swear.

There is hope for him.

"Don't beat yourself up too badly," Molly said. "She had me fooled as well."

She felt sorry for Paul. He really was a decent guy, not a snake like Sharpe.

"I think you're a pretty good investigator," she said. "I reviewed all the cases you handled while I was away. You did good work. However, you're still a bit naïve and need to learn how to think more creatively."

She paused to let her words sink in.

"This brings me to the revolver Desirée used the other night." Molly rubbed her sore chest reflexively. "It was a Smith & Wesson .38 filled with wad cutters."

He froze.

"Now, who uses wad cutters? I can't, because they don't work in automatics. Besides, the only time you use them is for shooting targets," she said. "I carry a Beretta and you carry a Sig Sauer, right?"

He nodded.

"But I also carry a .357 as backup." Molly opened her bag to show him the butt of the Smith & Wesson nestled in its special side pocket. "What do you carry as a back-up?"

Paul rubbed a spot over his left eye.

"I'm guessing it isn't registered so you could use it as a throw down in case something ever went bad," she said. "Where'd you get it?"

He sighed.

"During the last gun amnesty an old timer dropped it off and didn't want to hang around while I did the paperwork. The gun never made it to the crusher," he said. "But how'd you know it was mine?"

"You gave it away by leaving an empty chamber – that old cop trick."

Arnie had showed it to her years ago. Leave a chamber empty so if anyone got your gun and turned it on you, nothing would happen when they pulled the trigger. That would buy you a split second to get the gun back.

"She probably took it when you were sleeping."

He looked away in embarrassment.

"So what now?" he asked sheepishly.

"You could go to Sharpe and explain where her pistol came from but I suspect that would limit your career opportunities.

"Let's keep the gun's provenance our little secret. It'll be one of those loose ends we never managed to tie up."

She offered her hand. "Deal?"

Paul shook it with gratitude and relief.

"Thanks for saving my life back there at the bridge," Molly added with a smile.

~

Paul pulled the cruiser into her driveway and helped Molly from the car.

"Are you going to take the job Arnie offered you?"

"I don't know. Right now, I'm just going to get some rest and let my body heal," Molly replied.

Paul had a new respect for Molly Parsons. He realized he'd hitched his horse to the wrong wagon. Kenton Sharpe was a fool.

He waited until Molly was safely inside before he backed slowly out of the driveway.

FORTY NINE

The kitchen had a faint odor of stale bacon. Molly remembered she'd made a bacon and tomato sandwich for breakfast a couple of mornings ago. The dirty plate still sat on the counter above the dishwasher. She would do the dishes in the morning. Right now she was too tired and sore to think about anything but sleep.

After a restless hour in bed Molly decided to give up. She went back to the kitchen and got a beer. She knew she shouldn't have alcohol while on pain medication but at this point she didn't care.

She kept coming back to Paul's question about whether or not she would take the job with the sheriff's department. It would be great to work with Arnie once again but it would only be short term. He was tired and his heart didn't seem to in another campaign. From what he'd told her there was a good chance he might lose.

That would mean Kenton Sharpe would probably be elected sheriff.

She smiled at the irony.

Then he would get to fire me all over again.

That would no doubt bring him great joy.

It's time to move on.

Maybe it would help put the ghosts to rest if she left. At least she would leave on a high note after solving this case. She should have been elated about that but only felt an overwhelming sadness. Too much damage had been done to too many lives.

Coming back to Sunset was a bad idea.

She should have made a new start somewhere else. It wasn't as if she had any wonderful childhood memories to hold her here. For her Sunset meant only cruelty – no friends and a family who lived on the margins of society.

231

She escaped as soon as soon as she'd been able to but fate lured her back.

For a while she'd fooled herself that it was different, that she could have the things she had only dreamed about – a beautiful home, a loving husband, a family, and the respect of the community.

That was the cruellest joke of all.

The beer tasted bitter and she set it down.

She would leave this place. There was no reason to stay. She could get a good price for the house – it was prime lakeside property. If she was lucky she might even get something for Steve's packing plant and boats. There would also be a settlement from the department unless Sharpe found a way to stop it. She would be okay financially.

But what would I do?

The combination of beer and pain killers finally took their toll. Molly yawned. Tomorrow she would spend some time online researching possibilities for her future.

~

There's someone in the house.

Molly had been sleeping soundly. No dream plagued her tonight yet she woke up to find herself huddled in the corner clutching her pistol.

The medication had worn off and the pain from her wound was unbearable.

The house was silent around her.

This nonsense has to stop.

She had to get control over it. There were no ghosts here, only half remembered nightmares and shadows.

If I didn't have a dream why am I awake?

Puzzled she set the gun on the floor.

What was that?

She knew the ambience of her house intimately – each tick of the clock, creak of the joists, buzz of the refrigerator's compressor. Molly had internally catalogued every explainable sound and tuned into them each sleepless night.

This is a noise I don't recognize.

Molly closed her hand around the grips of the Beretta and flicked the safety off.

She heard it again, closer now, a soft liquid dragging that sounded like something heavy being pulled along the floor.

Is this a dream? Am I still sleeping?

If she was this was her most vivid one yet.

Adrenaline coursed through her body. Her rising panic forced her to draw in shallow gasps. Each one set off spasms of pain in her chest. She fought to control her breathing.

Jesus.

She could see the pale outline of a figure. Someone was standing in the bedroom doorway.

Is this real?

Nothing moved. The house remained silent.

Have I finally gone mad?

Fear bit into her.

It's nothing but shadows.

Something dark stepped into the room. It moved past her unaware she was on the floor. Molly didn't breathe.

Who is it?

She strained to penetrate the darkness, to see who had invaded her room but the shadows were too deep.

Less than three feet away the figure hesitated at the end of the bed and looked down at the bunched up blankets.

It raised its hand high and she could see the outline of a large knife.

She pointed her pistol.

The figure flung itself on the bed striking a series of quick blows into the mess of bedding and pillows. Feathers filled the air.

There was a scream of rage.

"Drop it," Molly shouted.

The figure whipped around and lunged toward her.

Crouched on the floor Molly had nowhere to go.

She squeezed the trigger.

A flash of light from the muzzle lit up the room.

It briefly illuminated the enraged face of Desirée Platt.

Desirée gasped in surprise as the bullet whizzed past her ear and shattered the bedroom window.

Desirée? How?

Desirée's face was like a chalk white Halloween mask.

Molly saw the knife arcing down toward her.

She steadied the gun and took careful aim. This would be her only chance.

The shot hit just above the bridge of Desirée's nose. It blew out the back of her head.

Death was instantaneous but her body continued its forward momentum, her hand still holding the knife.

Molly rolled to the side.

The blade flashed by her and buried itself in the wall an inch from her right eye. Desirée's lifeless body slammed into her. A searing pain exploded in Molly's chest as it took the brunt of the weight.

She passed out.

~

Consciousness returned slowly. Molly couldn't move and struggled to understand why.

What's on top of me?

Memory flooded back.

She was pinned under Desirée's lifeless body.

Oh my God.

She tried to wiggle out from under it but agony forced her to stop. She could feel the broken ribs grinding against each other. Her chest felt like it was on fire.

I can do this.

She gritted her teeth and with all her remaining strength pushed against the dead weight that had been Desirée. The body flopped to one side and Molly slid free.

Her BlackBerry had been knocked off the bedside table and lay on the floor nearby. She inched toward it trying not to aggravate her injuries. She picked it up and punched in 9-1-1. After she spoke to the operator Molly slumped over and lay on her side.

She looked at Desirée. The shot had destroyed her once beautiful face. Molly turned away but the vision of Desirée's ruined features stayed with her.

She can't hurt anyone ever again.

Molly felt it boiling inside her – the anguish of her physical injuries and the torment of her psychic ones. It increased as her sorrow grew, like pressure building dangerously in a boiler.

Finally it became unbearable.

She threw her head back and screamed into the darkness.

The dam burst. A lifetime of inadequacy, fear, guilt, sorrow, and regret spilled out of her in a single scream which felt like it would never end.

When it finally faded away there was nothing left inside. She was empty.

Hugging her knees Molly rocked gently back and forth.

She realized that she'd survived everything – Steve's uncontrolled rage, her overwhelming guilt about his death, Sharpe's political machinations, and finally, Desirée's frenzied attack.

Yes, she had survived it all.

But it was more than just survival.

She was alive in way she'd never felt before.

Molly began to weep, her tears carrying away the final vestiges of grief.

Somewhere off in the distance she heard the faint keening of a siren.

Taste your tears upon my lips
On smoke shrouded field
Cry no more my love
Let shadows yield.

~ Aubrey Colgate Jones

FIFTY

The following morning Arnie Voxx drove Molly to Jonathan Drake's house.

It was time to keep a promise.

She clutched a copy of the manuscript in her lap. The original was safely locked up in the crime lab.

"Did you read it?" Arnie asked.

"I'm not really interested."

"I read it last night. It's great."

This surprised her.

"I never figured you for a poetry fan, Arnie."

"Oh yeah, I love all the greats – Shelley, Emerson, Frost, Dickinson, Simon."

"Simon?" Molly looked at him, perplexed.

"Yeah, Paul," Arnie replied with a grin.

Molly didn't smile.

"You okay?" he asked gently.

"Yes. I am," she replied firmly.

And she was.

~

Molly thought back to the morning's events.

After a trip to the emergency room to have her ribs taped she insisted that she be allowed to view the post mortem.

Desirée Platt was lying on a steel table.

"She was one tough woman," Dr. Ronnie Kolmenn said looking down at the bullet wounds in her body.

237

Her skin was pale under the harsh lights. The blood had been washed away and the bullet holes could be seen clearly. They were small with slight bruising around them. There was also a large bruise under each breast.

Ronnie pointed to a wound on the outside of her hip.

"This one bled a bit but wasn't too bad. It's older than the others so I'd say she got it at the bridge the other night. From the size of the entry wound it was a rifle shot."

Ronnie next pointed to the two bruises on her chest.

"It looks like you weren't the only one wearing a vest. It saved her life. But like I said, she was a tough one. She must have swum down the channel after you shot her."

Molly shivered at the thought of swimming any distance in that frigid water.

Ronnie stood on a small stool and leaned over the body. He tapped his pen on the ragged edge of the forehead entrance wound.

"This one finished her off. You hit the jackpot."

Molly stared at Desirée with detachment; just another cadaver in a long series.

"If it makes you feel any better, she died instantly," Kolmenn added.

Too bad.

She fought the cynical desire to say it out loud.

It was true Desirée had lived a rough life but that was no excuse for all she had done.

Molly felt no remorse about stopping her.

~

They arrived at Jonathan Drake's home on Cufflink Hill.

He smiled at her as she held out the manuscript. He took it reverently and read the first page.

Drake could barely contain his excitement.

"Magnificent," he whispered in awe. "Thank you so much."

Molly left him holding his treasure.

Jonathan Drake would make sure it was shared with the world.

She smiled at the part she'd played in making sure that Aubrey Colgate Jones' last poem finally found its audience.

~

In the car Arnie passed Molly a deputy's badge.

"I thought you might like to get started."

She stared at the badge.

"I don't know, Arnie," she said. "I think it's time to move on."

"Had enough of Sunset?" he asked.

"Yes, I think so," she replied quietly.

She stared down at the badge.

"There are a lot of good people here," he said, "and they deserve the best protection we can give them."

She had a thousand reasons not to take the job.

"But what about the election," she said. "This could hurt you politically."

He started the car.

"I'm not going to run again," he told her.

She started to protest, to urge him not to give up.

"I'm going to nominate you instead," he continued.

She looked at him in surprise.

He nodded. "You'll make a damn fine sheriff," he said. "Anyway, you can't just walk away and let Sharpe take over, can you?"

Molly was stunned. She didn't know what to think. This was a bolt from the blue.

What do I really want?

Up to a few minutes ago she thought she knew – put Sunset behind her and go somewhere else to make a new life.

Arnie was right. Sharpe would be a disaster. His bad judgement and inflexibility would tell every crook in the state that Sunset County was a great place to set up shop because they had an idiot sheriff.

The badge seemed to have grown heavier in her hand.

Sheriff Molly Parsons.

Her ego was calling to her.

She knew running against Sharpe was the wrong reason to stay. She was wary about being swept away by emotions.

She thought about Steve.

Look how that turned out.

"I don't know, Arnie," she said.

"I can't help you decide, Molly. I know this town hasn't always been kind to you … "

If only you knew …

"But they sure could use you now," Arnie said.

He's right.

Arnie put the car in gear and pulled away from the house.

She'd lost so much but at the same time had gained something very important – respect.

And a second chance.

If she walked away now all she'd have would be bad memories.

Can there be more than that to Sunset?

Molly Parsons pinned on her new badge.

Maybe I'll stick around and find out.

ABOUT THE AUTHOR

After receiving a degree in film, Peter worked on various movie and television productions. He was head writer and show runner on two popular Canadian entertainment shows and also wrote and produced numerous radio and television commercials. His career took him all over the globe and he used this experience as senior writer for two travel guides published by Baffled by Travel Press. Peter has finished the second Molly Parsons novel, *Bloody Sunset*, and is currently working on a third book in the series. Peter lives in Toronto with his family.